THINGS
LEFT
UNDONE

ANNE LOVETT

WORDS
OF PASSION

THINGS LEFT UNDONE

Published by Words of Passion, Atlanta, GA 30097.

Editorial: Nanette Littlestone
Cover and Interior Design: Peter Hildebrandt

ISBN (print book): 978-1-958904-09-1
ISBN (e-book): 978-1-958904-10-7

Library of Congress Control Number: 2023915994

DEDICATION

To Virginia, who taught me so much.

We have left undone those things which we
ought to have done,

And we have done those things which we
ought not to have done.

—The Book of Common Prayer, 1979

Chapter One

S ometimes Liberty thought that if she'd had her daddy's dark old gun when it all started, the story might have ended a lot sooner and she'd have had a long, long time to think about it.

It started on a dark and stormy night, a gullywasher gurgling over the eaves and dashing down the downspouts, lightning cracking and flashing. Tomorrow was Thanksgiving. Her in-laws were coming. And Dallas wasn't home.

When a crash of thunder shook the house, Emmy wailed. The poor child hated the thunder and lightning, and maybe it was because she was born the way she was.

Maybe, sadly, it was because she'd been exposed to too much fighting in the house.

Liberty set down the glass of wine she'd poured to help her jitters and hurried up to the child's room. She knelt by the bed, flipped up the dust ruffle, and peered underneath. "Baby?"

"Mommy." The little lip was quivering.

"Come on out, sweetheart."

The child wriggled herself out and into her mother's arms. "I'm scared, Mommy."

"Hush." Liberty held her and smoothed the silky hair. Emmy was eight and a beautiful child with silky blond hair and dark blue eyes, creamy skin and a rosy smile. People would stop on the street and remark on her prettiness. Some couldn't tell that she wasn't normal.

Liberty couldn't forget the solemn face on the doctor in the delivery room. She didn't know what he was talking about when he tried to tell her. How could she, being from a small town in Florida where there wasn't anybody like that? For two weeks, she mourned the loss of the perfect child she'd expected and then pulled up her socks to love the child she had been sent.

Mama Jean was proud of her. Her grandmother was like that.

Emmy looked up. "Can I s'weep with you tonight?"

The rain was coming down harder. "You're a big girl," Liberty said.

"Juth tonight? Pleath?" The girl could talk pretty well when she tried, but when she lisped it was hard for anybody to understand her but Liberty, Mama Jean, and her teacher at school. Her daddy didn't try.

"You crying, Mommy?"

"It's nothing. All right, come on with me." The child grabbed the quilt Mama Jean had made and dragged it after her, and Liberty tucked her up in the big bed with it.

Liberty reached over and switched on the night light, kissed Emmy goodnight, and walked downstairs. Did she hear a car in the driveway? Dallas at last? He'd better have that turkey, the roast turkey he said he'd pick up from the deli that he passed on his way home. She closed her eyes. *And please, please, don't be drunk.*

If Dallas came home drunk one more time, Liberty was ready to pack her bags. If Dallas cussed her out one more time . . .

But. There was Emmy. And Emmy loved her Daddy. And Emmy hated change. Liberty kept hoping he would keep his endless promises, and just when she thought maybe he really meant it, just when life was better—it was back to Square One. Thunder muttered discouragingly beyond the window.

Waiting for Dallas to come in, Liberty finished putting away the pots and pans from all the food she had cooked that day. She thought about Father Sam. She'd tried to return his call today, but he hadn't answered, and she was worried. Still, he was just a friend. Maybe her best friend, except for Vivian.

A car door slammed in the garage.

Dallas swaggered through the door, hair flopping over his forehead. He dropped his briefcase in a corner and threw his coat over a chair. "Ah, my beautiful wife."

"Where's the turkey?"

He grinned maddeningly.

Drunks call it *high*. Never mind skunk-drunk, wasted, blasted, stoned, ossified, three sheets to the wind. Not even sobriety challenged. No. *High* makes a smirky, snaky, crocodile smile. She'd seen murder suspects smirk like that on TV cameras. That smile was on Dallas's face.

Liberty took a deep breath. "I'm leaving you.

"You what?"

"You heard me. I've been busting my butt all day to make a nice dinner for your folks tomorrow, and this is how you treat me? You forgot the turkey, and they're closed tomorrow! I've had it, Dallas!"

"Stupid bitch!" Dallas stared at her, jaw sagging, leaning into her space. He took a step forward, steeped in alcohol fumes.

Maybe she shouldn't have swung the spatula at him, but nobody was going to call her a *bitch*.

She barely grazed him, and then she saw his hand coming at her head. She tried to dodge, too late. Pain shot through her face and her knees buckled. She dropped to the ground and lay there, breathing hard, a big lump in her throat.

God. He'd really hit her.

"Get up, dammit," he growled. "I didn't hurt you."

She wasn't about to get up. She lay still next to the flimsy spatula, too angry to be hurt. All the fury that she had suppressed for the sake of her little one seethed in her gut. Let him think about what he did.

"Play possum if you want to." He stalked off.

She listened, her cheek cold on the vinyl tile floor, while he lumbered into the family room and opened the bar cabinet. She heard the scratchy opening of a bottle top and liquid gurgling into a glass. She heard an *oof* as he sank into his hideous marshmallow chair.

The TV gave a loud electronic belch.

She picked herself up, one arm at a time, like a puppet rises, then she picked up the spatula and laid it in the sink to wash. She padded to the downstairs powder room. The soft pink light revealed a puffy eye that would turn into a shiner.

She tiptoed out into the hallway. Her back plastered against the wall James Bond-style, she peered into the family room. Dallas was asleep, head back in his hideous marshmallow chair, the TV blaring.

She could have shot him then. If she'd had a gun.

She tiptoed upstairs, feeling guilty for the thought. Oh, how she had loved him once—before she knew how much he loved the bottle. He'd seemed glamorous then, far away from sleepy rural Florida, this cool, good-looking sales rep.

She crept upstairs to her room, where Emmy was still sleeping, and peered in her own bathroom mirror. She dragged a comb through her tangled curls, smoothing the hair into dark blond waves that fell across her puffy eye, and then she broke down, snuffling into a fistful of Kleenex.

The rain was still drumming on the roof, rushing through the gutters. She took a deep breath and straightened. She needed to get hold of herself. First, Emmy needed to be in her own bed in case Dallas woke up and staggered upstairs. Liberty drained a glass of water from the tap, then went to gather her little girl in her arms.

Emmy's innocent, snub-nosed, tilted-eyed face lay against the pillow, and Liberty was overcome with the unfairness of it all. She sobbed again, grabbed another pillow, and punched it. She punched it again and again, until all the feathers burst out, making a snowstorm in the middle of a rainstorm. Emmy would have giggled, but it wasn't funny.

There was nothing to do but leave. Now. Before he woke up. And she had to see Sam. She had to ask him if she was doing the right thing. It was all just so impossible.

She pulled her battered old duffel from the closet—not even considering the fancy tapestry set Dallas had bought her—and filled it with jeans, shorts, and T-shirts, and one plain cotton sleeveless dress. She crept into Emmy's room, laid out a lavender warm-up for her, and packed her clothes. Then she went back to her own room and shook the child gently awake. "Emmy," she whispered, "come with me. Be really quiet."

Emmy opened her eyes, sat up, and looked around, confused.

"We're going to Mama Jean's house for Thanksgiving."

"Why?"

"I'll tell you all about it later," Liberty said in a hoarse whisper. "Come on, honey. We've got to go."

She wasn't dumb. "Daddy mad again?"

Liberty nodded.

"I hate that." She followed Liberty and let her mother help her into a purple top and joggers and picked some favorite toys to pack. Liberty added an mp3 player and some coloring books and crayons. She'd already bought Emmy a portable DVD player for Christmas, but she didn't want to spoil Santa's surprise.

Holding the duffel bags, they tiptoed downstairs. Dallas was still snoring in the recliner. The remote had fallen to the floor, changing the channel, and a wavy-haired TV preacher was shouting, whipping the faithful into frenzy, calling on them to *repent*. Shouts of "amen" came from the congregation.

Liberty grabbed the clicker and turned the program off. She took Emmy's hand and they slipped out the back door to the open garage. Cold wet wind lashed in. The storm was getting worse.

Liberty buckled Emmy in. They'd stop by and see Sam on the way out. He knew something of her marriage difficulties, and he was a good man. Liberty prayed he wouldn't try to stop her.

Chapter Two

All Liberty had wanted was a happy family.

And now she was running away in the rain. When she and Emmy hit the expressway in the 4Runner, the storm had not abated. The wipers flailed at the torrents, and raindrops clattered like hailstones on the roof. Emmy whimpered and pulled the quilt, her blankie, over her head. The rain swished in front of Liberty like a silver curtain, and the night was black as the background of a velvet Elvis. She pressed her lips together and focused on the smeared red taillights in front of her.

Trucks like speedboats throwing up wakes roared past, while lightning sparked and laced the sky. "Mommy," Emmy whimpered. "I'm scared." She'd always been terrified of storms. Maybe because she was the way she was, and maybe it wasn't. Nothing about their life was normal, and it hadn't been normal for a little more than eight years. When Emmy had been born with Down syndrome.

"There, there, precious," Liberty said. "We're going be out of the rain soon. And then we're going to see Mama Jean. Won't that be fun?"

Not when the child's loving father was passed out drunk in his hideous marshmallow chair and Liberty's right cheekbone was throbbing dully where he'd hit her. The only time and the last time. They were fifteen miles away from him, and they had four hundred and fifty miles to go before she felt safe.

Was she doing the right thing in leaving? Her chest tightened when she looked at Emmy. Would Father Sam say she was wrong? They were close to the subdivision where he lived, and the green exit sign for Westbury Parkway loomed on the right. Liberty veered onto the off-ramp, heading toward the Westbury Plaza shopping center.

She needed to talk to Sam anyway. He'd tried to call her earlier, and she'd missed it. His message puzzled her. "Liberty, I need a friend to talk to, and I'd like it to be you. There might be a bit of trouble and I want a woman's point of view."

Sam was no stranger to trouble. That's the business he was in, you might say. And maybe he didn't want to bother Alicia with some kind of problem with his project, the one Liberty was helping him manage.

Just past the Waffle House a jumble of office buildings lined the road, and just past there, the road plunged into a string of subdivisions. In one of those subdivisions, Sam lived with his family—Alicia and two teenagers, a boy and a girl.

Liberty pulled into the Waffle House parking lot, asphalt glistening in surreal yellow light.

"Can we go home, Mommy?"

"No, sweetie. Come give me a hug." The child unbuckled and climbed into the front seat and Liberty held her and soothed her. Emmy buried her face into Liberty's shoulder and sobbed.

Liberty had to remain strong. It was easy to give Emmy what she wanted, but this time it wouldn't be good for either one of them.

"Now back to your seat," she said. "I need to make a call."

This time Emmy did as she asked.

Liberty drew her cell phone out of her bag and stared at it. The battery marker was sitting on one-quarter, and she'd lent Dallas her charger. How stupid could she be? She glanced over at one of the last pay phones in the city, scrabbled for some coins, and told Emmy she'd be in the phone booth. Rain pouring around her, she dropped in the coins and punched in Sam's number. Much to her relief, it rang. His voice mail answered, saying to leave a message.

The rain whipped against the door while she considered her options. Sam used voice mail to screen his calls when he was working, and she didn't want to record her quandary. No telling what she might say in her state of mind.

She hung up the phone and raced back to the car. What to do now? She wouldn't see him Saturday at Shadrach House and felt awful about leaving him in the lurch. He counted on her to keep the paperwork straight, and there was a lot of it these days. Grants, requests, twisted arms, anything to keep that center for fatherless teenage boys going. Anything to keep them out of gangs. She hated letting the project down, but she had to leave the city, go back to Maysville, the tiny town where she'd grown up with her grandparents. She hoped he'd understand. He already knew about her handsome, successful husband who could duck into a phone booth in his business suit and come out as Lex Luthor.

You think you know somebody—and then one day you find out you don't. Small-town girl gets dazzled by city boy, girl looks at floundering acting career, tires of Ramen noodles, and sees a safe harbor with one who cares. It had been wonderful at first. Had the wonder faded when Emmy had come along?

Had she been too busy with the child to pay her husband the attention he craved? Or had he felt angry because she had given him a child that wasn't perfect? Liberty didn't know. She struggled with her own understanding, was still trying to figure out just what Emmy had come to teach her. Sam had helped her understand.

Despite the steady downpour, the thunder had gone, and Emmy clutched her quilt for comfort during this strange car trip. Liberty wished she had something, someone to hold on to. If she could just have Sam telling her everything was going to be all right, she could face anything.

She pulled out of the parking lot, wipers beating, the car heaving sheets of dirty water.

She made her way toward Sam's house. As she turned into his driveway, a light flickered in one of the upstairs windows, and then the window went dark. Her heart quickened. He was here! Maybe he'd heard her car, spotted her, and was heading down to meet her. A space for the family minivan was gone, but his black Honda was parked in the garage. He'd told her that Alicia had planned to take the children to her parents' for the long Thanksgiving weekend. Sam planned to drive to Charleston to join them after tomorrow's ecumenical service at St. Chad's. Liberty pulled into the garage next to the Honda and doused the headlights.

"I'll be just a minute, Emmy," she said.

Emmy didn't say anything, but she looked resigned.

"I have to talk to Father Sam."

She wrinkled her nose, not understanding.

"In a minute. I promise." Liberty leaned over, kissed her child, and picked up the portable CD player from the floor. "Put on the headphones and listen to your Disney songs." She'd explain things to Sam at the door and then they'd be on our way.

Liberty's arms and legs felt like lead as she pushed herself out of the car. What would he think when he looked at her swollen face? What would he say?

She pressed the doorbell next to the laundry and mud room, hearing it chime inside, but all she heard in return was the drip of the rain. She leaned on the bell again, noticing a damp, oily, chemical fug. The shelves beside her held a jumble of garden tools, hedge clippers, lawnmower oil, and antifreeze. Clay pots of every size and shape jammed the corners, along with bags of manure and potting soil. Alicia must like gardening.

Maybe Sam was still upstairs and didn't hear the bell. She peered through the door glass and rapped firmly. A door that led to the kitchen gave a view of a black table lit by a geometric chandelier. The modern décor surprised her and didn't seem to fit with what she knew of Sam. On the table sat a white sandwich bag, a bottle of Schweppes tonic, and a Bombay Sapphire gin bottle.

Whoa. Surely Sam wasn't in there getting drunk, tonight of all nights. Okay, they joked about "Whiskey-palians" the term given to members of a church, unlike some, that accepted drinking, but she knew Sam didn't have a drinking problem. He'd had company earlier, surely, and the bottle was over half full.

He had to be here. She'd seen that light upstairs go off and his car was in the garage. Now what should she do? Was something wrong?

Liberty looked back at Emmy, under the spell of the headphones. No sense disturbing her. Rattling the doorknob, Liberty shouted, "Sam!" To her surprise, the door swung inward. She walked through the laundry room into the bright kitchen. "Sam? *Sam?*"

The black and white decor, the stillness, made the room colder and quieter. The dripping kitchen faucet sounded eerie.

On the left, a thin sliver of light sliced into the family room's darkness. She walked across the kitchen and tightened the faucet without success. Beyond the kitchen, living-room light revealed the dining room, where typed pages littered a glass-and chrome table. Stepping in, she noticed that some pages lay scattered on the floor. No one would give Sam any prizes for neatness, but something was wrong here. The hair prickled on the back of her neck.

She shrugged the feeling away. The pages most likely had to do with the Joshua grant they were desperate to win for Shadrach House. Neatness, drummed into her by Mama Jean, made her long to pick up the pages and square them, but she didn't have time. She didn't want Emmy to be frightened.

"Sam?" She stepped into the lamplit living room, where Sam's favorite picture hung—a street kid lounging against a wall watching a kickball game—out of sync with the rest of the decor. A teen-sized windbreaker lay crumpled on a white nubby chair; a forgotten coffee cup anchored a pile of magazines on the chrome sofa table. A black baby grand ruled over the room. Alicia had given up a dream of being a concert pianist to marry Sam, and now she taught music in the schools, as well as helping out on occasional Sundays at church. Would there ever be a day when women didn't have to choose between marriage and an artistic career?

"Sam?"

Liberty flicked on the hanging lamp in the entrance hall just as an unexpected boom of thunder shook the house. Was more rain coming? The suspended fixture shimmered; light from its beveled facets danced across the muted wallpaper, creeping her out. Liberty didn't know what was going on, but it was time she got back to the car and her child.

She stepped into the family room to take a shortcut back to the kitchen. Beyond the patch of light she tripped, pitching forward. She yelped in pain as her knee whammed the floor, and she looked to see what had thrown her.

A black running shoe, the kind Sam wore.

Her gut clenched, and in the dim light coming from the kitchen beyond she made out a dark-haired figure in T-shirt and black sweatpants sprawled on the wooden floor. Gin-drunk? No. His hand stretched forward, reaching for something.

"Sam!"

No answer.

She swallowed hard, crawled over to him, and touched his shoulder. His flesh felt rubbery, unresponsive. She watched for the rise and fall of his chest.

He was still, stone-still, still as . . . as death.

She struggled for her next breath. Sour liquid rose in her gullet as she set herself back on her feet. She was swimming through molasses and burnt matches, her mind dancing like water on a grill. Maybe she could do CPR, kiss him into life. Oh, God, was it too late?

She tried to roll him over, but the feeling of the cool flesh told her that it was much too late.

An involuntary scream tore into the dark room. A sea of black water was closing over her, and she was gasping for breath.

Emmy appeared in the doorway to the kitchen, blinking. "Mommy?"

"Emmy!" Liberty struggled to her feet and lurched to the child's side, murmuring soothing noises, and she hugged her daughter close to keep her from seeing Sam's body. How much would Emmy understand or remember?

"Emmy," Liberty said as calmly as she could, despite her trembling limbs. "We're going now."

Emmy pushed to see around her mother. "Who's that?"

"It's Father Sam. He's had too much to drink," Liberty mumbled.

"Like Daddy?"

"Ssh," Liberty said, and didn't know why. Nobody was listening. "Come on." Just then, the unmistakable squeal of a foot on a loose board upstairs made her stomach lurch.

Without pausing for breath, Liberty hustled Emmy out to the car, barely closing the door behind them. Was that a dog? A cat? Not even a St. Bernard would make that noise. Dear God, could it have been a person in the house?

Had Sam been murdered?

Liberty settled Emmy in and made sure her seat belt was fastened. Her little flower face scrunched up. "Mommy? Why did you scream?"

"I was scared by the lightning, little one." Liberty watched her trembling hand put the key in the ignition and turn it. Her mind roaring like the engine, she put the car into gear, backed up, and turned around. The sky opened up once more, pelting down, and she stared at the lights in the neighbor's house across the street. She couldn't go there for help. A strange woman at Sam's house when his wife was out of town . . .

She had to let someone know. Still, it would be awful if anyone got the wrong idea. They might have even thought she'd killed him, and she already had enough trouble on her plate. She gunned the car out of the driveway, headlights picking out rain-filled tire tracks muddying the grass. She knew she hadn't made them. She headed back to the Waffle House.

She ducked into the phone booth there and called 911, avoiding the dispatcher's efforts to get her name. When Liberty was sure she'd given the necessary information, she hung up and left, imagining a squad car right around the corner.

When they were many miles down the highway, city lights far behind, she told Emmy, "You must never, never say anything about our going to Father Sam's tonight."

"Why?"

"Because Daddy wouldn't like it," Liberty said. "He doesn't like Father Sam. He doesn't like for us to go see him."

Emmy considered this. "Okay."

Liberty worried. Did the child really get the message not to talk to Dallas about their visit? Would she make some slip later? Liberty knew she had to take the chance.

Dallas had frightened Emmy with his drunken tirades, with his lurching around the room. One of the most frightening things for a child is to see a parent out of control, and this child would never be able to reason her way out of it. Liberty didn't want Emmy to grow up afraid of her father. The memories of her own father shifted in shadow, but in the bright spaces were laughter and hugs, ice cream and air shows. Bedtime stories about brave girls who could do anything. The memories of her mother were more complicated.

Emmy lay down in the back, buried her head in the pillow, and pulled the quilt over her. When she was good and asleep Liberty stopped for a cup of coffee, bottles of water, and orange juice for when Emmy woke up.

Liberty plowed on through the rain by sheer force of will, wondering how far the storm clouds extended. Hands clenching the wheel, she made her way south to Florida down I-75, past Tifton, past Adel, past orange and pink Day-Glo billboards promising porn shops ahead.

Along about midnight the rain slacked off and then rippled away, and they were all by their lonesome on long highway stretches with just the moon and clouds overhead, a bright, full moon, a harvest moon. A big rig rumbled peacefully by from time to time.

Worries crept in. Should she have gone back home after she'd found Sam's body? Back to the man who'd hit her? And the next day, greeting her in-laws with a black eye? No. She wanted a pair of loving arms around her, telling her everything was going to be all right.

She wanted Mama Jean.

She tuned the radio to a late-night station: anything to keep her awake. Four hours had passed since she'd found Sam.

The police would have called Alicia by now. Or they'd call the senior warden first, and he'd be the one to call her. Liberty felt sad for her. She hoped Sam's wife had made him happy. Sometimes she felt he had some deep sadness within him, something that made him wary, but that was something he never talked about.

Tears welled in her eyes, and she choked them back. She had to keep going, though her muscles were cramped and her neck was aching.

She drove on through the black, black night with the lonely radio playing country songs, he-done-me-wrong songs, old-time songs. Patsy Cline sang "I Fall to Pieces" as the tires sang down the highway, the air outside getting warmer, Emmy sleeping to the rhythm of the rolling, a cup of truck-stop coffee steaming into the haze of the middle of the night.

A long dark tunnel with only a faint star at the end: that was what Liberty felt. What she had to do was keep driving—away from Dallas, away from any connection with Sam Maginnes, and away from the knowledge that someone, somewhere, wanted him dead.

Chapter Three

How could she explain her escape to her grandmother? The main thing now was to let Mama Jean know she was coming. When Liberty pulled off the exit to the state road after Gainesville, she gave her grandmother a call. Even at four in the morning, Mama Jean sounded awake, and very concerned. "I'll be there in about an hour or so," Liberty told her. "I'll tell you everything when I see you."

"I'll set the coffeepot on," Mama Jean said. Bless her big heart. She was used to setting the pot on for people, because she never knew who was going to come dragging in at five a.m. needing help and advice.

At last, head aching, Liberty steered the 4Runner into the sandy drive past her grandfather's shop, where he repaired TV sets and pre-computer electronics, up to a familiar white bungalow that stood under a live oak tree heavy with Spanish moss.

She was glad Mama Jean had turned on the porch light. Emmy, still sleeping, shifted and whimpered in the back seat. Liberty rolled down the window, took breaths of loamy Florida air, put her head down on the steering wheel, and cried.

The next thing she knew, her grandmother's hand was resting on Liberty's shoulder. Mama Jean's pale blue eyes crinkled with worry, but the rest of her—the tanned outdoor face, the permed gray hair, the flowered top and jeans, the Daniel Green Comfy slippers—looked the same as always, and Liberty was glad.

She blinked, foggy with lack of sleep. Had it all been some bad dream? Would she blink again and find herself on the kitchen floor at home? She sucked in a deep breath.

"What is it, honey?" Mama Jean's strong fingers stroked her shoulder. "What made you drive all this way? It must be bad."

"It was Dallas," Liberty choked out. She couldn't tell Mama Jean the rest—not yet.

The older woman shook her head. "I don't know what he did, child, to make you run off like that, but come on in the house before the skeeters get you out here. This is home, sugar. Let's get your bags in the house. You can tell me when you get ready." She pulled open the door of the SUV.

Emmy rose from the back seat and rubbed her eyes. She saw Mama Jean, broke out with her wonderful giggly laugh, and pushed herself out of the car. into Mama Jean's arms. Mama Jean grinned, just as delighted to see her great-granddaughter.

When they were under the porch light, Mama Jean caught Liberty's arm. "Let me see that face."

Liberty pushed her damp curls away from her face, exposing the puffy red welt beneath her eye. "Look."

Mama Jean drew a sharp breath. "He did that?"

"Uh-huh."

"Oh, honey." Mama Jean shook her head. "I never expected *that* kind of thing from him."

"You didn't like him," Liberty said slowly, realizing it for the first time. Her hands trembled with the effort of holding herself steady. She didn't want to come apart now.

Mama Jean shook her head. "Never did. Full of himself as an egg, that one. But you were so crazy about him, I thought it best to hold my tongue."

Emmy tugged on Liberty's hand. "Come on, leth go in!"

Mama Jean opened the door. "We'll talk later," she whispered. She nodded at Emmy. "She's still got that lisp?"

Liberty nodded. "She's had some speech therapy but could use more." She got out of the car into the woodsy early-morning smell, the scents conjuring up childhood. Insects chirred, and her throat caught. This was the place she had wanted to leave. Wanted to be sophisticated. Wanted to act in plays, maybe even by Shakespeare. Wanted to be a city girl.

The coffee was on in the kitchen and Papaw was waiting. "Hey, girl," he said, wiry white eyebrows shooting up. "Get you a cup of this. Ground them beans myself." He gave Liberty a bear hug, set her back, and narrowed his eyes. "Who have I got to shoot?"

"Later, Charley," said Mama Jean. "She'll fill you in later. Let the child be."

There was another smell coming from the kitchen, a warm, thick, oven smell. "I just put in the turkey," Mama Jean said. "Got up early to do it."

Of course. It was Thanksgiving Day. Her mind was still on the night before. "Mama Jean, did you have plans—?"

"George and Lucy are coming over," she said. "There'll be plenty for all."

"George and Lucy? I'd love to see them, but . . ." Liberty adored the couple that had been friends with her grandparents practically forever and hated for them to see her like this.

"You ran into the door? "Mama Jean said.

Liberty smiled. "I can think of something better than that." Papaw winked at Emmy and reached for a red-brown canister. "How 'bout some hot chocolate, princess? Let your momma get settled in?"

"Cool!"

"Come on," Mama Jean said, leading her granddaughter to the sewing room. Mama Jean had squeezed in a queen-sized bed for her and Dallas to visit, although he hardly ever came to see them. He fit their house awkwardly, like a giant in a woodcutter's cottage.

Mama Jean swooped some quilt fabric off the bed, folded it, and stacked it on top of the sewing machine. Liberty parked her bag on the floor beside the bed. Being there felt strange: it was home, and yet it wasn't. Not any more.

She sank to the bed as her grandmother waited, arms folded.

"Mama Jean, I made a mistake." Liberty felt a dumb need to defend her choice. "I never knew he drank like he did. He gets mean when he drinks. He's all right when he's sober. He's good to Emmy—he does love her, I know he does—"

The retort came fast. "If your daddy was alive he'd have gone up there and shot him."

Liberty shook her head, trying to recall the fuzzy memories of her daddy. If he'd ever raised his voice with her, she didn't remember it. "No, he wouldn't, Mama Jean. You know that." And then she smiled. Over the years her father's skill with a firearm had grown to be as legendary as Davy Crockett's.

"Your daddy would've made Dallas sorry he'd been born." Mama Jean gazed out the window, and Liberty followed her gaze to the moon hanging low in the lightening sky. "Your Papaw drinks too much from time to time, and when he does, he's just like he is when he's sober. Except for being a little stupid." She looked again at Liberty's cheek and ran healing fingers over it, fingers that could charm a dead plant back to life. "Is this the first time, baby? Has he ever hit you before?"

Liberty shook her head. "Only with words, Mama Jean. Words can make you feel you don't matter. Or no words. When he's, well, in his cups, it's like I don't exist."

She was a nobody to him then, just an irritation. Here, she was loved. Here, she felt warm and safe again. Here, in the little house.

She closed her eyes and tried to see herself back in Maysville, just Emmy and her in a trailer, or in a condo or duplex. Mama Jean was saying, "Maybe you ought to talk to somebody. There's a counselor in Gainesville that helped Lucy's daughter when she was going through a bad time. I'll ask Lucy for the woman's phone number if you want me to."

"I did talk to a counselor, Mama Jean." Her throat caught, and she felt tears coming. Sam had been the one she'd taken her problem to, and he had been so understanding, giving her recommendations for books about alcoholism. Suggesting she go to Al-Anon. She coughed and swallowed, trying to compose herself. "Mama Jean, I've read a lot of material." She told about the books she'd read on living with an alcoholic, of taking the steps they'd advised. She hadn't gone to Al-Anon, afraid she'd meet someone she knew.

Those books told her to make a life for herself. She'd started substitute teaching and doing volunteer work, looking for a full-time job as a drama teacher. The closest she'd come was a couple of after-school classes for kids with the county arts council. Acting for herself was out. Rehearsal schedules didn't mesh with Emmy's school, extra speech therapy, mainstreaming activities, and Dallas's traveling, not to mention the dance class for children with special needs.

What she didn't tell Mama Jean was that Sam's friendship had saved her sanity, had made it easier to stay with Dallas. And now Sam was dead and the waters were swamping her. She felt sickness rising in her throat, choked it back, and rested her head on Mama Jean's shoulder.

"I don't want to do anything for a couple of days. I just want to rest. Mama Jean, it's been so awful."

Her grandmother stepped away and placed both hands on her shoulders, inspecting Liberty. "Did that fool hurt you worse than you've told me?"

"No." She shook her head. "We've had fights, but he's never laid a hand on me before."

"Maybe that's just the start," said her grandmother. "Well, you just rest here for a while."

Liberty gazed around the room. On the wall, on the table, pictures were everywhere—pictures of her father as a child, pictures of him in uniform from Vietnam days, a citation from the Bureau for courage. Her mother, an autographed head shot and a promo photo of her on stage—Titania, from A Midsummer Night's Dream.

Liberty rose. "Let's get Emmy's things unpacked."

Memories of childhood Thanksgivings rushed back as Liberty carried Emmy's bag to the room where she'd spent her own young days. The glow-in-the-dark stars she'd stuck on the ceiling were still there, and on the bed was the same wedding ring quilt of Mama Jean's, and a shelf of books—Nancy Drew mysteries and *Stuart Little* and *James and the Giant Peach*—that brought her back to her upended childhood.

Mama Jean walked over and picked up a plush blue teddy bear that had tumbled off the bed. She arranged it along the pillows, among a collection of old stuffed animals. "Are you going to call him?"

Liberty set down Emmy's small blue bag. The unspoken question was whether Liberty really meant to leave Dallas. "I can't talk to Dallas. Not today."

"Mommy, Mommy," Emmy called from the kitchen. "I've got two marshmallows!"

"Great, precious," Liberty called back. She fingered the ear of a shabby brown teddy named Aloysius. Her mother had given him to her, already named after a character in some play or movie. Liberty had almost dragged the poor bear into shreds, like Emmy and her blankie, the baby quilt.

Aloysius had accompanied Liberty everywhere: to camp, to the doctor, to the hospital when a mysterious infection had laid her low, so low that her mother had made one of her rare trips from California to sit by her bed. The nurses hadn't liked Aloysius, called him smelly and germy. Mama Jean had washed him and brought him back.

Emmy, smug as a bandit, appeared at the door with her cup of cocoa.

Liberty praised its cap of gooey melting marshmallows and walked back to freshen her much-needed coffee. She took the steaming mug back to the sewing room, unpacked her clothes, then made space in the closet among her grandmother's old frocks.

How could she tell Mama Jean about finding Sam dead? She lived down here in her safe and tidy little world, growing her flowers, tending her son's memory and her husband's whims. She hoped Mama Jean didn't think Liberty was a runaway like her mother, Pamela or Paloma, as she now called herself.

Mama Jean had never quite forgiven Paloma for running off to Hollywood after Gavin McNamara died and then elbowing her way back—or perhaps having to sleep her way back—into her acting career. All those men she'd dated since becoming a widow, and not one lasted. Mama Jean never told friends when her widowed daughter-in-law was in one of those Lifetime movies, calling herself Paloma Morgan instead of Pamela McNamara, which Mama Jean considered a darn sight nicer name—and Liberty did, too.

Liberty finished her coffee and hung up a yellow knit top. Lord, what had she been thinking? Yellow was the last thing she wanted to wear. Black was more like it. She lay down on the bed to rest her eyes and her throbbing head. The next thing she knew, a phone was ringing. She blinked and rolled over and glanced at the bedside clock. It read noon.

Mama Jean appeared in the doorway, phone in hand. "It's Dallas. I think you need to talk to him."

Liberty shook her head and mouthed No, but Mama Jean nodded Yes, with one of her you'd-better-do-it stares, laying the handset on the bedside table.

Liberty struggled to sit, her mind jolting like a ship colliding with a large hunk of ice. Mama Jean turned to go. "Stay," Liberty waved. Her grandmother perched in a chair by the door and folded her hands.

Liberty picked up the phone. "Dallas?"

He cleared his throat. "Libby. I, uh, well, your friend Vivian called, kind of hysterical, if you ask me."

"Vivian hysterical?" *Yeah, uh-huh*, Liberty wanted to say. A real estate agent who wore designer suits was not usually the hysterical type.

"Said that preacher was dead. Wanted you to know."

Dallas always referred to Sam as *that preacher*. Liberty's mouth felt as if it were stuffed with cotton. She took long shallow breaths. What could she say? She squeezed her eyes shut. She was an actress; therefore, she would act. She shook out her hands, shimmied her shoulders, and said her lines. "You mean Sam Maginnes?" She sounded concerned. "Was it a car accident?"

"Oh, heart attack or something. You know Vivian. The woman rattles on so fast you can't understand half of it."

"Are you sure it was a heart attack?"

"I dunno. Not sure I heard it right."

Liberty felt faint with shock. The footsteps upstairs. No sane person would leave a heart-attack victim lying on the floor while they hid, turning off lights. Would they? Hadn't anyone suspected murder? She'd have to talk to Vivian herself.

"What else?"

"Nothing. Libby. I—uh, I want to say I'm sorry."

"You want to say you're *sorry*?"

"Well, ah, maybe I had a little too much to drink last night. You get to talking with these guys and you don't notice how many. When are you coming home?"

She took a deep breath. Could she do it? She glanced over at the bedside photo of her father and straightened her back.

"Dallas, I'm not coming back."

Eyes closed, she waited for him to explode.

Chapter Four

GIVING THANKS

"Libby, dammit, it's Thanksgiving Day."

Liberty could hear familiar voices in the background. Her in-laws, for whom she'd worked all the day before, cooking a Thanksgiving dinner. With recipes from Martha Stewart. All except the roasted turkey from the deli, thanks to Dallas.

Somebody else took the phone. "Let me talk to her." And then she heard the chirpy tones of her mother-in-law. "Hello, Libby, Happy Thanksgiving, dear."

This was insane, and also unfair. "Happy Thanksgiving, Marlene. Please let me talk to Dallas again."

Marlene ignored the request, as usual. "Please give your grandmother our best wishes for her recovery. How serious is it?"

Liberty blinked with surprise. So Dallas had invented a story to explain her absence. Okay, she'd improvise. "Pretty serious," she said. "The hospital discharged her this morning, but she's not out of the woods."

"Oh, dear."

Liberty heard muffled voices and then Dallas got back on the phone. She was fuming. "So you told them Mama Jean was at death's door?"

"What else could I do? So when are you coming back?"

"When she gets better, Dallas," Liberty said through her teeth. "And it's not looking very good. In fact, I think there's going to be a funeral pretty soon."

"A funeral?" Dallas blurted, and Liberty smiled. Somebody in the background, probably Marlene, gasped.

"Our marriage," Liberty said. "It died yesterday."

"I'll talk to you later," he said in clipped tones. "I'm taking them out for turkey."

And he hung up. So he was unwilling to serve the dinner she'd cooked for them—because she wasn't there to set the table and clean everything up afterwards.

"So?" Mama Jean said.

"I hate him. He told his parents that I'd come down because you were . . ."

"Yes, I heard. I don't blame you for being mad." Liberty's grandmother sized her up with one of her famous looks and shrugged. "I've got to get back to the kitchen. You splash some water on your face and come help. Lucy and George'll be here in half an hour." She was fond of Lucy and George, almost like an aunt and uncle to her. Their daughter was teaching abroad and their only son, Parker, her father's childhood best friend, had been killed in Vietnam.

"Oh, Mama Jean. I should have been helping you." The mouth-watering aroma of roasting turkey and dressing made Liberty feel guilty for sleeping the morning away.

"You needed your rest, honey. You drove all night." Her grandmother cocked her head like a curious bluebird. "I've got a feeling there's more on your mind than you've told me."

"No, Mama Jean," she said softly. But Jean McNamara had a keen intuition. That first awful summer Liberty had come to live with them, her grandmother had walked with her on the beach. Mama Jean showed the youngster how to tell there was a creature beneath the sand from the bubbles coming up. That intuition was detecting bubbles now, something below her granddaughter's spoken words.

The older woman slanted her eyes Liberty's way. "You'll tell me in your own good time, I suppose. Well, make yourself useful. Come slice the cranberry sauce." Then she winked. "Your favorite kind." Straight from the can with the little ridges on it, that was tradition. Not for her were fancy new recipes with fresh cranberries and stewed oranges.

"Give me five minutes to get decent for George and Lucy."

"Hmph. This is Maysville, and you don't need to primp."

Liberty pointed to her face, the shiner just beginning to turn, and Mama Jean nodded before she left.

Liberty blotted the area with cool water and combed her hair, and then applied make-up to the blueness beneath her eye. She cast a critical gaze at her handiwork. Maybe Lucy and George wouldn't notice.

Sam had once told her that her eyes looked sad when she talked about her marriage, and he hoped that someday he'd see them happy.

Strangely enough, Dallas was the reason she'd met Sam. Feeling isolated because of the drinking, she'd joined a women's group at church, hoping to make new friends. Her best friend Vivian, once her drama coach, lived on the other side of town and was always busy with work.

Sam Maginnes, a priest at Vivian's church, came to talk with the group about his Shadrach House project to help disadvantaged teenage boys by providing father figures, often missing in their lives. He wanted to recruit some men from as many churches as he could and hoped the women would convince their husbands to help. He could also use donations, and he passed out brochures.

He was interesting-looking rather than handsome, with dark hair and brown eyes, of medium height, and with a smile that overrode his seriousness. Curious, she'd asked him whether they worked with disabled boys. She had heard that a lot of marriages had broken up because of the strain of having such a child. He said they hadn't considered such boys so far, but he'd give it some thought.

She'd enjoyed talking with him, but she had to explain that Dallas traveled a lot and she knew he wouldn't be interested in that project. Sam nodded in understanding. And then, a month later when she saw Sam in a bookstore near the Cathedral, she was surprised when he recognized her.

"Liberty?" he'd said. "Liberty Chase?"

"Well, it's Father Maginnes," she'd said. "You remember me? I'm impressed!"

"Your name's hard to forget."

She shrugged. "It sounds like a subdivision in Philadelphia."

He looked at her with a winning smile. "It's a beautiful name. I'd have remembered you if your name had been Jane Smith. You paid attention and asked questions."

She shrugged. "Everybody scrambles for funding. I'm always interested in programs for kids who need help."

He raised his eyebrows, inviting her to tell more, but she decided to stay quiet. There was no reason to tell him about Emmy.

"So why don't you volunteer with us?"

"Me?" She put a hand to her chest. "Don't you need men?"

"We have some good men," he said. "But we need help with the paperwork, too, and I need all my men to work with the boys. It wouldn't be much—a few hours a week. I'll bet you're good at it. Did you say you were a teacher?"

She considered his friendly smile. He had a persuasive way about him, for sure. "Are you a politician?" she said. "Mainly I teach drama. But my daughter has Down syndrome. She keeps me pretty busy."

"Oh, we're all too busy." His tone was easy. "My wife teaches full-time, chauffeurs our two around, and helps out with the church music."

"Bully for her." Liberty turned away. "She's not married to my husband." Aghast, she realized what she'd let slip. Her cheeks flamed.

Now it was his turn to blush. "I'm truly sorry," he said. "I didn't mean that the way it sounded. I just wanted to encourage you." He touched her shoulder, and when she saw his rueful smile, she felt somehow comforted.

"Forget I said that." She smiled in return. "I'll ask Dallas for a donation for your shelter. He'll give money, but don't ask him for time. He travels for work."

Sam didn't leave then—he stood there radiating kindness. "Is there any way I can help you?" He swept his hand toward the shelf of religious books. "Were you looking for anything in particular?"

She'd been looking in the self-help section for books about alcoholics, but she'd read most of them. Was he— wasn't he—what are the signs—is it a game—what can you do—wife and children starve while hubby drinks the livelihood away—memoirs—the kids suffer. But her problem wasn't *that* bad. Hers was a genteel suffering, the sob-in-the-nicely-tiled-bathroom kind.

The books told her that nothing she could do would change Dallas's drinking habits. She could only work on changing herself, and the problem was, she was already so much Play-Doh. She'd wandered down to the religion section, looking for a way to stop changing and become who she really was. But who was she? The joy of acting was that you never had to be your actual self. She wasn't going to blurt out her agony to this Pied Piper. He'd probably tell her to take up her cross and bear it. Or even worse, tell her that she was the one with the problem, just as Dallas liked to do.

She told Sam Maginnes what she thought he wanted to hear. "Maybe I'm losing my faith."

Sam raised his eyebrows. She wondered if he could tell she was lying. Saying she was losing her faith wasn't exactly a lie: she wasn't sure if she'd ever had any. "I guess you hear that a lot," she murmured.

There was that smile again. "I'm more worried when I meet someone who's too sure." Almost like a conjuring trick, a copy of Thomas Merton's *The Seven Storey Mountain* appeared in his hand. He held it out to her. "This would be a good book for you."

"So now you know what's good for me? What's it about?" He looked so earnest, and also as if he *knew* something. Maybe she should listen.

He began to tell me of Thomas Merton's search for faith.

"But you said he was a city boy," Liberty interrupted. "You ought to see Maysville, where I was brought up. It's plumb eat up with religion, as they say there."

"And you've rebelled against the faith of your fathers?"

"Grandmother, actually. Staunch Methodist. I didn't rebel all that much," she said. "St. Ninian's was kind of a compromise. A good friend grew up in the Episcopal church and told me she thought I'd like it."

"Excuse me." A hefty man in a white shirt wanted to get by, and she sucked in her tummy to let him pass to the entrepreneurship section.

"How about a cup of coffee while we talk?" Sam gestured in the direction of the coffee shop. "I think we're blocking the aisles."

She glanced down at her watch. She still had forty-five minutes before she had to collect Emmy from school and take her to speech therapy. Maybe she could spare twenty minutes. "Just one, then," she agreed.

First, he convinced her she was going to like French Roast, then he convinced her to read the Thomas Merton, and then he told her a little of his work. He liked to use books and films to get lessons across to the kids he worked with.

"I showed them the film *Antz*," he said, "so we could discuss the desires of the individual versus the good of the social order."

"But it's a cartoon," she said. "With Woody Allen of all people. Hardly a good example."

"I don't see how Mr. Allen's personal failings . . ."

"He's ruined for me," she said.

Sam Maginnes raised his eyebrows. "That's something to explore, Liberty. Does a genius owe it to his public to conduct an exemplary life? Or do the very quirks that make him a genius somehow make it hard for him to behave as we would wish?"

"When the behavior was repulsive? Please clarify." She glanced down at her watch. "Oh, gosh, it's time to get Emmy. I should have left five minutes ago."

She jumped up from her chair, flushed with a coffee buzz and feeling almost drunk. It had been a long time since she'd had an intelligent conversation with anybody, and it was life-giving.

He rose and lifted her sweater from the back of her chair. He held it for her outstretched arms. "I should be getting along too."

She wriggled into the sweater and grinned at him. "Your flock needs tending. There are cliffs to fall off and wolves to eat them. The flocks, I mean."

He raised an eyebrow. "I have some good shepherds in my church, but yes." He reached into his jacket and brought out a card. He pressed it into her hand. "Call me if you have any more questions," he said. "I could recommend more books."

"Thank you," she said. "It's been refreshing."

She couldn't imagine talking like that with Father Pryor, the gentlemanly rector of St. Ninian's.

They walked toward the door. Liberty stopped to pay for the book, and Sam waited beside her.

"Hello, Sam!" she heard. And then two women were approaching them.

Sam greeted them and made introductions, telling Liberty that their husbands were two of his best volunteers. "I'm hoping that Liberty will join us," Sam said.

Liberty smiled. "We'll see. But I have to go now and pick up my daughter from school. Thank you for everything, Sam."

She had no intention of further complicating her life with another project. But Sam seemed so dedicated, so nice.

Still, she wasn't going to change her mind.

She fled before she could say any more.

Chapter Five

S he needed to find out more about Sam's death. And, probably, his life. Maybe that would explain what had happened to him. But how?

Mama Jean was happy to look after Emmy while Liberty went to Gainesville to buy a car charger for her phone and maybe hit the Black Friday sales early.

She also stopped at Barnes & Noble, where she found a couple of children's picture books on the sale rack. She thought Emmy might like them, and she did want the child to love books, not just TV cartoons and children's programs. Then she looked at newspapers. No Atlanta paper. As Liberty swiped her card at the register, the aroma from the coffee bar wafted her way. She glanced over and time went into freeze-frame.

A bristly senior citizen in a Hawaiian shirt was leaning across a booth toward a chunky woman in a yellow pantsuit, three-strap sandals, and buttercup hair. He was looking into her eyes, coffee growing cold. His hand gripped hers as if he was afraid she was going to bolt, but her face held a look of rapture, like an *aura*. Liberty's heart fluttered and twisted like a windsock. Would she have someone to love when she got old?

"Is everything all right, miss?"

The cashier, willowy as a mythical Asian princess, was holding out her package.

"Sorry. I'm okay. A dizzy spell." Her hand closed around the bag. "Would you tell me where the library is?"

"Of course." The young woman smiled and gave her directions.

Liberty nodded, thanked her, and stepped aside for the next person in line. When she found the library, she was heartened to see the paper she wanted on a shelf and took it to a table, almost trembling.

Then she drove away, back to the place she called home, her mind on what she'd read, and forgot to buy a charger. When she arrived, Mama Jean was spading the flower bed, while Papaw was propelling Emmy up and down the driveway, grasping the handlebars while she wobbled on her mother's old blue bicycle. He'd kept it oiled and greased and painted, waiting for the next child to visit. "Look, Mommy!" Emmy called out, with that infectious giggle.

"Short trip," Mama Jean said, her eyebrows raised.

Liberty waved her bag. "Got a couple of things. Just wasn't in the mood to shop."

Her grandmother nodded, but with a worried look.

"Good going!" Liberty called to Emmy. Would her daughter ever learn to ride by herself? Even so, she was having fun. Liberty walked inside, sat at the kitchen table, and poured herself a cup of coffee, brooding.

On the newspaper obituary page she'd found MAGINNES, Rev. Samuel H. in tiny type. It said only that the funeral service would be held at St. Chad's Saturday at 4:00 p.m. Survivors: wife, two children, father, two sisters, two brothers-in-law, a niece and nephew.

She'd plundered the metro news like a burglar but found nothing there, no mention of a crime. Maybe Duff Mowbray, the senior warden, had managed to keep it out of the paper—or perhaps she'd just dreamed the person upstairs, the light going out.

She caught a glimpse of her awful reflection in the pop-up toaster. The black eye had faded to yellow at the edges. That horrible night seemed unreal here in this familiar homeplace, with white clouds galloping across blue skies, fresh mornings that smelled of grass and trees, land that stretched on without views of yellow or red plastic.

Shoulders slumped, she slowly got to her feet.

Her throat was dry, so she poured a glass of water, cracked open an old-fashioned ice cube tray, and plunked three cubes in the glass before she filled it from the tap. She glanced out the window while she sipped. Mama Jean was planting bulbs, and Liberty thought of the bags of daffodils she'd just set out in the back yard at home, dreaming of a yellow spring carpet to cheer her while she sponged white plates at the kitchen sink. Whose flowers would she be admiring in March?

Mama Jean's phone rang, and Liberty reached for it without glancing at the Caller ID. "Hello?"

"Hey, baby!"

She nearly choked on a sip of water. "Hello, Dallas."

"So when are you coming home?"

"I'm not."

He cleared his throat. "Let me talk to Emmy."

"You're not going to use that child to get to me."

He sounded almost hurt. "I'm her father. She misses me."

She let some silence sink in. "You hit me, Dallas."

Now he roared. "You started it."

"I'm hanging up right now. You called me a bitch because I got upset about the turkey you forgot for dinner with *your* parents, and I did not appreciate your derogatory language. Yes, I swung at you with the stupid spatula but you came back with your big hard hand."

He finally took a couple of slow breaths. Then he said, "Jesus, Libby. Sorry. I did act kind of like an asshole. I didn't mean to."

Yeah. Uh-huh. She felt he was weighing his words, wondering how to string them together in the proper order, like a sales rep's trick he'd use to sell her The Remorseful Husband.

He sounded so sincere. "My daddy told me never to lay a hand on a woman. I just reacted without thinking. Just like then, I talked without thinking."

She let out a long sigh.

"Libby. I love you."

"Low blow, Dallas."

"I mean it. I'm concerned about you and Emmy. How will you live? What will you do?"

"We can stay here for the time being. She can go to school here. I can get a job."

"So will she have resources? The special ed? The speech therapist?"

Liberty was prepared for that. "We're not far from a major university. Maybe they'll have a program."

He paused and said slowly, "What about *The Nutcracker*?"

Oh. She'd forgotten about *The Nutcracker*. She hadn't mentioned to Emmy that they might not be going back. The kids in the Lorna Luna Dance Academy's class for special students were going to play baby mice in a production. They'd been rehearsing since September with the other classes, and Emmy was over the moon about performing on stage. Like Mommy. Like Poma, the way she said Grandma Paloma. Liberty had already sewed the costume, ears and all. Drama majors had learned how to sew, and she was a little proud of her work.

"*The Nutcracker.* I don't know," she muttered, feeling sick.

He turned slicker, smoother, full of patter. "I'm sorry, honey. I miss you. I miss Emmy. I want you home. I don't want Emmy to miss out on something so important to her."

"Do you miss me enough to change?" she snapped back.

"Change what?"

"I'm through talking." She hung up the phone. It rang again, and she turned her back. He'd try again later, but maybe by then she'd think of a way to let him know she meant business.

She drank the rest of the water straight down.

The Nutcracker. She felt as if a lead weight had settled on her chest.

Could she really stay here in Maysville? They didn't even have a school any more. There was a consolidated school a good hour away by bus. She'd need Florida teaching credentials for a job, and until she could earn them, there wasn't even a burger stand in town. This wasn't some romance novel where a cushy job house-sitting a local manor suddenly opens up for the distraught heroine. For one thing, there were no manors. And if there should be such a thing, there surely wouldn't be a wise and studly master arriving back from inspecting his holdings in Scotland. No such luck. Maysville had lost its last wise and studly young man when Gavin McNamara left town for college.

Right now what she needed was advice, and the source was out in the sunny yard. She'd just stepped out into the sunshine when Emmy hopped off the bike and came running. "Mommy! I can go with Papaw? Pleeease?"

"*Star Wars* film festival. Thought it would be a treat for both of us." Papaw rested the bike against a tree. Any and all electronic special effects were his catnip.

"Fine, princess. Now go wash your hands and brush your hair." Liberty ruffled Emmy's tangles. The princess squeezed her eyes shut and giggled.

"Liberty?" Mama Jean turned from hosing the new plantings, their fresh-earth smell tempering the heat. "I think I'll head into Gainesville to the mall for a couple of hours while they're at the movies. Christmas will be here before we know it. Want to come along?"

Liberty shook her head. "What if I run into any of my classmates?" She touched her eye.

Mama Jean gave Liberty a look she might give to a weed in her petunias. "Pshaw. Not likely. You don't need to stay here and stew in your own juice."

"I'm still wasted from that drive, Mama Jean. Maybe I'll take a nap."

Mama Jean stripped off her flowered gloves with the dirt-stained fingers and gave Liberty a skinny smile. "Good idea." She laid the gloves in the fancy gardening trug Liberty had sent her for Mother's Day. She'd sent Paloma, her official mother, a card and a silver-framed photograph of Emmy.

Emmy bounced down the front steps, shaking her hands dry. "Ready to go!"

After they'd left, Liberty hunched at the kitchen table and thumbed through the Gainesville want ads, the blue pansies on the wallpaper closing in on her. When she was little, she'd imagined the flowers' faces had watched her with pursed, disapproving mouths. She loved Mama Jean, but her grandmother had scary taste in wallpaper.

Didn't Thomas Wolfe write *You Can't Go Home Again?* The moment of appreciation for her homeplace was dissolving. Why did she suddenly miss her roomy house in that swim-and-tennis neighborhood, not too far from walking trails? Okay, in the city there was traffic and smog, but she'd loved decorating her house with yards of yellow linen and cotton and refurbished antiques. She missed her yard, where she'd dug and planted azaleas and pansies and impatiens and lilies-of-the-valley. If she stayed in Florida, she'd miss her daffodils coming up next spring. And oh, golly, *The Nutcracker*.

Shoving the paper aside, she picked up the kitchen phone and punched in Vivian Clark's number. Her husband, Romulus, taught at Westbury University, near

Sam's church, St. Chad's. Vivian had been Liberty's acting coach once, and they'd kept up over the years through long lunches, despite Vivian's giving up the greasepaint for real estate. Her friend loved both her job and her teenage step kids, and she'd encouraged Liberty to work with Sam. Vivian supported his project and thought the world of him.

"Where have you been?" her friend shrieked when she heard Liberty's voice. "I've been trying to reach you to tell you about Sam Maginnes."

"Dallas called and told me." Which was the truth.

"Hmph. He told me you'd gone to see about some sick relative. Wouldn't give me the number at first, saying the situation was bad. I bullied it out of him, of course. Where's your cell phone?"

"I left the charger at home. I ran off in a hurry and clean forgot to ask my granddad if I could use his."

"Your granddad?"

"I'm at my grandmother's in Florida. I've left Dallas."

The line went quiet for a moment. "Do you want to talk about it?"

"Maybe later." Liberty wished she could have a good heart-to-heart with Viv, but now wasn't the time.

"What are you going to do?"

"Try to knit back the raveled sleeve of life," she said. "Alone."

"Honey, life comes at you fast. It's not easy on your own. Rommy saved me from myself."

"Not everybody's as lucky as you, Viv."

"Or as determined to make things work."

Was this the beginning of a lecture? Another reason not to talk about it. "Tell me about Sam," Liberty interrupted. She had to know what had killed him. "What happened?"

Vivian breathed out, a *chuff*. "They think he had an asthmatic attack. They said if he'd only been able to reach his EpiPen, he might have survived."

"*Asthma?* So there was no question of foul play?" Liberty knew about the asthma. Sam had told her about it, joking about having to look out for bees among the flowers in cemeteries. He'd kept an EpiPen at Shadrach House, too.

"Foul play? What put that into your head? Come on, Lib. Who'd want to kill Sam? Smart, a little hard-headed, bullied people into doing good, yes, but *enemies?*"

"For one thing, wasn't it bees? How was there a bee in the house? In November? And as for enemies, you know there were those NIMBYs against Shadrach House." She'd opened a few of their angry letters and answered a few of their angry phone calls.

"Those people use other kinds of weapons," Vivian said. "Lawsuits, political wheeling and dealing."

"Maybe not all of them." Liberty, heart racing, tried to think. Just who were the people who called? Did she ever write down their names? Of course, and then she gave the notes to Sam.

Vivian was quiet for a moment. "I can't believe you'd go away and leave Shad House," she finally said. "You and

Sam talked me into donating a chunk of my last commission. What's going to happen now?"

Liberty's stomach dropped. "I was too involved in my own drama to really think about the boys. What my leaving might mean for them."

"Surely you don't think any of those *boys* harmed Sam?"

"No! They loved him," Liberty said, unwilling to tell Vivian about the night she and Sam had been working late at Shadrach House late and Rico had shown up with a knife.

Vivian was saying, "I'm sure that if there were any questions, the police would've investigated. Of course, they'll do an autopsy. Rommy says it's routine when someone relatively young dies suddenly."

"An autopsy! Will they test for poison?"

"Liberty, what on earth are you thinking? Somebody took him a batch of poisoned cookies?"

"Something's wrong here," Liberty blurted out. "Can people really die from asthma?" She had to stop herself from saying *when there are other people in the house.*

"Oh, yes, they can and they do. When I was in school, there was a boy in my class who died of it."

"Oh, my God . . ."

"You're *really* upset, aren't you, Lib?" There was a note above concern in Vivian's voice.

"Why shouldn't I be?" Liberty fought back the lump of nausea rising in her chest. "I liked him. I worked with him. We were getting somewhere with that project. We had a very good chance for that grant. We'd networked with all the right people; we knew what they were looking for . . . ." She took a deep breath. "How's . . . how's Alicia?"

"I heard she's a bit numb."

"It's bad enough when someone you love dies, but when it's sudden and unexpected..." Liberty felt tears rising in her throat.

She'd met Alicia only once. Sam had mentioned that his wife was having a hard time settling in at St. Chad's. Their last church, a large one where Sam had served as assistant rector, had been a place where Alicia'd had friends like herself, while St. Chad's, with a lot of academics and elderly faithful, hadn't been a place where she felt she fit in. "She grew up among social people," Sam had said cryptically and did not elaborate.

Vivian went on, "The funeral's set for four o'clock tomorrow afternoon. There's a wedding scheduled for noon. Those poor kids couldn't put the wedding off—everything ordered, tons of money spent. Josie Robillard will have to struggle through the service. Luckily, the wedding reception's elsewhere."

Liberty pictured the associate rector—petite, dark-haired, serious as an owl. She'd barely been in the job a year. "Poor Josie."

"She's strong," Vivian said. "Don't underestimate her. What about you? Will you be at the funeral?"

"I told Dallas I wasn't coming back, and I meant it. So I can't be there."

"You ought to be," Vivian said firmly. "You were his right-hand woman at Shad House. People will expect to see you. What does Emmy think about staying in Florida?"

"I haven't asked her, but she's basking in all the attention she's getting."

The silence grew, and she knew Vivian was thinking. "What are you running away from, Libby?" she finally said.

"I don't really know," Liberty mumbled. "Let's talk later."

She didn't want to go back to Dallas. She didn't want to go to the funeral. She might break down. But would it look strange if she didn't go? And the Shadrach House boys might expect her to be there. They liked to joke with her when they came, and they knew she liked them. What should she do?

Tears stinging her eyes, she stumbled to her old room and flung herself on the bed. It had been a long time since she'd prayed. She hadn't felt worthy of talking to God. But she thought about Sam and hoped he was with God.

Once he'd told her about lying in the desert at night, when he'd been in the Holy Land. There was no blackness like desert blackness, and it was cold in the desert. He felt small and knew why God loomed large to those early people. Civilized people don't believe in God, he said once, because they have nowhere to put him.

And what had gone through Sam's mind in those last moments, when he was choking, trying to breathe? Did he know he was dying? She tried to pray, and her prayer slipped away, and her mind slipped back into the afternoon when a group of adults had taken the boys on a hike.

Absorbed in conversation, she and Sam had fallen behind the others going up the trail and for a few moments it was as if they were all alone on the mountain. The sun was dancing through the leaves, and the trees high above hushed the forest on that fall afternoon. They could hear the boys ahead laughing and complaining as they tackled the steep, rocky terrain to the summit.

"I wish I'd had someone to take me on a hike," he said. "That's why I do this."

"What was your childhood like, Sam?" Liberty had always wondered.

"One day I'll write a book about it," he said. "I think you'll understand."

She looked at him, questioning.

He stared straight ahead. "It might be the end of my career."

"Sam, what do you mean?"

He turned and gazed at her with tiger-tiger-burning-bright eyes. "One day I'll tell you."

A shiver ran up Liberty's spine. Should she be a confidante? Ever since he'd disarmed the boy on drugs that night and she and Sam had hugged each other in thankfulness they were still on God's earth and breathing, they'd trusted each other enough to talk seriously. Would he tell her this secret?

She closed her eyes. She wasn't sure she wanted to know.

She awoke with her grandmother's hand touching her back. "Liberty Jean, I've been worried about you. Your grandfather took Emmy to see George and Lucy's new puppy so we could have a talk."

Liberty stirred then and rolled over and rubbed her eyes.

Mama Jean sat down on the end of the bed. "Something's bothering you besides Dallas, isn't it? I can see you coming down here on a tear, but the Liberty Jean I know would have been mad enough to call the police—or at least a lawyer—and put the fear of God into that man. You've been drifting here as though you're in shock."

She read the love and concern in her grandmother's eyes. "Maybe there's a lot you don't know, Mama Jean."

The older woman quietly waited.

Liberty sat up, gazed down at her hands, and then blurted out everything that had happened to make her leave home. The way Dallas had treated her, his drunkenness, her friendship with Sam, about stopping to ask his advice, about finding him dead. Mama Jean listened, not moving a muscle, not giving anything away. Liberty was afraid to look her in the eyes. "He's dead. And I'll never have another friend like him."

"Did you compare him with Dallas?" Mama Jean was sharp.

"Of course. Who wouldn't? But he would have tried to talk me out of leaving, I know he would've." She sighed. "Or at least urged me to see a marriage counselor. Again."

"Not bad advice," her grandmother said. "And I'll be sorry to see you go, but it's clear to me you've got to go back."

Liberty recoiled as if she'd been punched. "What? I can get a job here. I can find a place for Emmy and me so we won't have to disturb you and Papaw. "

The older woman frowned. "Liberty Jean McNamara, what are you talking about? You loved that man Sam, maybe good Christian love, but you loved him. Now he's dead, and you think somebody killed him. You've got to go back and find out what happened, or there will never be any peace for you. Tell the police what you know."

The tiny glimmer of light Liberty had seen on the horizon flickered out. She shook her head. "I can't let anyone know I was in his house that night."

"Why not? You were the one who found him. That would make you a witness."

She took the Kleenex her grandmother held out and swiped at her face. "What if they thought I . . . I killed him?"

Her grandmother shook her head. "They can rule you out. Do DNA testing, time of death, all that."

"Mama Jean. I touched him to see if he was alive. But it's not just that. It's his reputation. It's mine, if I want to divorce Dallas. What was I doing at his house at night?

People will assume the worst. Including child neglect for leaving Emmy in the car. A church scandal—that's the last thing St. Chad's needs, and Sam's family. And what about the grant for Shadrach House? That would sink it for sure."

Mama Jean considered, and then said, "You'll have to work just a little harder to find the truth."

Liberty looked at Mama Jean in wonderment. The pert woman with the determined expression was the same woman she thought she knew: wiry body, permed hair, strong arms, nimble fingers, flowers on everything. "Excuse me. Are you my grandmother?"

Mama Jean crossed her arms. "Right now, I'm Gavin McNamara's mother, and she knows this is what he would have wanted his daughter to do."

"But—"

"I'll be right back." She left the room and Liberty heard her rooting around in her closet. A few minutes later her grandmother came back, a folded white dish towel in her hands. "This was Gavin's," she said. "I want you to keep it."

Liberty took the towel, felt something hard and unyielding beneath. She folded back one flap, then another, and then she stared at the dark gray metal. "Mama Jean, I don't want a gun."

"Take it, learn how to use it," her grandmother said. "If Dallas touches you again . . ."

"I might shoot him and wind up in real trouble." Liberty shuddered and rewrapped the firearm. "It would be better if this thing stayed here, Mama Jean."

Mama Jean shook her head. "Take it."

Liberty laid the gun on the bedside table, the gun that had belonged to her father, and was relieved to hear the back door open. She slid out of the bed and walked out to meet her grandfather and her daughter, who were coming in the door, singing.

Chapter Six

T he house that Liberty had loved, the one she'd missed, seemed like a stage set now.

She guided the 4Runner to a halt in the garage, sweating like a marathon runner, aching as if she'd been hacking weeds and shoveling fertilizer all day. Her head buzzed with too much truck-stop coffee, and she was in no mood to play the Forgiving Wife or even the Show Me the Jewelry Wife.

The Nutcracker had won.

She'd hauled herself out of bed before the sun was up, and even so, had left later than she'd planned. Despite Mama Jean's advice, she'd refused to call Dallas to tell him she was coming back or that she was going to Sam's funeral. Emmy bounced up and down on her seat the last few miles. "I'll thee Daddy, Daddy."

When Liberty unlocked the door, Emmy dashed into the house and beelined to her own room, calling to her stuffed animals and dolls. In the kitchen, Liberty gritted her teeth at the red numerals on the microwave telling her that she had exactly forty-nine minutes to make it across town to St. Chad's for the funeral.

She didn't have any grown-up funeral wear, since she'd been just a child when her father died. She did have the gray suit she wore for meeting public officials and school principals, and that would have to do.

After swishing with a washcloth and spritzing with cologne, she tugged a black knit cami and the gray skirt over her damp body, then dragged a comb through her hair and slid her feet into pantyhose and well-worn black pumps. Next, she got on the phone and begged her next-door neighbor Netta Roberts to keep Emmy for an hour or so. Then Liberty put on her suit jacket, grabbed her bag, and propelled a squirming Emmy out the door.

"I wanna thtay home." Emmy tugged on Liberty's hand and kicked Mrs. Roberts' cypress mulch out of the pathway. "Where you going?"

Liberty didn't want to say that Sam was dead. It would just confuse the child, and besides, she wanted Emmy to forget about that night.

"I'm going to church."

Emmy considered this. "Ith not Thunday."

"It's a special church service," she said, "to say goodbye to somebody."

"Oh," Emmy said, furrowing her brow. "Father Tham?" They were standing in front of Netta Roberts's door before Liberty could choke out a reply.

Netta opened the door, smiling. She loved Emmy, because Emmy was always ready to play with Netta's grandson when he came over. "Come on, sweetheart," she said. "I have a surprise for you in the kitchen."

Emmy's eyes rounded as if Netta might have been beckoning her into her gingerbread house in the woods, oven heating up.

"Go on," Liberty urged. "I'll be back soon." Netta reached out and took Emmy's hand.

"Mommee!" Emmy looked back, wailing. "I wanna go home!"

Liberty shrugged, glanced at Netta apologetically, and hurried to the car, praying Emmy would settle down.

She gambled on the expressway and came up short. Halfway there, traffic ground to an inchworm's pace around an overturned tractor-trailer. Sweat crawled down her forehead and she licked it off the corners of her mouth. Maybe she should turn back. Maybe she shouldn't go after all.

It occurred to her that there might be a killer at the funeral.

They always said to look at the spouse first. Unthinkable. Maybe Alicia wasn't happy at St. Chad's, but that didn't mean she didn't love her husband. She surely wasn't a suspect. Yet if Liberty was going to find out if anyone had wanted to kill Sam, she needed to see who took his death without emotion.

In any case, Alicia wouldn't throw herself on the casket, or anything of the sort, because she was so ladylike. She wouldn't want to make a scene. Liberty needed to see the other people at that funeral, hear what they said.

Adrenaline and denial and sweat were her co-pilots. Her camisole clung to her ribs, even though a cool front was plowing in. Her hair was frizzing from the humidity. She didn't have time to be vain.

Arriving too late for the service, she hurried up the church walkway just as mourners spilled out of the church's side door and flowed toward the historic cemetery in the back. She wondered why Alicia had chosen to bury him at St. Chad's instead of in a family plot somewhere. A lot of this didn't make sense.

Liberty crossed the parking lot to the cemetery. The associate rector, Josie Robillard, walked beside a tanned older man with a mane of white hair and a craggy face, wearing clerical garb. Was this Sam's father?

Alicia, looking stoic in a Chanel-style black suit and pearls, walked behind them. Fifteen-year-old Katharine followed, hugging a black coat-sweater over a short skirt, and twelve-year-old Andrew in navy blazer and school tie walked along, chin up, hands in his pockets.

Just as Liberty caught up with the crowd, Alicia looked up. Her eyes widened for the length of one breath, as if she wanted to say something, and then she leaned toward a stout old lady in a hat.

Liberty was puzzled. Why on earth would Alicia have looked at her like that? All Alicia knew of her, if she knew anything at all, was that Liberty worked at Shadrach house.

And the one time Liberty had ever met Alicia was at Shad House, and then, not in the best of circumstances.

Now, at the cemetery, Alicia had gazed at her for a minute thoughtfully. Why?

A piney aroma wafted from the trees beyond the fence, blending with the scent of freshly dug red clay. Liberty scanned the crowd until she spotted Vivian, smartly dressed in a navy suit, her short red hair and pearls catching the afternoon sun.

Her friend was talking to Gracelyn Rodgers, the church secretary. Tall and slim, fiftyish, Gracelyn wore her silver hair in a side-parted pageboy, and she clutched her black-and-white tweed coat to her chest with black-gloved hands.

The mourners took their places and the graveside rite began. A light damp wind stirred. Someone coughed in the heavy silence. A small boy in red suspenders, a nephew perhaps, held the hand of a tall copper-skinned woman in black. Liberty spotted three boys from Shadrach House who'd been special to Sam—Jesse Everly, Cedric Jackson, and Rico Santiago, the boy whom Sam had counseled that day, the boy who'd tried to rob them once. Rico was now almost like one of Sam's children.

When the service ended, the family members walked in procession back toward the church. The tall woman, still holding the hand of the boy in red suspenders, walked directly behind Alicia, who wore no hat or veil, the wind whipping her pale hair across her pale face. When Alicia saw Liberty she gave her another look, more intense, and then Sam's widow walked on.

Liberty took a deep breath and walked away from the coffin on its straps, away from the pile of earth under the fake grass mat. Tears spilling, she swallowed the lump in her throat and pressed a damp tissue to her face.

When a friendly hand rested on her shoulder, she felt her knees go weak.

"Libby? Are you all right?"

She forced a weak smile. "Vivian!"

"Sorry," said Vivian. "You looked a million miles away. I didn't see you at the service."

"I just got back from Florida," Liberty said, with a grateful warmth. "I would've made it on time except for a wreck. Not mine," she hastened to add.

Vivian gave her friend's shoulder a comforting squeeze. "It must be awful for you. All that drama with Dallas and now this . . ." She gestured, waving her hand at the bier. "You must be exhausted. When did you last eat?"

"Sometime on the road." Liberty gestured vaguely. There had been a McDonald's along the way, a chicken sandwich for her and a burger for Emmy.

"Come to the reception in the parish hall. You need some strong coffee."

Liberty nodded. "I ought to speak to Alicia." She had to find out what Alicia's strange look meant, if it meant anything at all.

"Of course." Vivian patted her friend's shoulder as they joined the receiving line in the church hall. Facing Alicia, Liberty took the outstretched hand, warm and damp from the pressure of many others. "I'm so sorry," she heard herself say. "He was a wonderful man to work with."

"Liberty Chase," Alicia said unevenly. "I'm so glad you came."

"If there's anything I can do . . ."

"Oh, yes. Yes, there is." Alicia gazed at Liberty with brimming eyes.

What could it be? Her stomach clenched. "Of course. What . . ."

"That's so good of you." Alicia squeezed Liberty's hand. "Can you come by the house Monday, around ten? I'll explain it all then."

"Yes, but . . ."

Alicia was already glancing toward Vivian, so Liberty moved on to Sam's children, Katharine and Andrew, and to

Sam's father, the Rev. Aubrey Maginnes, the white-haired man she'd seen earlier. He nodded at Liberty's words of condolence and gave her in turn to his wife, a sweet-faced grandmotherly figure in a mauve dress. It struck her that Sam didn't resemble either of his parents.

"What did Alicia want you to do?" Vivian murmured, hot coffee at last in hand.

Liberty sipped at her steaming cup. "I have no idea. I've only met her once." She tried to keep her voice level. Had Alicia found out that she'd been inside the house the night Sam died? Did the widow suspect Liberty had anything to do with his death?

She couldn't tell Vivian about that horrible night. She couldn't tell anyone.

Instead, she gazed around the room at Sam's flock, most of whom she didn't know. "Who's that?" She nodded toward the tall woman she'd seen earlier, noting the long black hair braided down her back. Her black skirt swept the floor, and a black shawl covered her shoulders. Her silver earrings gleamed in the overhead light.

Vivian frowned. "I'm not sure. Someone told me she's Sam's sister."

"Yes," Liberty said slowly. "He told me he had an adopted sister. He didn't mention she was Native American."

Vivian nodded. "I think he said something about her in one of his sermons." She reached for a lemon square and held it out to Liberty, who shook her head.

"No appetite." Liberty sipped at her coffee.

"I know I encouraged you to work with Sam," Vivian said. "But don't you have your hands full with Emmy?"

"I know people think it's weird," Liberty said. "But I didn't want that child to become my whole world. I've seen some parents spend all their time, money, and energy trying to make their special child into a "normal" person. I decided to accept Emmy the way she was and go from there. It was good for my sanity to help kids with different concerns. Those boys. Without fathers. You know. They're susceptible to gangs, to cults, to radicalization."

"Cults?"

"Religious cults. Mind control. The one we're fighting right now tells poor white boys that they were chosen by God. Next thing you know, it's abuse, radicalization, or poisoned Kool-Aid. Then there are the Black and Hispanic kids that suffer from being marginalized and want to join gangs to *belong* somewhere. Sam was just so fervent . . . ."

She stopped when saw a familiar figure approaching.

"How are you, Liberty?" The Reverend Foley Manning, his salt-and pepper-beard matching his gray suit and black clerical shirt, hugged her, and then he reached over and took a brownie from a doily-covered plate. He'd partnered with Sam to found Shadrach House.

Liberty shook her head at the proffered brownie. "Vivian, do you know Foley Manning, from Apostles?"

"Vivian Clark. I'm happy to meet you," she said as they shook hands. "I've heard about your good work with Sam."

"This is a sad day, honey." He folded his hands in front of him. "I don't know what we'll do at the House. Well, Libby, you and I can talk later; I've got to round up the boys I brought." He shook his head. "They're the ones who'll suffer if the House goes under."

"Foley, we'll be in touch," Liberty said. "The program mustn't die." She glanced over at the boys hunched awkwardly by the door in jeans and clean shirts.

"It was Sam's baby. Without him . . ." Foley shrugged, palms upraised, and took his leave. He walked over to a red-eyed Rico and clapped a hand on his shoulder.

"I guess I'd better be going, too." Liberty set her empty coffee cup on a tray.

Vivian slid her cup beside it. "What were you going to tell me earlier? You started to say something, then stopped."

"No. Forget it. It was nothing."

"Nothing? You had a look of panic. Was it to do with Dallas?"

Liberty let out a long breath that she didn't realize she'd been holding. "It's like this. I really meant to leave him when I went to Florida, but then there was Emmy. She adores him. I still don't know what I'm going to do. He's Dr. Jekyll and Mr. Hyde."

"Would he go to counseling?"

"Maybe," Liberty said. All she knew was that if she was to have any chance of finding out what had happened to Sam, she had to buy some time. Time to get her head on straight. Time to let Emmy perform in *The Nutcracker*. Time to find out if Dallas would change.

Time to find out who the real Liberty McNamara Chase might be.

Chapter Seven

ROSES

As she drove the miles toward home, Liberty, still wondering why Alicia wanted to see her, recalled the day Alicia had fluttered through the door of Shadrach House with a desperate look. "Where's Sam?" she had asked. "I can't get him on the phone!" Her voice held the slowness of coastal South Carolina.

Liberty smiled, hoping to calm the flustered woman. "Hello, Alicia. I know you from your picture on Sam's desk. I'm Liberty, or Libby, if you like. Sam's in the office with Rico, and he must have turned his cell off."

"Your office phone is busy too," Alicia accused.

Liberty gave her an apologetic smile. "We let the boys use it. Sometimes they don't have one at home. Can I help you in any way?"

"Oh, I don't know . . ." She frowned and glanced around the room. "So here is where he spends all his time?"

"Well, a lot of it, I guess, "Liberty said. "You haven't been here before?"

"There hasn't been a reason." Sam's wife must have felt the boys at the pool table looking at her and turned her head away. Of course the boys would look. Alicia was pretty, with pale fair hair and long elegant fingers. Liberty wondered about the piano. Did Alicia regret giving up her career?

Sam must have heard Alicia's voice, for he poked his head out the door. "Well, this is an honor, Allie."

"Sam, I need to talk to you."

He nodded. "Come on in." Rico slouched out of the office and over to the Coke machine.

Sam closed the office door behind them. When Liberty heard the raised voices, she felt surprised. She walked outside and watched the traffic. She didn't want to know their business.

Alicia hurried out, face set, without saying goodbye.

He never explained why Alicia had come that day, and Liberty never asked.

Dallas still wasn't home when Liberty arrived at six-thirty. A good thing. Emmy was happy as a fat frog, a tiny smudge of chocolate in the corner of her mouth, when she was picked up from Netta Roberts's house.

"Mrs. Roberts spoiled your supper," Liberty chided, and the child giggled. And then frowned.

"What for thupper?"

"Well, young lady, we're having take-out." Dallas didn't deserve any home cooking, and anyway, she was tired. She'd stopped on the way home at Raoul's Deli.

That evening, the take-out food in the fridge, Liberty dumped her uneaten Martha Stewart Thanksgiving soufflés and casseroles down the disposal, then scrubbed the bowls while Emmy bounced on the back yard trampoline with Bianca from across the street. The bouncer was a sneaky way to get the neighborhood kids to play with Emmy, and Dallas had sunk it into the ground so no one would get hurt.

The kids were out in the back yard belly flopping, little-girl energy on high. Liberty had just finished scrubbing the last bowl when Dallas strode though the door, carrying a huge bouquet of red roses.

Liberty ought to have been touched by the flowers, but she was afraid the gift was just another empty gesture. Still, she raised her hand from the suds in greeting and shucked off her gloves.

"Hello, baby." He flashed the smile that had once turned her to mush. He leaned a kiss toward her, and she presented her cheek. He pretended not to notice and planted a smack on her lips. And then he stepped back with a look of concern. Of solicitude.

"You're beat, aren't you?" he said. "I called Florida from the office and found out from Jean that you'd headed back. I tried to call but you didn't answer. Guess you were driving. I'm so glad you're here, honey."

Liberty bit her lip. He thought his famous charm had worked. He presented the roses with a flourish. "I mean to make it up to you, sweetheart."

Taking the bouquet, she sank her nose in the petals and thought about the flowers at Sam's church: wedding flowers and funeral flowers, all on the same day. "Thank you, Dallas, but . . ."

"But what? Libby, I . . ."

Emmy slammed through the back door with Bianca, leaping into Dallas's arms. He was a good daddy when he was sober. He bantered with the two girls while Liberty found a vase and arranged the roses, snipping the stems underwater the way Mama Jean had taught her.

"Stay to supper, Bianca?" she asked casually. Anything not to be alone with Dallas right now.

He shot Liberty a look, but the little girl said she had to go. She gave a gap-toothed grin and sprinted out the door and across the street to her own house.

"I've made a decision," Dallas said. "We'll talk later."

Liberty spread out fried chicken, coleslaw, and potato salad on the table and heated canned vegetable soup. Dallas, now in jeans and sweatshirt, made himself into Fabulous Hubby: pulling out her chair, filling her water glass when it became empty. She stayed quiet, while he talked like the

Energizer Bunny on steroids, outlining where he thought they could go from his new starting point. "We'll go places, take family trips. Why don't we go out west? See Yellowstone? Or, if you want to stay closer to home, Take Emmy to Disney World?"

First things first. Liberty said slowly, "Those are good suggestions. But first, what about nights right here at home? Any change there?"

He flashed his winningest smile. "I'll stop going out with the guys," he said. "You and I can have a date night. Take in a movie."

"Mm," Liberty said. She wished she could believe him.

Emmy plowed through her food like a good little trooper, keeping an eye on both parents, watching them like a fox waiting for a chance with a chicken.

Dallas grinned at Emmy. "How was Florida, sweetheart?"

"Fun, fun," she said, so excited that she forgot her easy speech. Sometimes she had to repeat herself before going onto the next word. "We saw, we saw, we saw, *Star Wars*."

Watching her husband pay fond attention to his daughter, Liberty felt that this Norman Rockwell family scene, after what had happened, was unreal. She might as well be outside, peering in at strange people through the bay window by the kitchen table.

"You're mighty quiet tonight," Dallas said.

"Sorry," she said. "I've been to a funeral. It was so sad."

"That preacher."

"Uh-huh."

He shrugged. "Guess you'll have to find something else to do with your spare time, huh?" He shoveled a big forkful of potato salad into his mouth.

"The shelter will go on," she said, tight-lipped, "and I'm going to be right there helping."

He pointed his fork at her. "Listen. I know about these things. Without your preacher friend, it'll fold, and things will get back to normal."

"What do you think is normal?" she shot back, getting a glare in return. So Sam was gone and they would get back to normality? Their lives would close around the empty space Sam left like a lake does when you pull out a dead body?

The two of them silently finished their food, letting Emmy do the talking.

That night Liberty curled up in the king-sized bed, her back to Dallas, staring out at the black night at a solitary star. He leaned over and kissed her neck.

"Dallas—"

He smoothed her hair, and she quivered like a horse. "I want to make it all better," he said. "I want to start over. Talk to me, baby. Wasn't it good, one time?" He stroked her back, kneading into the muscle, rubbing the touchiness away as you might massage a cramp. He put his arms around her and hugged her to him, spooning.

He held her there, speaking slowly, seductively, not forcing anything. Comforting her.

He was all she had right then between her and the big, black, empty space out there beyond the sky. She turned to him and buried her face in his warm shoulder. He murmured, "I'm going to make it up to you, baby."

She closed her eyes and imagined Dallas so many years ago, when they were just married and she thought he hung the moon. Tenderness sometimes could do what lust could not. The waves washing over her were like the breaking of a dam. She had cried that day, and now the tears had all been spent.

She did not sleep. Dallas beside her slept on. He was going all-out to get her back. He had brought her roses, red roses. Blood-red roses.

Why? Was he really saying he was sorry? Did he want her undivided attention that much? Maybe enough to *kill*?

Chapter Eight

A licia seemed too composed to be a grieving widow.

That was Liberty's first impression, as the widow guided Liberty to the back yard deck, saying that her mother was busy in the house. The fog rose off the grass under a partly clouded sky, the air cool. Alicia wasn't in black but wore a white silk blouse and black slacks with flats, a pale blue cardigan over her shoulders. Today her fair hair still looked perfect, expertly cut so it would fall into place without trouble. Her hand held a lighted cigarette.

Liberty couldn't hide her surprised look, and Alicia gave Liberty a rueful smile. "Now you have my secret," she said. "I don't let anyone from church see me."

The widow took a long, grateful drag, smoke drifting into the wind. She gazed into the distance, and then waved the cigarette toward the sliding doors that led into the house. "Sam hated it. They all do. But I *enjoy* smoking." She glanced down at the withered grass. "Lord knows I need *something*. Please sit down, Liberty." The cigarette swept toward wrought-iron patio chairs.

Liberty sank down in a damp chair, chilling her jeans. She didn't like smoke but understood the need for comfort, especially now. Alicia settled across from her, left elbow resting on the chair arm, and flicked ash into a small clay pot.

"What a lovely ring!" Liberty blurted. Alicia's ring, its artistic pattern of golden twigs and deep green emeralds reflecting the sunlight, was far from ordinary.

"Pretty, isn't it?" Alicia gazed at the stones. "We had it made by a custom jeweler. Emerald's my birthstone, and we were married in the same month, May."

Liberty gazed beyond the deck, where tan lion heads of spent hydrangeas bobbed in flower beds heaped with pine straw, and a brown winter lawn stretched under the twisted dry vines of a shaggy arbor. "What did you want to talk about, Alicia?"

"The manuscript," she said.

"What manuscript?" Liberty froze. Had Sam written something—maybe something that someone wanted to suppress?

Alicia drew her brows together. "Didn't you know about it?"

"No," Liberty said, and then she remembered the hike with the boys where they'd talked. "Come to think of it, one time he mentioned he was writing something. He didn't talk about it."

Alicia tapped her ash into the clay pot. "He was writing a memoir."

A memoir. About himself, which he hardly ever talked about. "So why are you telling me this?" She looked squarely at Alicia, blood pounding in her ears. "How does this concern me?"

The widow took a drag of her cigarette. "Oh, dear. Maybe it wasn't you at all."

Liberty froze. "Maybe it wasn't me *what*, Alicia?" Had he been having an affair with somebody? Was his touchy-feely manner not just his caring nature?

"He told *someone* about his writing." Alicia shook her head. "I used to hear him on the phone talking about it. He'd stop when I came in."

"He didn't talk to me about it," Liberty said. "And I don't have a clue who he might have talked to, unless it was Duff Mowbray."

Alicia dismissed Duff Mowbray with a swipe of her hand. "Maybe it wasn't the memoir at all," Alicia said. "Maybe he was having an affair." Now the bereaved woman gazed out toward the garden bench, cigarette smoke spiraling toward the sky. "After all I gave up for him."

"Please, Alicia," Liberty said, eyes closed. She was beginning to shiver from the chill in the air and the dampness under her derrière. "I'm afraid I can't help you."

"No, of course. Sorry." Alicia lowered the cigarette to the clay pot and stubbed it out. "I hoped you knew about the manuscript. You see, I want to ask you to finish it."

"Me?" Liberty squeaked. "Why?"

Alicia lifted the box of cigarettes from the table, inspected it, and set it back down. "He sold the book. A friend of his at Dove Books—religious publishers—wanted it, gave him a contract even though it wasn't finished, and paid him a small advance. Of course, he spent it right away on those boys."

Liberty remembered the time he came to the center, jubilation in his eyes, waving a check he'd received that would buy a computer and accessories. A donation, he'd said.

Alicia leaned forward now, speaking softly. "I'd prefer to fulfill the contract than have to repay the money. After all, I'd like to find out what was in that memoir, too. Someday."

"He never showed it to you?" Liberty blurted.

Alicia shook her head. "He always told me he didn't want me to see it until it was ready. He was afraid I'd object to letting him tell his story, and he'd be unable to finish." She paused. "I didn't want to insist. And now, I'm afraid of what I might find."

Liberty understood, but if his story was that dreadful, she didn't want this task at all. "Don't you think, under the circumstances, the publishers might just forgive the advance?" The big question to her was why the memoir of a forty-five-year-old suburban priest should be worth the telling, interesting enough to attract a publisher. What had he done? He'd never told stories from the pulpit about himself, unlike others. She felt a chill run down her back.

"I'd like to help, but . . ."

Alicia interrupted, "Maybe they wouldn't ask for the money back. But you knew Sam. He worked hard on this. It meant a lot to him. So I felt a duty to put it out there. It will be his memorial."

"I can understand that, Alicia, but I still can't understand: why me? Surely there are those more qualified."

"Look, Liberty," she said, worrying another cigarette out of the pack. "You teach English, don't you? Surely you can string words together."

"No," she said. "I mean, I'm a drama teacher. I teach English sometimes, but as a substitute. Look. You can hire a ghostwriter. I know a good one, and I can give you his phone number." He was one of the few writers she knew who could support a family with his books.

Alicia managed a weak smile. "Well, this is dramatic, wouldn't you say?" She took a small silver lighter out of her pocket and turned it over in her hand a couple of times. "You worked with Sam, you knew the project, you knew the people. Oh, surely you can write. How much would you charge?"

"I'm sorry . . ."

Alicia flamed the lighter, took a long draw, and got up from her chair, lost-looking as she contemplated the leafless trees. Liberty unfolded herself and rose too. Shivering, she was ready to run to her car.

Alicia kept her gaze on the skeletons of the trees. "People ask me if I'm going to carry on with the project, with Shadrach House. It isn't up to me. It's up to the people of St. Chad's and Apostles, though it was very much Sam's personal vision. But one thing I can do for Sam is to see *this* commitment carried out."

"I hope you do."

Still Alicia gazed into the dead garden at the rising fog. "Are you saying you won't do it?"

Liberty chose her words carefully. "Maybe somebody more qualified . . ."

Alicia pivoted to face Liberty and burst into tears, choking out, "I want to get *rid* of this manuscript. I want to *forget* about Shadrach House. He was *absorbed* in it. He was *fanatic* about it. It was worse than any *mistress*." She hiccuped and dropped the unfinished cigarette into a deck flowerpot, where it hissed out in the dampness.

Liberty's face warmed enough to take the chill out of the air. She realized that Alicia was overwrought, maybe finally letting go after keeping her feelings suppressed for the funeral. Good Southern ladies always kept their poise. She stared down at the deck, at the lines and whorls of the planking, at the knuckles of her useless hands, at the dead cigarette. When she looked up, Alicia was facing her, arms by her side. *"You* cared about it. He talked about you, you know."

Liberty sucked in a deep breath and trailed it out. She wasn't about to ask what Sam had said about her. "Foley Manning cared about it, and he's the one who'll be carrying the project."

Alicia shook her head. "Foley, bless his heart, is well-meaning and sincere, but he's not very good at writing. At least that's what Sam told me. Say you'll do it, Liberty. Liberty closed her eyes, seeing her grandmother. Mama Jean would be asking her if the cat had got her tongue. Mama Jean would say there might be clues to his death in the manuscript.

Alicia caught Liberty's gaze and gave her a winsome smile. "There's no need to be creative. All you need to do is to collate the material, edit it, and fill in anything else that he wanted to go in. I'll give you the pages he left here. Gracelyn Rodgers has more at the church. Honestly, she thinks she owns the book because she organized his rough drafts and typed them. You might have trouble with her, but I don't want her to complete it."

Liberty wondered why not. She might find out if she said Yes.

All that was left of Sam was this manuscript, and it scared her. Maybe she didn't want to find out. Maybe she just wanted to remember the Sam she'd known, didn't want to know about feet of clay. But maybe she needed to see those feet. Maybe that's why he wrote the book, so people would know the real Sam.

She swallowed. "Okay," she said. "I'll do it."

Now Alicia smiled for the first time that day. "Thank you very much. I'll give you what I have now. Good luck with Gracelyn."

Alicia had just taken a step toward the sliding door to the kitchen when the door rumbled back, and Alicia's mother, in a purple silk warm-up ensemble and thick gold jewelry, stepped out, frowning. "Honey," she said, "Mr. Milton's here to see you."

"All, right, Mother." Alicia's shoulders slumped and her face fell. "The next-door neighbor," she waved her hands. "He once accused Sam of trying to poison his dog. You know Sam. He wouldn't hurt the dog's *fleas*."

"Alicia, maybe this is a bad time. I can get the manuscript later." Liberty put her hand on the rail of the deck steps.

"Wait, Liberty. Mother, tell Melvin I'll be right there. Wonderful news! Liberty's agreed to finish Sam's manuscript."

"How nice," Alicia's mother said blandly.

Liberty got the feeling the older woman wasn't mourning Sam. Why?

"Just wait here, and I'll get the pages." Alicia and her mother disappeared behind a curtain, and Liberty, alone on the deck, felt as if she was on stage and the play was about to begin, and she had never even read the script.

She hugged her sweater to her in the chilly sunshine, watching two crows rock across the pine straw. Sam had mentioned the conflict with the neighbor, about the dog in question tearing up Alicia's flower beds. Upset, Alicia had threatened the neighbor with calling the police. When the dog had died some time later, probably of old age, Melvin Milton had accused Sam of poisoning his pet with anti-freeze.

Then Melvin had called the police and blamed Sam, but most people in the neighborhood had anti-freeze and the dog was old and tended to wander away so the police told Melvin to stop harassing Sam or Animal Control would be at his door to investigate negligence.

Sam hadn't taken Melvin seriously; thought he was just an old grump with not enough to do.

What was keeping Alicia? Maybe Melvin had cornered her after all. Liberty gnawed her lower lip. Had she agreed to a project that would keep her from having time to investigate Sam's death? The sun peeked out from behind a cloud and warmed her shoulders, but she didn't stop shivering. She stuffed her hands inside her sweater sleeves, just like the old man in the Chinese ancestor portrait Paloma had given them for a wedding present.

The sliding glass door rumbled on its tracks and Alicia, pulling a beige rubber band around a stack of paper, stepped out. Liberty straightened, remembering. Was this the work she'd seen spread out on the table the night Sam had died—or been murdered?

"Sorry," Alicia said and sighed. "I had to talk with Melvin. He had to tell me how sorry he was." Her eyes brimmed with tears. "I wanted to tell him he was a little too late to be sorry, but I didn't."

"You know Sam would think that was right." Liberty took the manuscript, as warm in her hands as a living body. She guessed it had been kept on top of the refrigerator.

It was time to go.

"Alicia," she said, her foot on the top step of the deck. "If you don't mind my asking, do they know what was the cause of . . .?"

Alicia looked blank for a moment, and then frowned. "Asthma. Surely you knew."

Liberty nodded. "I knew he was allergic to bees, but there weren't bees in the house this time of year."

Alicia gave a deep sigh. "We're still trying to figure that out. He reacted to penicillin, too, but there was no penicillin in the house. Andrew had an ear infection, but I made sure to pack all his medication when the children and I left." Her voice caught and her eyes teared. She'd been holding herself together for her visitor, and now she was breaking down.

"Be easy, Alicia. I'll help however I can. I'll keep you informed about the work." Liberty walked down the deck steps, across the yard, and through a wooden gate to the driveway. She headed toward her car at the curb. How long would it be before Sam's lab results came back? She knew it took some time, not like in the movies or on TV.

She'd read enough detective novels, seen enough crime shows, to know that trails grew cold and clues disappeared. Alicia seemed to be a frustrated woman, though she loved Sam. The comment about "what she gave up . . ." Didn't she know he was in the church when she married him? Did she really suspect him of an affair? Could she have been putting on a grieving act? But she struck Liberty as the kind of person who didn't want others to see her cry.

Crossing the lawn, she noticed Melvin Milton walking over to his house. When he spied her, a broad smile spread across his face. An *aha* smile. He changed direction and hurried towards her.

What on earth did he want?

Chapter Nine

MR. MILTON

The outstretched hand and toothy grin didn't make her feel better. She clutched the manuscript with one hand and took his hand with the other. Quickly.

"I recognized you. Melvin Milton, next door." Late fiftyish, maybe, Melvin had patchy gray hair covering his dome, a red complexion, and a beer belly.

"I'm Liberty Chase." She waited, willing herself to be calm. "I don't think we've met?"

"Huh," he said. "Honey, I've seen you around."

Honey. Ugh. "What do you mean? When?" The pit of her stomach clenched, and she held on to the manuscript like a life raft. Had he seen her come to Sam's house that night?

"That your car?" He pointed to the 4Runner.

Liberty nodded.

"I seen it over here maybe once or twice." He slid his eyes to see how she'd react, but she kept her face in poker style. He went on, "I got downsized a few months back. Gets pretty boring talking to wise-ass young jerks on the phone about a job. The neighbors are better than TV sometimes." He nodded toward the house. "I'm sorry the guy is dead. I wouldn'a wished it on him, even though he was a hypocrite." The neighbor's eyes a little shy of a leer, he waited for Liberty to give herself away.

She wasn't taking the bait. "What do you mean? I don't understand."

Melvin Milton made a spitting sound. "He poisoned my dog."

Liberty's shoes gripped the earth, her suppressed anger ballooning. "Look, I'm sorry about your dog, but Sam didn't have anything to do with it."

"You married?" His leer came on full force.

"Why do you ask?" She closed her eyes in exasperation. "Look, Mr. Milton. I've got to go." She choked out, "Sam loved all God's creatures." Tears flooded unexpectedly, running down her cheeks, dripping off her chin. She tucked the manuscript under her arm to reach for a tissue from her bag. The manuscript slipped to the ground. *Oh, spit.*

Melvin Milton's face got soft. "Aw, don't cry." He patted her shoulder, then leaned down and picked up the pages, still tight with Alicia's rubber band. "What's this?" He read the first page's heading. "Chapter Five?"

"It's a manuscript Sam wrote." Liberty took a deep breath and held out her hand, afraid he'd start reading. "Alicia gave it to me to finish because I worked with him. With the boys."

"Well, I'll be damned," he said.

Liberty hurried on. "If you saw me come here the other night, it was because I was bringing him some information," she lied. She wanted to keep this witness talking. Maybe he could be helpful. "Mr. Milton," she said, "the day before Thanksgiving, the day Sam died, did you see anyone else come here? Earlier?"

"What?" he asked, smiling conspiratorially. "Some other woman? You jealous? I know *she* left. I saw her leave with the kids."

Liberty closed her eyes and prayed for strength. Maybe she could play it that way, confirm his suspicions that hanky-panky was going on. It might come back to bite her, but she had to get the information. "Oh, gee," she said, acting worried. "So you did see a woman?"

He looked her up and down. "You're a cute chick," he said. "Maybe I did, maybe I didn't."

Now Liberty's muscles tensed, and she wanted to snatch the pages from him and slap him with the thick paper. This shifty-eyed lizard just wanted to have something on Sam. Okay, on with the act. She leaned forward a little and batted her eyes. "Mr. Milton, please tell me," she murmured. "Everyone who came."

"You poor, misguided kid," he said. "Three cars. A Lexus, a Chevy, and one of them little sports cars. Old one. MG or something like that. I don't know if there was any women."

"You didn't see the drivers at all?"

"Only the guy in the Lexus. I went out to get my mail about the time he came. I noticed him because he looked like David Niven. You know that old movie *The Guns of Navarone?* God, that was a great flick."

Just then, a Dodge Neon the color of a bluebottle fly pulled up to the curb and a red-haired woman of about forty-five, ample curves stuffed into a blue knit dress, slid out. "I gotta go," said Melvin. Finally, he thrust the manuscript at Liberty. "There's my girlfriend, Rhonda."

Liberty pressed the pages crossed-armed to her chest. "Girlfriend?"

His brows knotted. "My wife died a couple years back. Cancer. I know what you're going through. And even *her*." He nodded back toward Sam's house.

"I'm sorry," Liberty said. Melvin's sympathy was confusing her. Maybe the man had tenderly cared for his wife. "It's been nice meeting you," she said. "Goodbye."

"So long." He waved at Rhonda and walked a few steps toward her. Then he stopped, and a knowing look spread across his features. "Oh yeah. I didn't want to tell yuh."

"What?"

"There was a lady who pulled up right as I was leaving, but I was in a hurry because Rhonda gets pissed if I'm late, and I was late on account I had to see the end of the game."

"What kind of car?" He'd already seen a sports car, a Lexus, and a Chevy.

"Just a lady's kind of car, that's all I noticed. Avalon, something like that."

"Okay, Mr. Milton. Thank you."

"Any time. And call me Melvin."

"Melvin? What color was the Lexus?"

"Damned if I know. I'm colorblind."

All the way home, a big lump in her throat, Liberty slumped in despair about editing the manuscript, about trying to be a sleuth. She missed Sam. She wanted to talk all this over with him, ask him what she should do. More tears slid down her nose and she swiped at them, wiping her hand on her jeans.

She had to get hold of herself. There wasn't an Audi—that was good. Kind of hard for Dallas to attack him if he was in a bar after work. The David Niven man in the Lexus—a thought kept nagging. Was that one of the board members of Shadrach House? It'd be easy enough to check that one. Then there was the old sports car. She could ask Alicia, but she didn't want to bother the poor woman too much.

Someone else could've arrived after Melvin *said* he'd left for his date. She thought of the car tracks she'd seen beside the driveway. Someone had roared off in a hurry, careless about the grass. But who had the person upstairs been, and where was his—or her—car? Had the person parked down the street and walked or come over from next door?

There had been no signs of a struggle or a break-in. Sam had known whoever came to see him, and he was no tea-sipper. He'd swung hammers at Habitat houses and would have swung fists at the boys if he'd had to, so nobody overcame him and shoved a pill down his throat. Nobody suffocated him. The bottle on the table nagged at her. Penicillin in the gin? Or maybe anti-freeze?

Back home, she laid the manuscript on the desk in her kitchen where the telephone sat, under school papers and phone notes and coupons, junk mail and rubber bands and half-mugs of cold coffee. She'd need a free hour and a quiet house to read it. Good luck there.

The truth was that she was scared to death. Was she going to see a different Sam—not the Sam she would have gone to *war* for? She didn't know if she could stand it. The only way she could postpone the reading was to plunge into work. It wasn't hard to do, especially since flu was going around and she'd been called to teach the next day.

NOVEMBER 28

The students were deep in the study of *Julius Caesar*. The girls were fierce into cliques and the boys into sports teams and best buds, and they couldn't comprehend Brutus's betrayal of his friend.

Liberty explained that it was the central dilemma of Brutus's character—his personal feelings or to save Rome, for the Senators felt that the very existence of the Roman republic was being threatened by Caesar's dictatorship. One girl wanted to know how that related to the current administration, but that was a question Liberty wasn't prepared to discuss. She told the student to ask Miss Jones and turned to something she knew how to do well. She divided them into groups and gave each a scene to be performed in class.

While the groups were busy talking and planning, she had time to reflect on her situation. Caesar was murdered for wanting to be king. But why would anyone want to kill Sam? Dallas could be violent; she knew that quite well. And the flash of—was it anger, or just frustration? — that she'd seen in Alicia's face seemed to have deep roots.

Would either person kill to get Sam out of the way? Alicia because she was disappointed? Dallas because he was jealous? No. What about the boys Sam worked with? Did one of them have it in for him?

She thought again of the time Rico had come to the center, high on drugs, when she and Sam had been there alone. But Sam had calmed him down. No, the boys all respected him and liked him. Were there some toughs outside the group, who didn't want Sam to poach their potential gang members? Would they have gone after him? Risky.

And that mysterious past she had yet to discover, that odd feeling that something about him was a bit off. Had someone come to settle an old score?

Who was the person he'd talked with on the phone about the manuscript?

The classroom bell rang. "Homework," she called, as the students gathered their books. "Work on those scenes. Try to memorize your lines. We'll perform them tomorrow." They groaned as a matter of course, but she knew they'd have a blast.

At home that evening, even though she was tired after an afternoon of *The Nutcracker* rehearsal, she made a complicated gourmet dish, one that called for couscous and julienned carrots and shallots, maybe to make up for even *considering* Dallas as a murderer. Dallas drank his Diet Coke before dinner and complimented her on her cooking, something he rarely did. He was trying hard to please her, and she was trying hard to trust him.

For the next few days, Sam's manuscript had to wait. Friday there was *The Nutcracker* performance, then another performance on Saturday, then a Sunday matinée.

The first performance was magical. Emmy was ecstatic in her costume, proud to be a baby mouse, and Liberty watched the performance with growing pride and a lump in her throat. Dallas videoed the performance like all the other daddies and swore he was going to show it to all their friends and relatives.

During the last performance, the matinée, it was Liberty's turn to be stage helper in the wings, ready with needle and thread and encouragement and lipstick. She let her thoughts drift to the manuscript waiting for her back home. She'd have to face that stack of paper soon, and she didn't want to see another version of Sam. She wanted the one who had listened to her troubles and told her that she was stronger than she thought. Told her that she could handle things. Told her he believed in her.

Finally, that evening after supper, the sounds of TV football rolled into the air. Dallas, with Diet Coke and Fritos by his side, settled into the hideous marshmallow chair. Liberty fed Emmy, sent her for a bath, and then tucked the exhausted child into bed.

To the usual soundtrack of their weekends, she cleaned up the last of the pizza boxes and salad containers. "Forgive," said Jesus, "seventy times seven." She'd forgiven Dallas for his drinking and the mean things he'd said to her four hundred and ninety times, she was sure, before he'd hit her. Did she get to stop at 491?

She realized that she hadn't really forgiven. She'd swept it all under the carpet and the lump was getting bigger and bigger. She was perched on a pile of grief and regret, and Dallas was drinking Diet Cokes. Dear God.

She picked up the manuscript and peeled off the top sheet, a blank sheet of blue paper on which Alicia had scribbled MEMOIR. She walked with it into in the living room, among all of her favorites—the stone Egyptian head, the silk tassels on the old china cabinet, the leather-bound Shakespeare plays—the accumulations of a woman who'd tried to find comfort in pretty things.

Her heart pounding, she snapped off the rubber band, sank to the sofa, and peeled back the title page.

I am a liar . . . it began.

Chapter Ten

THE MEMOIR

I am a liar.

The Sam Maginnes you know, that the world knows—priest, husband, father, friend, colleague, citizen—all those labels by which one associates himself in the world—is a Sam Maginnes who was born some years after the boy upon whose frail shoulders he stands, born with the help of lies.

This book is the story of how the man became the man despite the fractured life of the child, perhaps because of that life. The story now told I hope, in some small way, will help Shadrach House carry out its mission. If Shadrach House had been there for me and my friends, three young people might have been saved.

Some people wouldn't have predicted a good outcome for those young lives, born in poverty, brought up on meaner *streets. But as wildflowers spring from sidewalk cracks, heroes and saints can spring from cracks in the human heart. A longshoreman philosopher once told us that the mass of people is rich with talent. And, I might add, with heart and possibility. It takes hope—a path out of despair—to make that talent bloom. Add faith and love, and miracles happen.*

Not many people gave me much of a chance, and the reason I am here today is because of a remarkable man, Aubrey Maginnes, whom I have always called my father.

He became my father when I was fifteen years old.

"I am a liar . . ."

It's all in this book, the truth behind all the lies. The lies that began when I turned up, a fourteen-year-old runaway, in the soup kitchen of a strange church in an unfamiliar town in Florida.

Liberty turned the page, heart in her throat, to see what came next. What lies had he been talking about? What lies? The chapter that would have explained what he meant was missing.

She flipped through the chapters, back, forth, searching for a mention of his early life. What had happened before he'd turned fourteen?

Hello! So he'd won a scholarship to law school? He'd worked hard and graduated second in his class; nothing surprising about that. That was the Sam she knew—charging ahead, overachieving, leading with his heart. Wait. What was this? He'd changed his name from Tony after hearing the biblical story of Samuel, who'd been dedicated to the service of God as a baby and chosen to lead his people?

As she skimmed the pages, she realized that in all the time the two of them had talked so much and had developed a lovely rapport, he'd told her nothing about his growing up. They'd shared disasters and dreams, but the past had been a shadow, an enormous cloud of fog.

She turned to the pages about Alicia. The brilliant law student had met the beautiful music major at a concert, and their mutual passion for Bach had spun out into more concerts, spring walks under the blooming dogwoods on campus, trips to her parents' summer place at Hilton Head.

Alicia's parents were cool to him at first. After all, he was a nobody from St. Augustine, even if, as the son of a clergyman, a respectable nobody. He didn't play golf or tennis. He did fish a little, and enjoyed running, especially on the beach. For her parents he trotted out all his charm, and starry-eyed Alicia made them come around to accepting him.

Sam's goal had been to work with the poor—legal aid work—but Alicia's father, a corporate lawyer, managed to convey the message that he'd approve the marriage if Sam would build up a substantial income before he ventured into pro bono work on the side. Working for the poor was all well and good as long as Alicia was provided for, and in fact, he was prepared to offer Sam a job.

Alicia, torn between the comfortable life she'd lived and the ideals of the man she loved, urged him to accept the offer. Didn't Jesus say ye have the poor always? He could surely get back to them later.

Thoughtful, Liberty returned the manuscript to the crowded kitchen desk. It was then she saw the stack of mail Dallas had brought in Friday and Saturday. She hadn't had time to go through it between *The Nutcracker* performances and the household chores.

Among the bills and junk mail she found a creamy envelope, postmarked California, the address in a familiar royal blue handwriting with its swirls and flourishes. Liberty grimaced. *Oh, spit.*

Emmy, freshly bathed, in pajamas and sleeping socks, had reappeared with her quilt and saw her mother with the letter. She gave a questioning look.

"It's a letter from your granny Poma."

Emmy's eyes shone. "She ith coming?" Her California grandmother, who usually appeared trailing clouds of scent and indefinable glitter, entranced her.

Darling, Liberty read aloud,

I was so sorry not to be able to spend Thanksgiving with all of you, as we couldn't take time off from the new project. Thank God I have one. I don't think I'll be able to come for Christmas, after all. (Liberty had invited her to spend Christmas in one of her less sane moments.) *You remember Bruce: things are rather precarious and he has proposed a Hawaiian cruise.*

I'd better take it, dear. Know I love you, and I'll send you and my precious baby some pretty things very soon.

Love, Paloma

"She's not coming," Liberty said.

Emmy's sweet face fell in disappointment.

Liberty felt relieved that she didn't have to deal with Paloma, but on the other hand, it would have been nice for her mother to put her own concerns aside for her family just once. Paloma had never wanted her daughter to call her Mother—it made her seem too old, Paloma said.

Angry, Liberty stuffed the awful letter into the trash. Why did she care? Maybe it was because of Emmy. "I mith Po-ma on Cwithmath," said Emmy and sniffled.

"Maybe she'll come later." Liberty gave her daughter a tissue and settled her at the kitchen table with some Play-Doh. Then Liberty edged out of the room and slipped into the living room with the manuscript.

Forgetting, for the moment, her gadfly mother, she settled on the sofa and read Sam's words. His day-to-day routine in his father-in-law's office—the deeds and deals and contracts that were his bread and butter—bored him and made him feel he was wasting his time. When he came home from the office, he endured rather than enjoyed Alicia's conversation about music and her friends, whom he thought were shallow. After dinner he buried himself in his study, rereading Plato, Augustine, and Jung. Alicia, feeling neglected, clamored for a baby. A baby would set things right, she said. A baby would calm his restlessness and give life the meaning he was seeking.

He had doubts about the power of fatherhood, but he loved Alicia and wanted to please her.

Liberty lowered the pages thoughtfully. What would Alicia think when she read this part? Would she be crushed? If she had known what was in the memoir, would she have asked Liberty? Or maybe she *did* know what was in the pages and didn't care.

Liberty read on. One winter Alicia had asked Sam to take her for a weekend at her parents' place at the beach, hoping that time away from the city might restore some of the closeness that had been ebbing away from their marriage, as certain as the tide carrying away the sand.

He'd agreed on going away for the weekend but suggested that nature might give him the answers he sought for his restlessness and proposed that they choose a wilder place. But Alicia wanted familiarity and comfort, arguing reasonably that her parents' beach house at Hilton Head would cost nothing.

They'd only arrived at the cottage an hour before his life changed forever.

While Alicia made a trip to the store for supplies, he'd been walking the sands alone, the vastness of a gray sky around him, fog blowing, and the water kicking up. He studied the sand as he walked, asking for guidance, asking for help with the direction of his life. Then the winds shifted, and the sand became golden with brilliance as the sun split the clouds, and his face became warm, and it seemed that the fog in his mind became clear too. He wanted to fulfill his childhood dream, one which he'd been afraid to pursue because he wanted to get so far from his childhood. Only then would he feel whole.

And then he wrote:

I came in from my walk, my clothes damp, smelling of the tide and my exertions, my face flushed from the chill. My heart was racing. I couldn't wait to tell Alicia of my happiness. She'd understand, of course she would. I flung open the door.

Alicia, wearing her favorite sweater, a pale blue cashmere, had returned and was sitting on the rug, her back to me, in front of a driftwood fire in the big stone fireplace.

"Allie, I . . ."

She turned with a smile on her face and said, "Darling, wouldn't it be heavenly to have a place like this of our own? We could spend every other weekend... smaller of course, maybe in one of those wild places you like . . . Daddy would help . . ."

I grew numb with apprehension, but I couldn't turn back. It was time to tell her. I knelt on that rag rug beside her, took her hand, and looked into her eyes. "Do you love me?"

"Of course I do," she said. Her eyes met mine but slid down to her hands, where she twisted the ring we had designed together.

"It would be nice to buy a beach house. But I'm afraid we can't."

Her head jerked up and she looked at me again with a hint of anger, or was it fear? "Why not? When you make partner . . ."

"I'm not going to. Allie, I . . ."

She interrupted. "Of course you are. Daddy . . ."

How could I make her see? I took both of her hands. I kissed her and said, "Alicia, my heart hasn't been in that job for some time now. I want to tell you something. Something I felt on the beach." Surely now she would understand.

Her face blanked in confusion. "What do you mean?"

My eyes must have shone. "Alicia, don't you see? I think I'm called. Like my father."

"Oh, my God," said Alicia.

"Yes," I said. "I need to talk to my father first."

We sat for a long time looking at the fire. After a while her body softened and she relaxed against me. I thought that meant she'd finally accepted it.

He followed that heartfelt paragraph with the notation that he'd called Aubrey, and they talked long-distance for an hour. Liberty wrote in the margins: *ask Aubrey Maginnes what they talked about.*

He didn't say what else had happened that night, but a little over a year later, when he entered the Candler School of Theology, both Alicia and little Andrew came with him.

Liberty's stomach ached with recognition. Alicia wasn't the first woman to marry a man she'd conjured up. And poor Sam—he'd misjudged Alicia too. *We see through a glass darkly, and then face to face.* Once she was face-to-face with the man she'd married instead of the man she'd thought she'd married, she must have been bewildered. And Sam? Perhaps he'd felt that love would conquer all.

But there had been enough love between them to go on, hadn't there? Or had it been pride, willfulness, unwillingness to admit making a mistake, a dogged determination to make the best of things? Maybe all of it. Had she never known his true background? Perhaps that was the reason she was so undone now. That's why she didn't want to deal with the manuscript. It brought back painful reminders of what might have been.

Liberty skipped to a later chapter, heart in her throat, looking for anything that might shed some light on his death. Any scandal? No scandal should touch him now. Nothing should discredit his work or jeopardize the funds for Shadrach House.

She found a chapter about the project, describing a house where boys who needed a helping hand, boys who might be attracted to gangs, boys who had no men in their lives, who'd been in minor trouble, could come and hang out, get counseling, find role models and advisers. He had so many wonderful plans. She found nothing out of order.

She shuffled through the papers and found a paragraph of credits, and there was her name, mentioned as one of the "many fine people" who helped with Shadrach House. Part of the story, the part that would tell his early life, tell about what formed him as a child, that would tell her about the Sam Maginnes nobody knew, was missing.

She had to know the rest for herself, whether it had anything to do with his murder or not. There were two puzzles—Sam's mysterious background and his untimely death. Were they connected? That night, these very pages had been scattered on the table, had fallen on the floor.

Had someone been looking for an inconvenient truth?

Chapter Eleven

Now, after a week filled with substitute teaching and *The Nutcracker* rehearsals and performances, a wonderful time for Emmy but an exhausting one for Liberty, she knew it was time to face Gracelyn. Maybe the secretary wouldn't be as difficult as Alicia feared. Surely Gracelyn would want to see Sam's book published.

After Emmy was in school, Liberty drove to St. Chad's unannounced. What greeted her was a cacophony of buzzing saws and pounding hammers, and her chest tightened with regret and sorrow when she saw the white Lopez Construction van. Workmen in jeans, jackets, and coveralls bent over saws in the parking lot, carried buckets and tools. One was taking a smoke break.

Sam ought to have been here to see that his plan was going ahead. He had breathed life back into the little church, raising enough money and enthusiasm to start the hammers. He'd planned to convert attic space into a workroom and two offices, freeing up square footage below for a conference room.

It gave her a funny feeling to be at Sam's church, knowing he'd never be there again. She passed a row of nandinas loaded with reddening berries, then walked past signs reading *Preschool*, *Parish Hall*, and *Office*. She stepped inside.

The musty smell of aged wood and a faint whiff of incense hit her as she entered the reception area, where Gracelyn Rodgers sat at her desk and, with perfectly manicured nails, flipped a Rolodex. Liberty supposed the woman was used to the old system and would sanction no newfangled computer address books.

A door behind the desk was half-open, and Liberty heard the whine of a copier.

"Gracelyn?"

The older woman's silvery pageboy didn't move as she turned. A fleeting shadow passed across her face, melting into a Southern-belle smile. "Oh, hello, Liberty. What can I do for you?"

"I need to talk to you," Liberty said.

The smile froze in place. "About Shadrach House?"

"About its survival. We can't lose it. It meant too much to Sam."

The secretary picked up a piece of paper and fingered it. "Well, you're welcome to try."

Outside, a saw whined and ground to a halt with a sputter. "Gracelyn?" Liberty leaned forward, stung, unable to hide her confusion. "We thought you supported us."

Gracelyn folded her hands primly. "I supported whatever Sam wanted to do." She left unspoken but *he's no longer here*. Her gaze trailed around the area but found no one else who needed her attention. Still, she lowered her voice. "This renovation is costly. I don't know if pledges will come in without Sam. We may have to cut back."

The smell of pine rosin drifted by, and the hammering, in violent syncopation, started again. Sam's office door stood ajar to the right of Gracelyn's desk, and Liberty half expected him to come out smiling, holding out both hands in greeting: "Liberty, *cara*, you're here . . ."

She swallowed the rising lump in her throat. She had a mission, and she must be strong. She straightened her shoulders and spoke. "Alicia has asked me to finish Sam's memoir. I've come for the rest of his chapters and notes."

The older woman stared with shock and set her jaw. She clipped her words. "I've done a lot of work on it. I don't know why Alicia didn't ask me."

Maybe because you two don't like each other? "I'm sure she didn't want to add to your duties." Liberty smiled and adopted a soothing tone. "Sam always said you were overworked. He wanted to hire an assistant for you."

Gracelyn's raised feathers smoothed just a little. "I don't need one. I can handle everything." Just then the door to the copy room opened fully, and Liberty froze where she stood, hardly breathing, half expecting Sam to come out.

Josie Robillard—her petite stature, dark hair, and round wire-rimmed glasses reinforcing the nun-like impression she made—walked out with several sheets of paper and a book in her hand. She gave Liberty a regretful smile. "Liberty, how nice to see you."

Liberty nodded. "You too, Josie. I came over to talk to Gracelyn."

Josie turned to the silver-haired woman. "Gracelyn, is this your book? I found it behind the copier. Would you mind if I borrow it?"

Liberty peered at the book that Josie held. *The Name of the Rose.* Wasn't that book about killing a monk?

Gracelyn shifted in her seat. "Not my book. I don't know who left it there. Go ahead and take it, and I'll ask around." Did she look uncomfortable?

Josie went on. "Thank you. Would you come to my office when you finish here?" Then the associate rector walked across the hall to her office, went in, and closed the door.

Gracelyn rose from her chair. "I'd better go now. The vestry's asked Josie to stay as acting rector until they can find an interim. It's so chaotic. I don't know how we're going to manage. Why don't you come back later, Liberty, and I'll have that material printed out and edited for you. Some of it's rough."

"I'd like the rough material especially. Now, please."

Gracelyn grimaced and tapped a pencil against the calendar on her desk. Liberty guessed the woman was trying to figure out how to refuse, but Liberty wasn't going to give her a chance to change any of Sam's words. She wanted his voice as it was, unaltered by Gracelyn's efficient hands—or maybe even an effort to suppress truth.

"It'll take time." Gracelyn nodded toward the office where Josie waited.

Liberty leaned forward. "The memoir needs to be finished and delivered to the publisher by next month." Okay, that was a lie. Alicia hadn't told her of any deadline, but she was giving herself one.

Instead of answering, Gracelyn opened her eyes wide and gasped.

"What is it?" Liberty looked around to see if the police were rushing in.

When she glanced back at Gracelyn, Gracelyn's hands went to her temples. "It's coming on. I can see it. I can feel it." She gave a loud moan. "A migraine."

"Is there anything . . ."

Josie's office door opened, and the young priest glided over and laid a hand on the woman's shoulder. "Gracelyn, are you all right? You can lie down on my sofa. Do you have your medication with you?"

The secretary shut her eyes, still holding her head. "In the bag."

Josie retrieved a capacious handbag from under the desk, dark brown with a pattern of entwined tan LVs. *Louis Vuitton? Expensive for a church's salary* was Liberty's fleeting thought. "Maybe you'd better come back later, Libby," Josie said. "She'll have to lie down until this migraine passes."

The phone on Gracelyn's desk rang. Josie picked it up, answered, and told the caller she'd get back to them.

Thinking quickly, Liberty wished the two women goodbye and walked toward the door. She lingered outside until she was sure they'd gone into Josie's office. How long did migraines last, anyhow? She'd assume the worst and hurry. She slipped back in, saw that Josie's door was closed, and wedged herself into the seat behind Gracelyn's humming computer.

The files she sought were marked simply *Maginnes* 1 through 12. Liberty jerked her key ring out of her pocket, uncapped her flash drive, and shoved it into the USB port. A couple of mouse clicks downloaded the necessary files. She leaned over and slipped the drive out and into her pocket, trying not to clink her car keys. Her heart in her throat, she hoped these were all the pages that were missing.

When she straightened, an elderly woman, short and chunky, wearing a navy print dress and red sweater, stood directly in front of the desk. A chill snaked down Liberty's back, and she made a supreme effort to recover her composure. The old lady in front of her knitted her brows.

"Oh, hello," Liberty said.

The lady's expression was a study in mourning, though powder dusted her wrinkled cheeks and she wore a sweet perfume. "I'm Ruby Drake. I'm here to see Josie."

Liberty smiled encouragingly. "Josie's taking care of a minor emergency. She'll be right with you. Won't you take a seat?" The second phone line rang and she wrote down a message for Gracelyn. The tall, thin organist strode in. Liberty pretended to pick up some trash from the floor but, as the organist strode toward the nave to practice, he never glanced her way.

Ruby Drake gave Liberty the who-are-you fisheye when Liberty popped up, and Liberty knew it was time to leave. "I'm going to lunch," she explained. "Josie will be right out." She walked as fast as she dared to the glass door. Directly in her line of sight, a dapper, mustachioed man wearing a gray-brown pinstripe suit reached for the handle and opened the door. He held it for her to walk out.

"Hello, Liberty," he said.

Boing. "Hello, Duff," she replied. The senior warden of St. Chad's, Duff Mowbray, served as president of the Shadrach House board. He looked just like David Niven.

Chapter Twelve

The Past Begins

"Duff, can I talk to you?" Liberty blurted. "About Shad House?"

"Of course, Liberty," Duff checked his watch. "Can you stick around? I have a meeting with Josie."

"I'm on my way home," she said. "Can I call you?"

"Call the office. My girl has my schedule. We'll have coffee." With those words ringing in her ears, Liberty rushed out to her car and left, noting Duff's black Lexus parked near the door.

She drove away, pulse racing, zipped past the shopping center, and sped down the highway toward home, darting in and out of traffic like a crazy squirrel.

Melvin Milton had seen a Lexus, and Duff drove a black Lexus. Duff Mowbray couldn't have wanted to harm Sam.

Duff had probably been Sam's drinking buddy that night. A plausible picture was the two of them talking at the kitchen table, glasses in hand, while Sam ate a takeout sandwich.

The fifteen miles back to her house passed in a blur of wind and skittering fast-food wrappers. A brown plastic bag sailed up, up, and away. When she pulled into the garage, dead leaves swirled in behind her.

The warmth of her house, its scent of home, enveloped her like a big hug. She took off her puffy down coat, hung it on a hook by the back door and headed to the refrigerator for a drink of water. Emmy's crayoned picture magnetized on the fridge stopped her cold. Stick figures: Mommy, Daddy, and Emmy, with half-moon smiles and too many fingers, standing in front of a box with a triangle on top.

A happy family in front of their house. Somewhere out there was the key that unlocked the secret of a happy family. Where was it? After she'd solved the mystery of Sam's death, could she reset the relationship with Dallas like you can reboot a computer? Would he ever understand her as well as Sam had? Would she learn to make peace with a relationship that didn't include her soul? Maybe real intimacy with another human being just wasn't possible. Maybe Dallas was the best she was going to get.

With nervous hands and dry mouth she walked upstairs to the tiny "bonus" room that served as her computer room and popped in the flash drive. She held her breath as the files downloaded. As she scanned them, her tension drained away. The chapters were different from those Alicia had given her.

She printed out them all before she allowed herself to read one. She picked up the first page and Sam's words grabbed her.

I'd learned to be a street kid in New York, to pick pockets and grab purses, break into cars. When the time came to leave, I rolled a drunk for bus fare to Florida. I rode through states with names I'd only read about in school.

I sat next to a bronze-skinned girl about my age on the bus. Her purple-red hair exploded from her head in plumes, and silver earrings tickled her shoulders. Her eye makeup telegraphed street hooker, and at first I thought that's what she was, so skimpy was her tank top, so short her flared skirt. I tried to make conversation, but she turned away with "fuck off" and stared out the window, chin in hand.

The miles ground away and I sank into the cocoon of the bus and its funky smell of packed bodies, but the silent girl beside me bothered me.

"It's a long trip. Talk to me. So where are you going?"

She waved me off with her arm, like a fly. "Home."

"And where's home?"

"Why do you want to know?" She looked me full in the face then, and I thought how much she reminded me of somebody I'd seen in a film, some up-and-coming hottie with dark smooth skin and wild midnight hair.

"Geez. Just being friendly. I'm going to Miami myself."

She didn't say anything for a minute and then said, "You running away?"

I looked at my hands, at the human bite on my thumb crusted over, puffy on the edges. I gingerly touched it. It was sore as hell. "You might say that."

"I ran away," she said, inviting me to tell more, but I could be closemouthed too.

"And now you're going back home."

"St. Augustine," she admitted.

"Your folks give you a hard time?" I asked, thinking of my old man, whom I never wanted to see again. Of my mother, who had become almost as bad.

She shook her head. "They're nice to me. Too nice sometimes. They adopted me from foster care. It wasn't easy. Some people thought I ought to stay with my own kind."

"Your own kind?"

"Seminole. Creek. You know."

My interest ratcheted up a few more notches. You didn't meet many Native Americans in my neighborhood. "So why'd you leave?"

She twisted her mouth in wry distaste. "You wouldn't understand."

"Try me."

She stared at me. "You ever had anybody expect a lot out of you?"

I snorted in disgust and looked at the ceiling. "You got to be kidding."

She settled back and started to fiddle with her nails, picking off flakes of purple-red polish. "My dad is a minister. Episcopalian." She got quiet. "And my mom is the kind that stays home and bakes cookies. Can you believe?" She waited for me to say something.

Could I tell her my old man always told me I was going to be no good, like him? No. I told her I was the illegitimate son of the mayor, and a few other choice lies.

"I don't believe you," she said, but she was smiling for the first time. "My name's Isabel. I guess we're heading in different directions."

"Call me Richie." Suddenly I wanted to kiss her badly, and I leaned over and touched my lips to hers. "For luck," I said, but her smile faded.

"I'm scared, Richie," she said. "You scared?"

"Don't ask me that," I said.

Her hand crept into mine and tightened.

We made love out of loneliness that night under a blanket in the back of the bus, and I slept the sleep of the blessed for the first time in weeks.

When she got off at St. Augustine, they gave the rest of us on the bus a short layover. I stood beside the bus, drinking a cold Coke, and watched her run to the loving arms of her parents.

Her father's collar threw me for a few minutes—I didn't know anything about Episcopalians. I'd grown up Catholic and at one time had been an altar boy. Before my mother took to drink when my brother died. Before my friend Robbie warned me to never be alone with a certain priest, and why.

The Episcopal priest I saw now was fairly tall, with steel gray hair and a long tan face. His eyes met Isabel's with stern compassion.

She looked back for me, just once. No one had ever looked back for me since I'd wept at my brother's grave. And then the tall man swung his arm around Isabel's shoulders, and the family walked off, together again.

I walked back to board the bus, my feet dragging. I looked down at the ticket for Miami in my hand. The bus was roaring, belching diesel. An old lady hurried up to the door of the bus steps carrying a paper sack, entered, and the door closed behind her.

The driver saw me then and gave me a questioning glance. I shook my head, thrust the ticket back in my pocket, and walked into the terminal. I heard the roar of the diesel as the bus left.

Liberty turned the page, her breath shallow. What came next? There was a lot of unmentioned life between his getting off the bus and going to college. And she hadn't seen any major lies, just minor ones—so far.

Time for carpool. She put away the manuscript, grabbed her coat, and left. She drove in such a fury, rattled by all she had read, that she almost nosed into a Jaguar in the carpool line of the small private school that accepted a few special-education students. The woman driving looked as though she'd stepped out of an ad in *Town and Country*, her streaked hair tousled, artful above her black fur collar.

She gave Liberty a look as though her fellow carpooler might be a pile of horse manure the woman had narrowly missed on her way to the stables. Liberty eased into line. Dallas had wanted this school for Emmy rather than the public one, but he didn't have to deal with some of the Momzillas.

Emmy and two other girls piled in, full of giggles and high energy, brandishing the day's artwork. This time it was animals, and Liberty admired the cats and dogs and horses. These kids were so excited, it made her forget her troubles for a time.

After she and Emmy arrived at home, Liberty was so eager to get back to Sam's manuscript that the hour she spent giving Emmy her snack and hearing about school seemed like three. And at naptime? Her daughter complained she wasn't tired. Liberty firmly told her that this was rest period and sent her upstairs.

She should have read the sly look on the child's face. After she'd picked up the new manuscript pages, she heard a rhythmical thumping coming from above. She ignored the noise, figuring that Emmy was just showing her tail, like Mama Jean used to say.

Liberty read that "Richie" had obtained a phone book and found listings for three Episcopal churches. At the first and largest, he arrived as churchwomen were clearing things away after a seniors' luncheon. Pretending to be lost and asking directions, he charmed his way into conversation, offered to help wash up, and was given a huge plate of food.

He ate it gratefully as he talked with the ladies. Innocuous questions revealed that the rector had two young children. Not the one he was seeking.

He left, promising the ladies he'd come back Sunday morning and meet the youth group. *Not freaking likely they'd have me,* he thought.

The second church was small, and the rector's name on the sign was The Rev. Barbara Conway, so he passed it by. The third church was some distance away, and it took him more than an hour of walking and goofing around before he arrived.

When Richie walked into The Church of St. Adrian of Canterbury and studied the staff photographs on the bulletin board, he identified the Rev. Aubrey Maginnes as the man he'd seen at the bus stop picking up Isabel. The rector had left for the day, the secretary explained, for hospital visitation. He'd be in the next morning.

Richie walked into the nave, where an elderly woman sat praying. He sat, bowed his head, and waited until she'd left, then he looked around the building for a place to hide. He found an unlocked janitor's closet in the hall just off the chapel and, hoping the cleaning was done for the day, slipped in. He remained still, breathing fumes of Pine-Sol and floor wax and furniture polish, until the building was perfectly quiet. Then he slipped out and roamed the building until he found the church parlor and slept on the sofa there.

When he was found the next morning by the sexton and ushered in to see Father Aubrey Maginnes, he didn't explain that he'd met Isabel on the bus. Now came more lies, lies within lies. He told the good father that his family had been wiped out by a tornado in Indiana and he had run away from his cruel uncle. He said that his father, before he died, had been a farmer. He said he'd had no religion. He had happened on St. Adrian's Church by chance.

My heart was in my throat when he placed a call to the juvenile authorities. They assured him that they'd had no runaways or dangerous teens on the loose, nor had any been reported in the past few days. I don't know why he didn't turn me in.

Father Aubrey, sympathetic to a runaway but not trusting his story, consulted his wife Hazel, and he put the boy to work around the church to earn supper and a bed for the night.

When he brought the boy in for dinner, Isabel, now dressed in jeans and T-shirt, her hair tamed and restored to its usual shade, didn't betray him, but her mischievous eyes couldn't conceal her delight.

Aubrey and Hazel Maginnes decided to take the boy into their rambling old rectory for the summer. If he behaved himself, and if he wanted to, he could stay longer. It was a risky move, but Aubrey believed in the goodness of human nature. He enrolled the boy in summer school and arranged some odd jobs for him.

Richie tried to kiss Isabel the moment they were alone. She rebuffed him, saying that if they got caught, they'd both be thrown out on their butts, and anyhow, she'd promised Daddy Aubrey and Mama Hazel she was going to be good.

She had been my savior on the bus, and I did not want to let her go. I hadn't changed my spots that much. I plotted and schemed how I was going to make her change her mind. She didn't feel anything like a sister to me.

Then Sam wrote:

It was on a summer's day after my odd jobs were finished. I'd come home to change and catch up on my summer reading assignments, maybe go shoot a few baskets with some of the guys I'd met in the neighborhood. Isabel, never a good student, was struggling with summer-school algebra in her room. Father Aubrey and Mis' Hazel had gone to have dinner with parishioners, leaving pizza for us.

Isabel called for me to help with some word problems.

I leaned over her with my pencil poised, solving for x, the heat shimmering in the back yard below, the ceiling fan stirring the room's filmy curtains, the lush smell of peach pits rising from her paper-filled wastebasket. My nose was close to her neck, and I breathed in the fruity odor of her brown skin. I kissed it then, that tender neck like a ripe fig, and she turned to me with a look that caught me and pulled me under.

Our foster parents found us asleep in Isabel's pristine white bed when they arrived home, the sheets awry, both of us naked.

There was a scene. Isabel and I were in powerful trouble. Aubrey searched his soul deeply. In the end, an alternative summer school was found for Isabel in Sarasota, where Aubrey's brother lived, and in lieu of being kicked out, I was placed at hard labor helping the church grounds crew.

Out in the pungent, dewy grass, the noise of the mowers clanking and clattering through broiling heat, I thought of her. Endlessly. I wondered if she thought of me, too. She had been forbidden to write to me, and I was afraid that when the summer ended, I might be sent away for good.

Isabel broke both my heart and Aubrey's when she ran away from the new school. Why did she do it? Aubrey could have given up on her, but he didn't. They found her again in Miami, high on cocaine. She went into a treatment center.

I figured that for her, I had just been another thrill in a life that needed unending thrills to keep the wolves away. I didn't see her pain at trying to fit into a white world. I saw my own past and felt that I couldn't help Isabel by following her back into it. I prayed for the first time since I'd quit the church. I prayed to stay. I was sorry. I pleaded with Aubrey to let me stay with them, and redoubled my efforts to succeed.

Liberty laid down the paper. There was nothing in these pages that would tell her what Sam had kept buried all these years. Maybe there was yet more to learn. Maybe he hadn't written it yet, but Alicia had told her it was complete, but then Alicia hadn't read it. Maybe Isabel knew.

Isabel had been the tall woman with Sam's father at the funeral. The Native American, his adopted sister. Had they stayed close? How much had he told her about his background? Would talking to her give Liberty the clues she sought? And would Isabel be willing to talk?

Chapter Thirteen

DETECTING AT HOME

"**M**ommee, look! Look!"

Uh-oh. When Emmy bubbled, Liberty knew there was trouble. She dropped the manuscript and hurried upstairs to the child's room, where the pillows and comforter, the pink-and white-striped sheets lay jumbled on the carpet. She'd been trampolining on her bed, which she knew was a definite no-no. One corner of the bed had caved in; the mattress sagged on the floor.

"Pretty!" Emmy gleefully held out her hand to show off her sticky, smudged red nails. Her mother's favorite bottle of Miss Scarlett sat on the bedside table, now streaked and smudged with red.

Liberty squeezed her eyes shut and took a deep breath to calm down. "Emmy. Good try, but next time ask for help. Come on. We have to clean up." In the bathroom, she cotton-balled Emmy's nails with polish remover. Then she cleaned the bedside table, applied spot remover to Emmy's clothes and the smudged sheets, and started a load of laundry. She propped the bed up and somehow managed to bolt it back together, then she put Emmy to work helping to make the bed with fresh sheets.

The manuscript had to wait. Lessons needed to be taught to children when misdeeds were fresh in their subversive little minds. And she now knew to stash the nail polish out of sight and out of reach. Together they tidied Emmy's room into spotlessness. The girl gazed around and sniffed with disapproval. "Ith organized." When had she learned *organized*? On one of her videos? On TV? Liberty stifled a laugh. Then, and only then, she painted the small nails pale pink.

The old clock on the living room mantel chimed five o'clock. Emmy would be wanting her supper at six, and Dallas would roar through the door looking for a Diet Coke. What an irony. Liberty's husband now came home on time nearly every day, stone cold sober, and she was too busy to care.

She settled Emmy in front of the cursed, reviled, but oh-so-handy electronic nanny and found Sesame Street. Then she decamped to the dining room and picked up the manuscript once again, seized with the enormousness of the task before her. She was no detective. Her job was detecting weak points in dramatic incidents, bad acting, and sometimes, dangling participles.

Sure, she'd taught students about Conan Doyle and Willkie Collins, liked Lord Peter Wimsey's adventures at the Bellona Club, and had gone down the Nile with Miss Christie. *But, really, Liberty Jean McNamara, who do you think you are?*

She needed a dose of reality. She tucked the pages into the drawer of the antique chest Dallas had bought her, checked that Emmy was absorbed in her show, and made a cup of tea. She called her best friend. "Vivian, I've got to talk."

"So talk," Vivian replied in a way-too-cheery voice. Liberty heard whacking and chopping in the background, and asked what was happening.

"I'm decapitating vegetables for stir-fry."

"Vivian," Liberty told her, wincing, "this is serious. Alicia Maginnes has asked me to finish Sam's book."

The chopping ceased. "He was writing a *book?* About *what?*"

"A memoir," Liberty said. "He's got a publisher already."

She could almost see Vivian's knowing smile. "That man always intrigued me. He had some kind of toughness behind that gentleness, I could tell. Is it a rehab story? Was he into drugs or something?"

Vivian was just being her usual breezy, irreverent self, but surprisingly, it struck a nerve, and Liberty's voice caught. "It wasn't substance abuse, Vivian."

"Then what was it? What happened to Sam that somebody would pay to read? Was he in the military or something like that?"

"No . . ." Liberty couldn't find the words. She was quiet too long.

Vivian's manner changed and her voice dropped an octave. "Lib, I've been worried about you. Sam's death has hit you hard." She paused. "Is there something you're not telling me?"

Liberty took a deep breath. It was time to tell somebody. "That's why I called you. Vivian, I think somebody killed him."

Her friend let out a long *whoosh*. "When you mentioned that before, I just thought it was your imagination running wild. I didn't give it any further thought. Why are you certain he was murdered?"

"I can't tell you."

Vivian's voice hardened with exasperation. "Liberty, we've known each other too long to play games. If you've got some kind of evidence, take it to the police."

Liberty's shoulders ached with tension. She blurted, "I can't go to them. It's the grant for Shadrach House. The Joshua Foundation will make a decision on it in a few weeks. I'm hoping we can keep the application alive without Sam. The woman in charge was impressed with him and the presentation. But if she thought Sam was mixed up in scandal or crime—well, you know, the competition for dollars is fierce. They'd choose a cause that wouldn't wind up in the National Enquirer."

"I know you two worked pretty closely," Vivian said. "You weren't . . ."

"No," Liberty said. "But besides you, he was my best friend."

Silence, thick and heavy, floated between the two friends. "Maybe you need to talk to a professional," Vivian finally said with a sigh.

Liberty choked the telephone in a death grip. "What, you mean a lawyer? I'm going to talk with Duff Mowbray soon as I can."

"No, I don't mean about the grant. I mean about you."

"I don't need a therapist, Vivian."

Viv's reply snapped like a rubber band. "Are you sure? What about this business with Dallas?"

Liberty cleared her throat. "We're working on it. Things have been calm at home."

"The calm before the storm, dear. I'm going to suggest a priest, a spiritual adviser. He's written inspirational books, gives talks . . ."

"I need inspiration?" The last thing Liberty wanted was to confide in somebody besides Sam. She took a sip of tea, but it had cooled.

"You haven't let yourself grieve enough. It hurts to lose a friend, and I think you could use some help."

Liberty opened her mouth and closed it again. Vivian went on, "I have one of Hartley Ford's cards right here in the drawer."

Liberty half-smiled, picturing the drawer crammed with scrawled phone numbers, business cards, messages, clippings, theater programs, classroom lists, the layers compressing like prehistoric sedimentary rock. Maybe she wouldn't find it.

"Hartley Ford," Vivian pronounced again. She gave Liberty his number.

"Vivian, I don't want it."

"He also used to be a private investigator."

"You're kidding, right?"

"I'm serious. He's an unusual guy."

It was worth a try. What else did she have? Liberty wrote down the number and thanked Vivian. She told her friend goodbye and let her go back to her unfortunate vegetables.

She stared at Hartley Ford's number, set it aside, and poured the dregs of tea down the sink drain. She changed her mind and reached for the phone. She had just pushed a number when the back door opened. The phone clattered down.

"Hi, honey." A peck on the cheek, a whiff of spearmint. "Got to get a run in before dinner. Where's Em?"

"Watching whatever's on PBS now. Send her in to set the table, please."

"Gotcha." He detoured through the family room, then went upstairs to put on running clothes. That was another change. The exercise.

She could hardly remember the athlete, the sexy stud, the hero he'd seemed when she met him. The one who'd sent her a huge bouquet of roses after their third date.

When had it happened? When had the magic soured? It hadn't happened all at once, in a blinding epiphany, the way she'd heard it did for some people. But does it ever? The tunneling is done underground—like water under a city street, unnoticed until a huge sinkhole appears and the cars start falling in.

Hope dies slowly. The marriage web unravels even as it spins, Penelope gone over to the opposition. Small disloyalties, unkindnesses, confidences broken, weaknesses exposed to others, requests refused, words used to wound. The wounding had become more frequent. Never had she dreamed he'd turn violent. Could it happen again? She hoped he'd seen a wake-up call with her leaving for Florida. She hated this in-between time, not knowing whether to believe him or not. Could love be rekindled? She wanted to try—for Emmy's sake. And for the chance for the happy family she had always wanted.

The teacup was empty. She wished it held leaves, leaves that could forecast the future.

Liberty turned on the tap, filled a pot with water for pasta, and set it to boil. She broke out a packet of frozen broccoli, found red peppers, cheese, turkey. She cut carrots diagonally into thin slices, gently, as Sam would have cut carrots. His gentleness had been devastating.

She called Emmy in to help set the table and handed her a fistful of silverware, and then she allowed Emmy to lower the pasta into the pot, wondering if the child would ever be able to cook alone.

"You're awfully quiet," Dallas said at dinner. Emmy was concentrating on twirling her linguine on her fork, trying to copy the grown-ups.

Reluctantly, Liberty told him of her new editing project.

"The man is dead and he's still got my wife working for him," Dallas grumbled.

That comment would have upset her before, but she'd learned about boundaries. "The man is dead. That's why I'm doing it," she said calmly.

Dallas just grunted. "Pass the cheese."

Liberty set a stalk of broccoli on Emmy's plate. "Ewww, Mommy." The girl stuck out her tongue and continued to roll the linguine into a huge ball.

"Broccoli looks like little trees," Liberty said, spooning cheese sauce over the broccoli, watching her daughter gnaw pasta off the ball.

Dallas snorted. "Can't you teach the kid some manners?" He grabbed his knife and fork and cut up Emmy's linguine. Then he sat back. "I'm having wine." He got up and went to the refrigerator, returning with a bottle of the cooking

Chablis. Liberty sat very still and willed herself to say nothing. He was testing himself, testing her.

Dallas fixed an eye on his wife. "You want any?" She shook her head *no*. He drank one glassful. *See, I can stop any time I want.*

Later that evening, he went to his basement office. When Liberty heard him on the phone, she stole out to his car, not sure what she'd find. She checked the sides for mud. The paint gleamed from a fresh trip through the automatic wash. She opened the door and felt under the driver's seat. Her hand closed around the neck of a bottle.

She left it where it was, feeling sick, and began to search the rest of the car. There was nothing in the glove compartment but an owner's manual, a batch of gas-station receipts, a couple of restaurant receipts, and a pair of sunglasses. Very faintly, she heard Dallas shouting for her. She stuffed the restaurant tickets in her pocket and hurried back inside.

He was at the top of the stairs. "Where have you been?"

"Meeting my boy toy." She paused. "Actually, taking out some trash."

"Sarcasm's not your style, Libby. I've got to go to Pittsburgh tomorrow. I've got an early flight. Where the hell are any clean socks?"

She went to the laundry room and took the whole basket of clean clothes upstairs. She picked out the socks and tucked them carefully in his bag.

"Have a nice trip." She made sure Emmy was bathed and tucked her in bed, then distributed the rest of the clothes and took the ones to be ironed back downstairs.

She curled up on the sofa with an Agatha Christie novel. Might as well get some pointers on detection.

After a while, she heard Dallas come up from the basement and clump upstairs. She didn't want to follow him, and he didn't call for her.

It was funny, wasn't it? When they'd first been married, she felt bereft every time Dallas had to leave for a few days. Now, a door to the world seemed to open whenever he was on his way to the airport. That was facing reality, wasn't it?

She stayed up late watching *Casablanca*. She thought a lot about the way it had ended.

Chapter Fourteen

L iberty picked up the phone.

Emmy had gone to school and Dallas had left with his suitcase full of clean socks. The house was empty and still. Liberty keyed in Hartley Ford's number and bit her lip, rehearsing what she might say to this detective.

The voice mail clicked on. *Hartley Ford. Nothing I'd like better than to talk with you right now, but I can't be in two places at once. Please leave your name and number at the beep.*

What? Vivian didn't say this paragon was a wisecracking Yankee. Liberty wasn't exactly looking for a good ol' boy, but she was hoping for someone soothing, grave, and kind, like Jimmy Carter.

She hung up and sat gazing at the handset, counting her choices on the fingers of no hands. She tried again, and when the message ended, took a deep breath. "My name is Liberty Chase," she said. "I'd like to talk with you. Please." She left her number, hung up the phone, and stared blankly out at the back yard she loved, now *wither'd leaves lie dead* with oncoming winter, the dried hydrangeas stiffly elegant, the evergreens dark and richly furred.

Hartley Ford called back half an hour later, while she was rinsing the breakfast dishes. "Is this Liberty Chase?"

Her breath caught; she choked out a Yes.

"This is Hartley Ford. How can I help you, Liberty?" The hint of impatience and brashness in the recording was gone. This voice was sympathetic.

"I'm not sure." She told him that Vivian Clark had given her his name.

"Vivian Clark?"

"She had your card. She said she'd heard you speak."

"What church?"

She hesitated. "St. Chad's."

He remained quiet a few beats too long to make her happy. "Yes. I did speak there." His tone ratcheted down a notch. "Sam Maginnes asked me to talk about my book."

Sam? A chill racked her body. "Your book?"

He gave a wry chuckle. "The thing came out a few years ago. It's called *The Paradox of Peace*. Sam was using it to teach a class."

She waited, hoping he'd elaborate, but he didn't. His voice softened. "Did you know Sam, by any chance?"

"Yes . . ." Her voice faltered. "That's what I need to talk with you about."

Anvil-like gravity crept into his voice. "Are you one of his parishioners?"

"No. I worked with him. Shadrach House." Her mind spun furiously. Might as well come out with it. "Vivian said you were a private eye."

"*Was* is the operative word here. I don't do investigations any more."

"But that's what I need." She struggled to keep desperation out of her voice. "For Sam."

His reply was quick and sharp. "Are you suggesting that something about Sam's death needs investigating?"

Her mouth went dry. "Yes."

"You have a reason?"

"I do. I'd prefer not to discuss it over the phone."

Pages ruffled in the background. "Believe me, dear lady, I'd like to talk to you, but my schedule's pretty full this week, and as I said, I don't do detective work any more."

Her stomach clenched, and she felt sick. He thought she was a nut case, no doubt, and was trying to let her down easy. It was a mistake to have called him. Maybe she should just forget the whole thing. But hadn't Mama Jean told her it was her duty to find out what happened? She visualized the gleam of her father's gun in her hand—the gun that was now locked in her glove compartment, the gun she had no permit for as yet. She'd screwed up the courage to send in the application the day before. "I'm not crazy!" she blurted. "I just need to talk this out."

And now she heard the smile in his voice. "I was going to say that I'm free this morning until ten. Do you live near Cheshire Cups & Books? Can you meet me there ASAP? I don't live far from there."

She felt as though the air had been sucked out of the room. That bookstore and coffee shop was where she'd met Sam. The world tilted on its axis a little, and when it righted, the clock read eight-thirty. She looked down at her morning robe, its blue lapels spotted with orange juice. She considered her frizzy curls, which needed a curling iron to tame them. Vanity, she figured, would have to wait. "I can get there," she told him.

Half an hour later, dressed in jeans, turtleneck, and boots, she stood in the Cheshire, where everything reminded her of Sam—the stacks of books crowding the shelves, the mind-bending coffee aroma, the hiss of the latte machine, the silvery clink of spoons, the conversational hum. The barista behind the counter winked at her, recognizing her.

A man touched her elbow. "Liberty?"

How did he know her? She nodded, turned, and her heart sank. This was definitely not Jimmy Carter. Here was a retro flattop, straight eyebrows, and Jeremy Irons mouth. She wasn't comforted by the houndstooth sport jacket with elbow patches draping his slim frame. For somebody who didn't want to detect, he dressed a heck of a lot like

Sherlock Holmes. She half expected him to take out a pipe. "Mr. Ford, or is it Doctor?"

Squarish strong hands caged hers warmly. "I'm Hartley, Liberty, but my friends call me Jack, and I hope you will too."

He escorted her to a booth by the window. "I'll get the coffee."

She looked out at the overcast sky, gathering her courage. He fetched steaming cups of French roast, dark and fragrant, and waved off her tentative move toward her handbag. She sprinkled sugar in her coffee and stirred cream into it. He sipped his brew black.

"Okay. Spill."

She studied his eyes, a topaz color, fringed with dark lashes. "I don't know where to begin."

He gave her a cockeyed grin. "I keep trying but, damn. Telepathy's hard to learn." He leaned forward, as if telling her a deep, dark secret. "Remember that line about learning to whistle? 'You just put your lips together and . . . blow?' Well, just open your mouth, and see what comes out."

"I expected you to be more serious." She turned away, uneasy. "I didn't come here to make jokes."

"I'm sorry," he said, "but I broke the ice, didn't I? Now tell me what it is about Sam Maginnes's death that concerns you."

She swallowed hard and met his eyes.

"We don't have much time," he continued quietly. "In an hour I'm talking with a recovering alcoholic."

That got her attention, fast. "Did you know Sam well?"

"I loved the man like a brother," he said, shaking his head. "He was all about making a difference in kids' lives. Asthma's a hell of a thing to die of."

Blood rushed to her face and she leaned forward. "I can't believe it was an accident."

"Can't you?" One skeptical eyebrow cocked.

"Before I go further, please tell me how long you've known him."

Jack regarded her thoughtfully. "I knew about his asthma early. I met him at a conference. He'd read my purple thing, and we got to talking. Just hit it off, I guess. Talked about all kinds of stuff. I was popping a penicillin tab after lunch—post-root canal—and he told me to keep it the hell away from him, and why." He paused and pinched the bridge of his nose. "Damn, I wasn't even here when he died. I'd gone back home for my uncle's funeral."

"What did you mean by *purple thing?*"

He gave me a rueful smile. "The book I was telling you about. It had a purple cover. My fifteen minutes of fame. *The Paradox of Peace.*"

Knowledge dawned. "Yes, now that you mention it, Sam talked about it. It was about religion and war."

"Unfortunately." He nodded absently, sipped his coffee, and appeared to be thinking. "Liberty, how well did *you* know Sam?"

She swallowed, hard. "Maybe I didn't know him as well as I thought. You know I worked with him at Shadrach House."

"That didn't answer my question," he said, but let it go. "Do you think anyone had a grudge against him because of his work?"

She shook her head. "He wanted a new shelter with room for boys to stay for a few days when they needed it, so we raised funds to buy a house in a transitional area. Some people didn't want the shelter near their neighborhood, but I can't see them resorting to violence."

"Do you think any of the boys had it in for him?"

"No way." Rico was the only boy who'd threatened him, and that was because of a gang.

"Did he speak of any toughs or pimps who wanted to exploit the boys? Who wanted to sabotage his efforts? Did he finger any criminals?"

"Not to me. Maybe to Duff Mowbray, the senior warden?"

"Then what reason do you have for suspecting that his death wasn't natural? What motive might anyone have had to kill him?"

She chewed her bottom lip. Blood rushed in her ears; heat rose in her neck. A cold, heavy chunk of rock settled in the pit of her stomach.

"Liberty?"

"I was there," she finally said, so quietly he might have missed it if he hadn't been listening intently.

"Where?" His words were gently spoken.

"At his house. I stopped by to see him on my way out of town." She paused. "I found his body."

Now Jack looked down at her hand resting on the table, at her wedding ring, at the engagement diamond sparking light. "Were you alone?"

Her breath caught, and she forced her reply. "My daughter was with me. She's eight."

He looked into her eyes. What was he looking for? Signs that they'd been more than friends? She couldn't take that sort of thing. She shivered, stifled a sob, and grabbed her bag, ready to bolt from the coffee shop.

Jack Ford regarded her with patient interest. "Liberty, calm down and listen to me. There was a storm the night Sam died. We'd buried my uncle that afternoon. My landlady called to tell me about the storm. She'd lost power, the creek behind her house was rising, and she was headed for her sister's place. She thought I ought to know, in case any of my things got soaked."

Liberty clutched the bag on her lap. Jack waited until she relaxed a little and then said softly, "Why were you out in that storm?"

Her shoulders slumped and her hands slipped off the bag. "My husband . . .we had a fight. A bad one. I left and took my daughter. He . . . had hit me. I was going to my grandparents in Florida."

"And you wanted to talk it over with Sam? You wanted to know if you were doing the right thing?"

"Yes," she whispered. "I tried to call him. He didn't answer his phone. I felt desperate and thought he might just be screening calls. I didn't have time to wait for him to call back, so I drove over to his house. The back door was unlocked. I went in and found his body in the den. "

"That must have been hard for you."

Tears rose and spilled from her eyes, stinging her cheeks. "I thought I was going to faint."

He waited while she wiped her eyes. "What did you do then?"

"My daughter—she was waiting in the car. She has Down syndrome and I had to go to her. I had just reached the kitchen when . . . when . . . I heard someone upstairs. I froze. There had been a light upstairs when I drove up. Then I saw Emmy in the doorway. She'd missed me and come to look for me, and I hustled her out before she realized he was dead. I was terrified that whoever was upstairs might come down to get us . . ." Liberty couldn't hold herself together any more, and she collapsed in muffled sobs.

Jack didn't seem fazed by the tears. He reached into his pocket and handed her a clean handkerchief. As she dabbed her streaming eyes, her shoulders heaving, he sipped his coffee.

"It's all right," he said. "You've had a terrible shock."

She let the tears flow into Jack's handkerchief.

Jack sat with his coffee, waiting. Though time was growing short before his appointment, he didn't seem in a hurry. When she had finally composed herself, she handed him back the crumpled, damp handkerchief with thanks. She knew she had to get up from the table and walk out, so she peered into her pocket mirror at her red eyes and nose. Useless. She slid the mirror back into her bag.

"Liberty, I've got to go," he said. "Let's talk again. Are you absolutely sure what you heard? Could the shock of finding Sam have caused your imagination to work overtime?"

"No," she said, fumbling the compact into her bag. "I'm certain I heard footsteps."

He nodded. "Can you be here by eight o'clock in the morning?"

She took in breath. "Yes. I can't thank you enough." She gazed at him with gratitude, aware that he was making time for her.

"I've got to eat breakfast. Why not here with you?" He clasped her hand warmly. "Keep your spirits up."

She walked out into the rising mist, watching as he widened the distance between them and disappeared behind a line of parked cars. She reached her vehicle and unlocked it. She had *told* someone. She felt as though she'd emerged from under a crushing pile of stones.

Little did she know what lay ahead.

Chapter Fifteen

COFFEE WITH JACK
DECEMBER 6

When she walked into the coffee shop ten minutes late, he was sitting in the same booth by the window, wearing the same houndstooth jacket, a pea-green cashmere turtleneck under it.

She slid into the padded booth, half out of breath. "Sorry I'm late. School traffic was impossible—a high-schooler with a car full of kids pulled out in front of somebody. Nobody hurt, but a big mess." She took a deep breath. "Now. About yesterday."

That raised eyebrow again. He held up a finger. "Wait. I'll get your coffee."

She struggled out of her windbreaker, and he brought her coffee as she liked it: one spoonful of sugar, one dash of cream.

"You catch on fast," she said. "I could get used to this."

He regarded her thoughtfully. "You don't have to explain anything to me about Sam, Liberty. He was happier in the past year than I'd ever seen him, yet he seemed deeply troubled. I felt he was conflicted about something."

"But . . ."

He touched her hand. "Sam was easy to love. You think you're the only one who's fallen in love with someone out of bounds?"

She shook her head. "Jack, it wasn't like that. We were friends. If he was happy, it wasn't because of me. It was the progress we were making with the boys. I think the conflict might lie in this memoir he was writing."

Jack nodded. "It's possible. But spouses can be jealous of friends. If you think Sam was murdered, do you think your husband was jealous? Or Alicia? I can't see that, but hell hath no fury, as the saying goes."

"Oh, no, not Alicia," I said. "And my problems with Dallas had nothing to do with Sam. They were building up before I ever met Sam. Marriage is hard with a special needs child. No, my husband had nothing to be jealous of."

"Are you sure?"

She sighed with impatience. "He's away half the time, selling. I'm the one who ought to be jealous of all the women he meets. But what I want to know, Jack, is why did the medical examiner think it was asthma? Couldn't someone have poisoned him? I saw glasses, and gin on the table . . . the remains of food . . ."

Jack shook his head. "The autopsy will reveal mucus in the airways. Anyhow, poisoning's not as common as you may think. Men prefer a more direct method. Phallic, you know. The gun or the knife. Poison's generally a woman's method. Maybe Alicia . . ."

"Alicia was out of town."

"She could have left something for him. One poisoner I know of gave her victims homemade lemonade with arsenic in it. Arsenic's not common for poisoners any more—too easy to test for."

She told him about the dog and the suspected antifreeze. "What about that? Could somebody have slipped antifreeze in that bottle of gin?"

He smiled. "Not antifreeze in the gin. Alcohol is what they give as an antidote to antifreeze poisoning. If it's suspected that someone's had antifreeze, you give them alcohol and try to make them drunk. Antifreeze—ethylene glycol—is, chemically, an alcohol, a triple alcohol, if you will. You simply fill up the body with a less poisonous alcohol to drive out the really poisonous kind. And anyhow, what about the green color? You'd have to have a daiquiri."

She shook her head. "It was Bombay Sapphire. And some antifreeze is blue."

"Let's run with that theory. Suppose something deadly was in that gin. And let's also assume that he did, indeed, die of asthma. Suppose some substance was in the gin that triggered his asthma."

"Penicillin," she said, feeling a chill. "But it's bitter."

"Tonic is bitter," Jack Ford said. "Alicia had opportunity. I'm playing devil's advocate here, mind you. I got the impression that when I met Alicia they were happy."

"There were complications," Liberty said. "She was upset that Sam had spent so much time with the shelter, and the manuscript says that she was disappointed when he decided to enter the ministry."

They sipped coffee and Jack looked up into the rafters where book banners hung with Harry Potter's likeness, black and blue and gold, ready to zap evil with his magic wand. Liberty wondered if her coffee companion had a wife. He wore no ring. She couldn't imagine a wife letting him leave the house in the kind of clothes he wore. Nor did she see him as gay. He would have a better sense of fashion, surely.

"Let's put Alicia aside for the moment," Jack said. "Penicillin is common. What would the police want to know? They'd want proof of the penicillin in the gin. They'd want to find other sources where the suspect could have gotten hold of penicillin. They would ask who knew Sam was allergic to penicillin, who had the opportunity to administer it, and the most important of all, who would want him dead. Motive and opportunity." He watched me keenly. "Maybe Alicia wasn't happy, but she wasn't in town. What was your husband doing that night?"

She felt herself go red-faced. "He came home late, drunk as a skunk. We had a fight. He hit me, and I felt it could only get worse. I played possum and he left me alone. When I heard sounds of snoring, I got up and found he'd passed out. That's when I gathered my clothes and my child and I left."

Jack considered this. "But he could have gone to Sam's, then hit a bar."

"No," she said. "No. I didn't talk to him about Sam. He couldn't have known about any penicillin."

Jack's face was keen. "Has he ever followed you? Snooped in your mail? Listened in on your phone conversations?"

"No. And he's always traveling."

"You sure?"

She considered for a minute. Was she sure? She'd never had a reason to check up on him, and he called in from time to time. "Dallas can be a first-rate son-of-a-bitch and we sometimes fight like junkyard dogs, but he's not the jealous type. He's pretty sure of himself. Or maybe he just doesn't care."

Jack shrugged. "Is there anyone else who might've had a reason to be in Sam's house?"

She told him about the conversation she'd had with Melvin Milton. The Lexus. The man with the David Niven look. The old MG. The "lady's car." She told him about the tire tracks she'd seen in the mud, as if somebody had left in a hurry.

"Hey, girl," he said approvingly. "Very good observations."

She blushed. "I was an actress once," she said. "I know how mysteries work."

"An actress, hmm?"

"Acting might come in handy. You never know."

"So what's your next move?"

"I'm going to talk to Duff Mowbray," she said. "He's the David Niven look-alike."

"What about the woman in the car?"

"That's pretty hopeless. It was raining. Melvin didn't get a good look and I don't see how I can question the other neighbors."

"I can deal with the neighbors," said Jack. "And Melvin could have been lying. Where was he that night?"

"Said he went out with his girlfriend." Then it hit her what Jack had just said, and her spirits soared. "Are you saying you'll help me?"

"Whoa, whoa. I know how to worm out information. I don't do investigations."

Liberty leaned forward. "I could pay you something, even if I have to write to my mom in LA and beg." Her spirits rose. Jack Ford was the exact kind of help she needed.

"Sweetheart," he said, "I'm through with that kind of work. What's this about a mom in LA?"

So he was curious? Maybe he would change his mind. Her voice catching a little, she told him about being raised from the age of five by Mama Jean and Papaw; about her father, Gavin McNamara; and what she knew of his life as an FBI agent. Her grandfather had been proud of him. Her father had been shot seven times while trying to investigate a cell of neo-Nazis that had bombed a synagogue.

"Well, I'll be damned," Jack said, "and me with my old man a cop. Killed in the line of duty, huh? It must have been tough on you."

She nodded. "I just have hazy memories of him."

"More coffee?" She shook her head, feeling jittery enough. Jack's cup was empty, and he went for a refill. When he came back he said, "My pop's still around, Chief of Police in a little town someplace in Illinois you never heard of. He's not easy to know." He paused and sipped his coffee, looking as though he was trying to chase a thought away.

"My father would help, if he were here," she said hotly. "I'll bet yours would too. You said you were Sam's friend."

He rubbed his chin. "You make me feel ashamed of myself. Sam was there for me when I was going through a rough spot."

"Rough spot?"

"We don't need to talk about my problems."

"Divorced?"

He nodded and went on quickly. "Aside from jealousy, why in hell would anyone want to kill Sam Maginnes? Not for money, that's for sure. He'd give you his last dime."

"Jack, in that book I'm editing, he hints at something or someone in his past. He never talked to you about it?"

Jack leaned forward and his voice went down a notch. "One night we'd had a few beers and he got thoughtful. He said, 'Jack, I'm not what I seem. I don't deserve what I've got.' And I said, natch, 'What the devil are you talking about?' 'One day you'll know,' he said. 'I'm going to write a book.' And then he shut up. "You know, Liberty, I think, with the book, Sam might have been trying to come to terms with his wounds."

"Wounds?"

Jack nodded. "Henri Nouwen says that a healer can use his own wounds to help heal the wounds of others. Sam knew that he would be a better healer if he came clean."

Liberty remembered Sam mentioning the spiritual thinker.

Jack gazed outside for a beat or two, and then turned back to Liberty. "Oh, hell. I may be crazy, but I'll help you, because it's Sam. I've kept up my license, and I'll just need expense money. Frankly, Liberty, I don't think it's going to come to anything. If we find anything, we'll have to give it to the police anyhow. Why not go ahead and talk to them?"

She licked her dry lips. "Please, not yet. There's no proof. What can I say? That I was there and heard someone? What then? I'm afraid the questions will start. You know how people talk. Even you speculated about him and me. There can't be any blots on Sam's character while that grant is pending. And what if they think I did it?"

"Liberty, I repeat, if we find out there was foul play, we'll have to go to the police."

"If we could wait a couple of months. Just until we're sure that we have the grant."

"Could they take the grant back?"

"I don't think they would. Not if Sam was murdered for something unconnected with his character. Not if the board has a plan to go forward without him."

"Suppose you find out the opposite?"

"It's a chance I'll take. I hope it didn't have anything to do with the project. Some people would love for Shadrach House to just go away. The people who live near the new facility look at our kids as dangerous."

"You're forgetting one thing. *Somebody* knows you were at his house, sweetie. Whoever was upstairs. You might be putting yourself in danger if you go poking around."

She shook her head slowly, feeling relieved that she had help, at last. Now the path didn't seem so impossible. "I can handle it."

"So you say," Jack said. "Let me ask you this. Is there anyone at all who'd be glad Sam's gone?"

"A couple of those neighborhood activists, maybe, but they're just afraid. He'd planned to go meet and talk with them."

"That would be like Sam."

"Oh, yes. It was impossible not to like him." Liberty was thankful she had someone to talk to. *The more you sin,* Sam had quoted from Jack's book, *the lonelier you feel.*

But now the detective frowned at her. "That gin bottle's been in the back of my mind. If that bottle was important, too bad. It's probably been thrown out by now."

"But I remember it as only half full. Maybe Alicia put it away."

"Or drank it." Jack Ford looked thoughtful. "If so much time hadn't passed, I'd ask you to steal the trash."

"Do *what?*"

"Steal the trash, love. It's basic. Get hold of that gin bottle."

"But what would we do with it?"

"Take it to a lab. They could find traces of penicillin."

"Wonder if the bottle's still there," she mused.

"Maybe, maybe not. I want to talk to the neighbors, see if anybody saw anything. You check one more time about what your husband was doing that night and talk to Duff Mowbray. Find out about Sam's last conversation. Can you meet me again Friday morning?"

She nodded. They rose and walked out together, and she had a quick, painful sense of déjà vu, of her and Sam leaving the coffee shop. Jack walked her to her car and patted it lightly on the fender, as you might pat a horse.

"You like this 4Runner?"

She sighed. "It does the job."

"My car does, too, when it wants to. I'm right behind you."

She turned around to see an elderly dark green MG, somewhat the worse for wear. "One day I'm going to restore it," he said.

Her eyes widened as she thought of Melvin's list of cars he'd seen that night. *"You* weren't at Sam's, were you?"

"I was at my uncle's funeral, remember?"

She nodded and met his gaze. "Jack, why are you helping me? Really?"

"Maybe," he said, "maybe it's for friendship. Maybe it's to see justice done. And maybe, just maybe, it's the look in your eyes when you talk about Sam."

He held out his hand. "Take care, Liberty."

"Thank you, Jack." She glanced back at the MG. She hadn't seen one of those in years. Why didn't he take better care of it?

Could she trust him?

Chapter Sixteen

The Senior Warden

Liberty trusted Duff Mowbray.

A dapper corporate lawyer, the Shadrack House chairman draped his well-tailored suits over a slim frame, favored polka-dotted ties, and listened more than he talked in meetings. When he did say something, you could count on its being useful, and he was Sam's staunch supporter.

She called his law office as soon as she got home, identifying herself to the secretary and explaining that she needed to talk with Mr. Mowbray about Sam Maginnes and Shadrach House.

"Wasn't it just awful?" The secretary lowered her voice. "I'll have him call you." She paused and murmured, "Just a moment. He's leaving the office. I'll see if he can speak to you before he heads out to lunch."

A moment later Duff came on the line. "Mrs. Chase. Liberty. Hello again. You seem to always catch me on the fly. We need to have that coffee."

"Just a quick word, now, please." She hoped he wouldn't mind. "I'm editing Sam's memoir. Alicia wants very much to see it finished, but she's too distraught to participate. I don't know if he told you about what he was writing, but I'd like to include anything you could tell me about his life—after he came to St. Chad's, or even before."

Duff's voice held surprise. "I didn't know Sam was working on a book."

"He was doing it to help the boys."

Duff replied firmly. "That project has to go on. Our church was just beginning to come alive again. Our old rector . . . well, he'd stayed too long and didn't make an effort. Sam was the best thing to happen to us in a long time, and now this. It's like a house under construction being wrecked by a tornado."

"I understand."

"I'll help in any way I can," Duff said and paused. "There's something you should know."

"Yes?" She sank down to the chair beside the phone, wondering if Sam had told his secrets to Duff.

"I may have been the last person to see Sam alive."

"Oh," she said. "Oh."

"Just a moment." She heard a muffled, "Yes, Elise, I know, I'm coming." Then, to Liberty, "He seemed preoccupied that evening. Not himself. We had a drink together." Duff gave a self-deprecating laugh. "I'm afraid I monopolized the conversation with my concerns. He listened and gave me some good advice but never mentioned anything about himself."

Then Duff spoke to someone else again.

How long could Liberty keep him talking? This Elise seemed hot to trot. "He never said anything about himself?" she prompted.

"Actually, he did, come to think of it. Sam was talking about one of those neighbors who opposes our new facility. Sam told me that the neighbor wasn't a bad man, but he came from a poor background and wanted to pull up the drawbridge behind him. And then Sam said, 'He and I have more in common than he realizes, except that I want to help them up and he wants to keep them out.'"

"Yes," Liberty replied. "The memoir explains that Sam came from a disadvantaged family."

"He never talked about it in sermons," Duff said, "like some of them do. Confessional, you know, that wasn't Sam."

"You were the last person, to see him, you say?" she asked Duff hopefully.

"Yes." The lawyer cleared his throat. "Gracelyn Rodgers dropped some papers off at his house and left. She, uh, she seemed to be in a hurry. Sam and I had maybe two drinks and then he said he'd had enough because he was going to do some writing and needed a clear head."

Liberty opened her mouth to ask a question but Duff went on. "Look, my wife's waiting for me; have to run. Why don't we have lunch Friday? I can tell you more then."

"All right, thank you so much." Liberty hung up. So Gracelyn had left in a hurry, and Duff seemed uneasy at mentioning it. Now Liberty would just have to wait for Friday for information. She needed to ask Duff which neighbors of the new Shadrach house particularly opposed the project.

Gracelyn Rodgers must have been the woman in the "lady's car." She must have been the one who arrived right as Melvin was leaving. And what papers had she brought? Were they the same chapters Alicia had given her?

That didn't explain why the papers on the dining table that night had been scattered. Should she call Jack Ford and forestall the door-to-door questioning? No. Any scrap of information might be helpful.

The thought of inspecting Alicia's trash intrigued her.

A car honked in the driveway, the doorknob rattled, and Emmy burst into the kitchen. "Mommy! Caitlin come home with me?" Liberty walked outside to a waiting green Ford Explorer and assured Caitlin's mother it was all right.

She gave the girls peanut butter and banana sandwiches and sent them upstairs, chattering about the Bratz dolls they loved. Emmy was expecting a new one for Christmas. Santa Claus would deliver the doll, because Liberty didn't want her to be the only child in the neighborhood without one. Still, Liberty had her reservations. She hoped Emmy wouldn't start wanting to dress like the bad-girl dolls.

She remembered well her fashionable Barbies, and Mama Jean's chagrin that she didn't appreciate the dull old dolls of Madame Alexander.

The younger generation has been driving their parents mad forever, Sam once told her. Even Plato said so, he insisted. Then he said, "Faith has to operate in the world, not apart from it. Faith means you don't seal yourself off. That means the faith is weak, not strong enough to stand up by itself. You have to meet the world head-on, not hide in a cave. We become stronger in our faith by embracing the world."

By embracing the world, he wanted to save his boys from the worst aspects of it.

His boys.

It came rushing back to her, that night Rico tried to rob them. She'd been helping Sam write up a report to give to the vestries of both St. Chad's and St. Ambrose's, in the hope that the donations they'd given would be repeated another year. Since Sam wasn't the organized type, work of that kind was usually done shortly before it was due, and this time was no exception. Everyone else, boys and volunteers, had left.

They were just finishing up when the outer door opened. They looked at each other. Neither of them had locked it after the last boy shut it behind him.

A young fellow, a wild look in his eyes and a switchblade in his hands, stood at the office door.

"Give me your money," he said. His hand was trembling.

Sam reached for his wallet. The boy pointed the knife at me. "You, too."

Liberty grabbed her bag off the table behind her, opened it, and took out fourteen dollars, all she had with her.

"Why are you doing this, Rico?" Sam asked calmly, wallet in hand. "I would have given you money if you needed it. Armed robbery is serious jail time."

"Deme, deme, come on," the boy said, scooping with his fingers.

Sam caught Liberty's glance. She knew he was about to do something, because she knew Sam. She held out her fourteen dollars, and when the boy went to take it, Sam lunged at him, grabbing the hand with the knife and bending it behind his back.

"You don't want to do this, son," he said. She held her breath at the way he'd taken control, as if he'd had martial arts training. Maybe he had.

Sam twisted more tightly. The boy dropped the knife and began to cry.

"It's a gang, isn't it? You want to be in the gang? Robbing is the first step?"

The boy dropped his eyes.

"How old are you?"

"Fourteen."

"Sit down."

Liberty picked up the knife and closed it. The boy hunkered miserably in the chair opposite Sam and Sam talked to him, and when he finished, the boy promised to come back the next day and join Sam's group instead. Sam kept the knife.

After Rico left, Sam locked the door behind him, and Liberty wondered why. Hadn't he calmed the boy down? But she was glad he did. Probably to make her feel better.

She'd been holding her breath, holding in all her fear, and now she let it out in long, racking sobs. Sam had held her and held her, and when she looked up at him, they both knew an invisible wall had been breached. They pulled away. Breathless. She unlocked the door and stumbled out. She drove straight home.

Her throat caught now as she thought of him, and tears spilled from her eyes. She took a deep breath. She had to hold herself together. There was work to be done.

She wanted to talk to the boys. She called Foley Manning at St. Ambrose's. She hadn't seen him since the funeral, and a call to him was overdue.

"Hi there, Liberty. I bet I know what you want to talk about."

She swallowed hard. "I'll bet you do." Why couldn't she have had a detective like Foley, with his sheepdog eyes, salt-and-pepper beard, and mind that could wrap itself around the most convoluted theological argument?

"Actually, I was fixing to call you," he said. "The Board's meeting Thursday night. We'll be talking about how to go forward with Shadrach House. I'd like for you to be there."

"Am I really needed?" She had so much to do with the memoir, and Emmy, and...

"We want you to join the board. We need another member."

Join the board? Could she really sit there at those meetings with people like Duff Mowbray and talk about Sam, about Shadrach house, without coming apart? "Me? I don't have money or connections or anything like that."

"We need you, honey. Commitment means as much as connections."

"Couldn't I just stay as administrator for a while?" She'd push herself to make sure of the grant, then she wanted out. Best to leave those memories behind.

"Well, come to the meeting, and we'll talk about it."

She bit her lip with frustration. "Dallas is out of town, and I don't know if I can find a babysitter on short notice. It's a school night."

"Heck, bring the little girl along."

The excuse well was running dry, and she hadn't gotten to the purpose of her call. "All right. I'll come to the meeting. One question, please. The boys who came to the funeral."

"What about them?"

She wrote their names on a pad by the telephone. "I want to talk to Rico, Jesse, and Cedric about Sam. For the book. He did tell you about the memoir, didn't he?"

"A little bit, yes."

"Will they talk to me?"

"I don't see why not. I'll mention it to them. They should be at the House Saturday afternoon. We're having lunch and a meeting, and they usually hang around afterward. Just go on over. And while you're there, how about checking for messages for me, in case I can't make it until late?"

"All right, Foley. By the way, do you know which neighbors have made noise about the project?"

"Sure. Sam and I made a list, and we were planning to call on each one personally. I don't know how that's going to get done."

"I have an idea that might help,' she said. "I'll tell you at the meeting."

Foley agreed. They said their goodbyes, and Liberty stared out into the back yard, at the rain misting down, the fog rolling in, the glistening black trees, and the brown and red oak leaves holding fast to their limbs by their dear, tough little stems.

Sam was gone, and they'd all have to carry on, while she was finding layers and layers of the unknown in the man she thought she knew.

She'd been prepared for Dallas to make noise and objections. She'd been prepared for people telling her she should work with the disabled.

She was not prepared for Sam to die.

She had to pull at least two things out of this chaos. She had to find out what really happened that night, and she had to help fulfill Sam's dream. She felt as determined as Scarlett O'Hara pulling that root out of the ground, vowing never to be hungry again. As for Dallas . . . she'd think about him tomorrow.

And now, she desperately wanted to pick up the trash from Sam's house.

Chapter Seventeen

O nline, she found that the garbage for that area was picked up on Friday.

But she didn't know what time. Could she arrive before the truck Friday morning? The kids would be at school, but what about Alicia? Melvin Milton might be watching. What if the truck came so early that she missed it? How could she be on time with all the traffic? Thursday evening, Alicia and the children would be home. Could she snatch the garbage out from under their noses?

She'd be heading to the board meeting then, so she'd be on that side of town anyhow. It was risky, but it might work.

She called Alicia with an excuse for stopping by that Thursday evening, but she wasn't home. Liberty spent the next three hours stewing. She left messages—for Alicia, for Jack Ford, for Blaine, the teenager who babysat for Emmy. She even took the precaution, just in case she ran into trouble, of moving her father's gun from the glove compartment into the house, safe from Emmy on a high closet shelf, hidden in a box of sweaters.

Caitlin's mother came to pick her up, and Liberty worked with Emmy on her reading homework before she let her daughter watch TV. The child was reading better than anyone had predicted, but just like her mother, she found numbers a challenge.

Since Dallas was out of town, Liberty made an easy dinner of hamburgers, baked potatoes, and tossed salad. Afterwards, she'd just run the water for Emmy's bath when Alicia returned her call, sounding less than friendly.

Liberty, her nerves like an over-tightened violin string, told her cover story. "It's the book," she said, as sincerely as she knew how. "Do you have any pictures, you know, of the boys, of Shadrach House, anything like that? I'd like to send them with the manuscript, just in case the publisher wants to use them for the cover or promotion."

"Sam didn't mention anything about pictures," Alicia said, "but then he didn't tell me everything." Liberty wished she had a picture of Sam, maybe one of him and the boys. She had two things to remember him by: a book of Yeats's poems he'd given her as a Christmas present, and a bookmark with a prayer on it like the ones he'd given all the boys.

She suddenly realized Alicia was saying, "I was in his study this afternoon, sorting out his papers to see if there was anything the church would want. I believe there were some packets of pictures—at church and with those boys at the house. Wasn't there a picnic or something when it opened?"

"Oh, yes," Liberty said. "That was the workday when somebody donated the space. We spent all day cleaning and painting." She wondered how Alicia could bear to go through his papers so soon. Maybe she just needed something to keep her busy, to keep from thinking too much.

"I can drop them in the mail," Alicia said. "And there's the picture of him for the church directory—it's the most recent."

A recent picture of him—perfect for the book jacket. "Alicia, that would be wonderful. I'll stop by for the packet, if that's all right. I'll be out that way for a board meeting tomorrow night."

"If you like. I'll be home."

"I'll return them when we're through with them," she said.

Alicia's next utterance blindsided her. "Liberty . . . you can keep the pictures."

She mumbled her thanks and hung up the phone. *Alicia didn't want them*. Did she hate the project so much?

Blaine, the teenager from up the street, called back and agreed to sit.

DECEMBER 7

Liberty's plans were clicking together, and Thursday she started the day with relief that the investigation was progressing. Then, shortly after lunch, Duff's secretary called and told Liberty he'd be unable to meet with her on Friday.

"Can I reschedule?"

The secretary hesitated. "Call back, maybe next Tuesday. I'll know more then."

Liberty assumed he had a logjam of work and didn't give it a second thought.

Late Thursday afternoon, she grated cheese for Emmy's favorite Tex-Mex casserole: taco-seasoned ground beef, rice, Monterey jack cheese, beans, half a jar of chunky salsa, mixed and baked at 350° until bubbly. She hummed as she set the casserole in the oven.

After Emmy had done a pretty good job of demolishing Liberty's creation and the casserole dish had been left to soak, the time was about seven, good and dark. The Shadrach House board meeting had been set for eight at St. Chad's, and it would take half an hour to get there. At least. She gathered her cold-weather gear and notes, but the sitter was running late.

Liberty paced the floor and gnawed her well-chewed nails. She called Blaine's cell number and got a busy signal.

And then a car screeched to a stop out front. Liberty flung open the front door, and in the moonlit night saw Blaine struggling to heave a wheeled book bag out of a car that seemed to be filled with boys.

"Sorry to be late, Mrs. Chase," she called, rolling the bag up the front walk. "I caught a ride with my brother."

Blaine came in and Liberty closed the door. Then she shrugged into her black nylon parka and picked up a pair of leather-and-spandex driving gloves. She smoothed them onto trembling fingers.

As the miles to the other side of town ticked away, her mind ticked off all the undesirable outcomes of this trash exploration. She would be discovered and humiliated, Shadrach house would be affected, the investigation would be stymied. But Sam had often said: "Courage isn't the absence of fear. It's going ahead despite it."

She nosed into Sam's subdivision and rounded the corners, headlights sweeping over front lawns and mailboxes. She recalled once when she'd had to deliver some materials he'd left at the office. It had been summer with subdivision lawns wildly green, and Sam had been alive and sweating and tramping after a mower, waving to her in greeting.

The lawnmower's shadowy outline in the garage startled her as she walked through the pool of light from the security floodlamp. Alicia's minivan was parked next to Sam's car. Guilt gave her gut a violent twist. Had there been anything, *anything* at all she could have done to prevent his death?

At the back door she rang the bell. No answer. She knocked. The garage light clicked on, and the back door opened. It was Sam's daughter, Katharine, her long dark hair swinging around her face, Sam's face, her coltish body echoing Sam's rangy one, her brown eyes like his. The girl held a manila envelope in her hand. "Mom said you were coming by for these."

Liberty took the package of pictures, hearing the TV chatter inside. "Please thank her for me." She turned to go.

"Mom's on the phone," said Katharine. "Or she'd have come. Wait, there was something else I was supposed to tell you. Oh, yes. Mr. Mowbray's in the hospital."

"In the *hospital?* What's wrong?"

Katharine shrugged. "I don't think they know."

"Thanks, Katharine. I'd better be going." Now she was really in a hurry. Foley would tell her more at the meeting.

Sam's daughter closed the door. Liberty walked to her car and tossed the envelope into the passenger seat. The garage light clicked off and a crazy notion swelled in her chest. The envelope made her think of the missing pages, the pages that told what he had done to make him leave New York, what he had lied about all these years . . . could he have left them in his car? She closed her car door gently without latching it and crept back to the dark garage, keeping to the far wall.

She quietly pulled on the rear door handle of Sam's Honda, making sure not to touch the dusty exterior. It opened, a lucky break. As she'd guessed, no one had felt like cleaning it out. Propped on the back seat, a cardboard box of donated footballs and basketballs waited for a trip to the center. A dark blue nylon windbreaker lay carelessly beside it. She picked it up, and underneath lay a brown envelope.

A sermon? More of his writing? *The missing material?* Whatever it was, apparently no one had gone looking for it. Before she could examine it, she heard a noise from the house, ducked, and nearly lost her balance. With shaking hands she threw the jacket down, stuck the envelope under her arm, and pushed the car door shut with a soft click. She still had a job to do, and she didn't think anyone would miss the envelope. She could return it later if necessary.

She crept out of the garage and lowered the window of her rear hatch. Then she swung herself into the car, tossed the envelope on the back seat, and started the engine. Lights off, she slowly rolled to the end of the drive.

She stopped when she drew even with the large wheeled bin looming by the curb. She glanced back at the house. The blinds were closed, the curtains tightly drawn. She jumped out and jerked two black trash bags out of the curbie and shoved them through the open hatch of her vehicle. Then she tossed two bags full of crumpled newspaper into the bin, just as Jack had instructed.

As she sped away, from the corner of her eye she glimpsed Melvin standing on his front doorstep.

Feeling sick, tense, and shaky, she stopped in the next block and closed the back hatch.

When she got to the church where the meeting was taking place, she parked in an inconspicuous spot and hoped the garbage wouldn't smell up her car. The next hour and a half went by very slowly indeed.

At the meeting she found that Duff Mowbray had been stricken by some sort of extreme stomach flu and been hospitalized while they ran tests. The meeting was chaotic with neither Duff nor Sam to keep control, and the talk was mainly about the Committee to Save Hollydale Hills, a subdivision edged with disintegrating brick ranches. All that Shadrach House wanted to do was fix up a long empty ranch on a nearby street where many of the houses had turned commercial. For some reason, the fatherless teenagers were less desirable than, say, a loan shark's office. It didn't make a whole lot of sense.

She took Foley aside and told him that Jack Ford had offered to help in any way possible, and that she might be able to convince him to talk to the Hollydale Hills people. She didn't want to tell the whole board until Jack had agreed. Foley gave her a list of the complainers and wished her luck.

She left the meeting with a headache. On the way home, the reek of garbage filling the car didn't help.

When she arrived home, she was shocked to see Dallas's car in the driveway. Her heart hammering, she grabbed the envelope with the pictures inside. Where was the other envelope? The one that might hold the missing material? She patted the back seat, searching for it.

The light in the garage clicked on. "Mrs. Chase?" The babysitter stood in the kitchen door. "I think you'd better get in here quick."

Emmy? Liberty leaped out of the car and hurried into the brightly lighted kitchen, heart in her throat.

Chapter Eighteen

GARBAGE

Liberty plunged through the door into sounds of thumping and gagging. What on earth?

Wide-eyed, Blaine fluttered her hands. "It's Mr. Chase. He came in just a little while ago and asked me to stay because he's sick. I tried to call you but you didn't *answer*. I was about to call my *mom*." The last was said accusingly, as if it might be a mortal crime to be out of reach for half an hour.

Liberty had turned off the cell phone while she was stealing garbage.

Now she gripped the envelope of pictures in her hand. She hoped Dallas wasn't drunk. "Do you need a ride home?"

"I'm cool," the girl said, hoisting her book bag. "I can walk."

"Be careful." Liberty opened her handbag and paid the sitter, adding a generous tip. A look of relief crossed Blaine's face as she headed for the door, glad to be out of the house.

Liberty opened the junk drawer under the kitchen phone, slipped in the pictures, and hurried up the stairs. She found Dallas coming out of the bathroom, his face a nasty shade of olive. He wasn't staggering and she didn't smell booze. He gazed at her with bleary eyes.

"So where have you been?" He didn't sound angry, just curious.

Liberty pushed damp frizz back from her forehead. "The Shadrach House board meeting. I told you I was going."

"I forgot."

"What are you doing here instead of in Pittsburgh?"

"Being sick."

"What *happened?*"

"Who the hell knows how I got this? Bad shrimp, oysters, whatever—can't trust anything these days. Hazard of the road." He looked away. "Plastic bag over there—that stuff needs washing."

She walked over to pick it up. The smell told her all she needed to know.

She crimped the bag shut and carried it downstairs and stuffed the items in the washing machine. She poured in a good dose of 20 Mule Team Borax and programmed the machine for the pre-wash rinse cycle.

She poured Dallas a big glassful of Gatorade and took it up to him.

He sipped the glass of green stuff. "Thanks, babe. I appreciate it."

That was a surprise. "Would you like anything else?"

"Yeah. Why don't you sit with me awhile?"

"Do what?" Liberty blinked.

"Sit. Talk. Converse. Or just hang out here while I cop a few z's."

Knock me over with a feather. "You don't want me to get your laptop?"

"This may surprise you," he said, "but I don't feel like working. Remind me why we don't have a TV in here."

"Bedrooms are for sleeping," Liberty said, "and making love. That's what we agreed." Well, not exactly. He'd given in so that she'd agree to the hideous marshmallow chair he kept in the TV room.

"Maybe I'll come downstairs and watch."

Liberty swallowed. "You need to be in bed, and I've got a few chores to finish up. Tell you what. There's a portable DVD player in the closet that was going to be one of Emmy's Christmas presents. I'll bring up a new movie—"

"You're always complaining I don't spend enough time with you. Well, here I am, hog-tied, and you're too busy?"

"I'm sorry," she said. "I'll come right back when I finish. Remember, the laundry?" Oh, dear God, he had to stay in bed while she went through the garbage bags. She plunged into the gift closet to retrieve the DVD player and prayed there was a film downstairs he'd like.

She slicked on a pair of new yellow rubber gloves and ripped a big green leaf bag off the roll in the storage room, and then found a knife to slice the toothed fasteners of Alicia's black bags. She nicked her glove with the knife, but she wasn't going to stop to change it.

She reached into the first bag and pulled out handfuls of paper. Her pulse raced; then she saw it was notebook paper—math problems, homework. Then she found tissues, more tissues, a tissue box. Aluminum pie pans, doughnut boxes with crusts of sugar, soft drink liter bottles, a baked beans can. Foam trays, meat wrappers, beginning to stink.

The smells got funkier, and she tried not to breathe. They say when you smell something you breathe in molecules of that substance. A mixed nut can, ice cream carton, coffee grounds.

Then: Disposable razors, cellophane. Cigarette packets. A half-gone can of shaving cream.

A lone black nylon man's sock with dust bunnies clinging to it. She closed her eyes and stuffed it into the bag. She found more dust bunnies and a full vacuum cleaner bag and stifled a sneeze.

A white deli bag. She dusted it off and put it aside.

The second garbage bag was much like the first. No gin bottle. She re-tied the trash bags and found that only one would go into her already stuffed curbie. While she was trying to decide what to do, she heard Dallas calling for her, and she had no choice but to hide the other bag in the storage room off the garage.

It was two in the morning when she sank, exhausted, into sleep.

DECEMBER 8

When she awoke at eight, she was horrified to see she'd overslept. Dallas's side of the bed was empty. And she was supposed to be meeting Jack!

She staggered out of bed and rushed into Emmy's room. The bed was neatly made. She hurried downstairs and found a note on the kitchen table.

Hey Babe—feeling much better. Gone to the office. I dropped Emmy by school so you could sleep. I took your car. Mine is a mess. Can you take care of that today? Love, D.

Dallas got Emmy dressed, gave her breakfast, and took her to school? Maybe he was really trying, for once.

She called Jack and he answered. "You sound bleary."

"I am, and I'm going to be late. Can you wait? "

"If you hurry. I have an appointment at ten."

She hung up, and then she remembered: Dallas was driving her car!

What about the envelope she stole from Sam's car? She sent another prayer that Dallas wouldn't find the envelope. Was she allowed to pray for things like that?

She rolled her now-empty trash bin away from the curb and stuffed Alicia's trash bags in. She grabbed some rags and set about cleaning up Dallas's car.

Fog was just beginning to lift by the time she'd cleaned most of the nastiness. She kept all the windows open while she drove to the coffee shop to meet Jack.

Wearing the houndstooth jacket with elbow patches, he waited in the usual spot, his hand cupped around a white mug. A plate of crumbs sat in front of him as well as a notebook.

He broke into a grin when he saw her. "Thought you weren't coming. Let's get you some java," he said, rising from his seat. "You look like death."

"Poor choice of words." She walked to the counter with him. "Sorry to be late. It's a long story."

Half-smiling, he glanced at her. "No worries. I recommend the chocolate croissant."

"What about my diet?"

He looked her up and down and shrugged, then went to the counter. "Two chocolate croissants," he told the barista.

At the table, the pastry looked good, all buttery gloss and oozy rich chocolate, but her appetite wasn't there.

"Jack, I stole the garbage," she said.

"You *what?*"

"I took two bags from Sam's house, and I went through them."

"I was half kidding! I didn't mean for you to do it."

She shook her head and shuddered. "It was awful, Jack. Not that it was garbage. It was bits of his life. Life that was cut short."

His smile faded. "I understand. What did you find?"

"No gin bottle."

"What else?"

"Food containers—aluminum pans, plastic dishes, paper plates. Dust and stuff. Notebook paper. Used Kleenex. Junk mail. One of his socks."

He winced. She took a bite of her pastry so she wouldn't have to talk any more. The chocolate melted on her tongue, and she felt guilty for being alive and eating chocolate while Sam was dead. "I ought to be eating ashes," she said.

"Don't let me hear that kind of talk," Jack said. His topaz eyes narrowed. "Let's concentrate on finding his killer. So the bottle may still be at the house, unless Alicia drank it."

"Or gave it to visitors."

A couple carrying monster lattes edged their way past their table and settled directly behind Jack. The man's elephantine shoulders and well-padded back spilled over against Jack's chair. He edged up and scooted the table forward, and she had to slide back.

"So what do we do now about the bottle?"

"Let me think," he said. "What did you find out from Duff Mowbray?"

"He's the one who had drinks with Sam."

"Did he bring the bottle?"

She shrugged. "He mentioned talking to Sam about the neighborhood opposition and a personal problem."

"What else?"

"That's about it, except he said Sam seemed unusually gloomy. He thought it was just the pressure of everything they were doing. And he mentioned that Gracelyn Rodgers came by."

Jack's eyebrows went up. "What kind of car does she drive?"

"An Avalon. I think that qualifies as 'a lady's kind of car,' as Melvin called it."

Jack sipped his coffee, thinking, and then said, "I didn't get much out of the neighbors." He'd told them he was investigating a burglary for an insurance company and wanted to know about strange cars or people in the neighborhood Thanksgiving Eve. No, said the neighbors, they hadn't seen a thing, and that included Melvin.

Liberty twisted her rings nervously. "Did Melvin say anything about someone stealing garbage?"

"What? No."

"I think he saw me. I've been waiting for the other shoe to drop."

Jack smiled. "You think he'd tell Alicia?"

"No," she said. "I think he had a grudge against Alicia. But it creeps me out that he might know I took the garbage. I have a feeling I'll hear from him."

"So what do you make of Melvin?" said Jack.

She hugged herself and pondered, then shook her head. "I just don't know."

Jack reached for the second croissant, and Liberty pushed it his way. "So there were no other cars there, but you heard somebody in the house. Melvin could have walked over, and you said he didn't like Sam."

She stared at him.

"I know this is hard for you," Jack said. "Go over what happened that night once more."

Liberty closed her eyes, gulped, and took two cleansing breaths. "When I drove up, I saw a light go off upstairs. That made me think Sam was home. I walked in and called him, but there was no answer. It started thundering again and I had to get back to Emmy, since she's terrified of thunder. I cut through the family room and that's when I stumbled over a shoe and fell.

"Then I saw Sam in the light from the kitchen, lying on the floor, one arm extended as though he was reaching for something. I crawled over and touched him. As soon as I felt his skin . . ." She stopped, swallowed, and waited a minute before she choked out the rest of the words. "It was cool to the touch. I saw the lividity and I knew he was dead. Then it gets all confusing. Emmy came in, looking for me . . . and then I heard the noise upstairs."

"You're sure about that noise upstairs."

Her eyes filled with tears. "I've never been more certain about anything in my life."

He touched her hand. "Maybe something fell off a shelf."

"Jack, I know the difference between a falling object and a footstep squeaking the floorboards." Her throat thick, she pulled her hand away and fished for a Kleenex while Jack waited. People walked by their table, happy people, bored people, people living everyday lives. How did anyone ever live an everyday life?

She was grateful for Jack's patience. He didn't become angry at her for being upset, the way Dallas sometimes did.

"You think it was a person up there," he said.

"Well, what else could it have been? What if I'd come just a little sooner? I might have saved him." Her tears started afresh, and she snuffled into her tissue.

"Liberty, look at me. We can go crazy with *what if.* What if Dallas had come home that night stone cold sober and you'd had Thanksgiving with your in-laws? If somebody wanted to kill Sam, he'd still be dead."

Her mouth opened. "Do you think God put me there to solve his murder?"

Jack shook his head. "Sometime when we have a couple of hours I'll explain how wrong that proposition is. If you want to bring God into it, let's say that God can use you to solve the murder, if there was a murder."

She nodded and wiped her eyes. She took a sip of her coffee. Outside, the fog rolled on by, thick, casting the parking lot into shades of gray.

Jack went on. "We don't know if it's murder. We're just looking into this, Liberty, to find the truth. I owe it to him as a friend who helped me when I was going through a bad time."

He withdrew a small notebook from his inside coat pocket. "Once again, tell me if there's any way your husband might have been involved."

Heat bloomed in her cheeks. "I know what you're getting at. Jack, my marriage is pretty shaky, and Dallas is no angel, but the thought of his hiring a . . . a *hit man* is absurd. He even took Emmy to school and let me sleep this morning."

Jack gave me a grim smile. "You're loyal, in spite of it all, and I like that about you." He jotted down something in his notebook.

"Are you making notes on me?"

He snapped the notebook shut. "Lower your hackles, honey, and tell me just a little more about Dallas."

Liberty felt that her hackles were as up as a hyena's. She remembered Dallas as he was last night—sick, human, depending on her. Dallas was a shit sometimes, maybe, but he was her shit, and she was not convinced Jack was wholly trustworthy. "Dallas is just about as devious as a water buffalo, Jack."

"He was violent with you," Jack reminded her, as if she needed reminding.

"He'd been drinking, and it was the first time he'd been violent like that. He swore he'd never do it again."

"That's what they all say, sugar."

She looked down at the table, at her hands. He didn't know the first thing about Dallas and her. He didn't know how gallant he'd been, how much fun he'd been, how well he could dance—and Jack wouldn't shut up. "Does he love you?"

"What does that mean?"

"I detect avoidance, Liberty. Does he cherish you? Are you important to him?"

A lump rose in her throat, and she fought tears again. "I don't know."

"Tell me about it."

She took in a deep breath and let it out slowly. "It's up and down. He drinks, he's awful to me, then he makes up with me, becomes warm and fuzzy and loving, so I drop my guard. Then, Jack, it's like the gate slams shut. He goes on a bender and turns on me."

Jack said, "This is your therapist talking. What keeps you there? Are you expecting him to change?"

She held her head in her hands. "Jack, I have to give him a chance, for Emmy's sake. For the sake of the happy family I always wanted. I never really knew my mom and dad. My grandparents are wonderful, but I want my little girl to have a mommy and daddy. She has enough problems as it is."

"You stay with Dallas for your little girl?"

"My grandfather told me my father was all about duty. He told me the importance of duty. Not only do I love my daughter, I have a duty toward her. And she loves her daddy. It isn't all bad. Dallas can be a real charmer. Lots of my friends think I'm lucky."

"I hear you about duty. But don't rely on charm. Ever hear of Ted Bundy?"

She placed two hands on the table. "Jack. I think I would know if Dallas was a psychopathic serial killer."

"They're very, very deceptive. Look, Liberty. You have to look after yourself as well." He reached out and took her hand.

She pulled it away, afraid that his concern would weaken her resolve. "Why are you picking on Dallas? What about Alicia?"

He leveled his eyes at Liberty. "I'm not ruling her out. Sam never talked to me about his marriage, but you said you found something in that material he wrote?"

"Only that Alicia had planned a much different kind of life."

Jack looked away. "That happens."

There was a silence, a long silence. Jack got such a distant look he might as well have left the room. She wondered how long ago he'd been hurt and who'd been the one to leave.

Whatever it was, it passed. "OK, kiddo," he said, "what else do you have?"

So much for the lonely romantic private eye. She riffled through her notebook. "During the board meeting, Foley Manning mentioned that Sam got two threatening phone calls about Shadrach House. Couldn't identify the caller but thought it might be one of the neighborhood group members disguising his voice. Sam didn't take the calls seriously. When he invited the caller to come over for a talk, the guy hung up."

"That could be significant," said Jack, scribbling in his notebook. Anything else?"

"Well, I had suggested to Foley Manning that I knew someone who might contact those people in the neighborhood group . . ."

"I'll call Foley," Jack said without hesitation, scribbling a note. "What did Duff Mowbray have to say?"

She took a sip of coffee. "Well, Duff didn't make it to the meeting. His secretary canceled the lunch we'd set up today. Last night, Alicia let me know that Duff was in the hospital."

Jack's eyes narrowed and he pulled out his cell phone. "Do you have Duff's office number?" he asked. It was written in her notebook, and she slid it over to Jack.

Jack keyed in the number, listened, and after a moment ended the call. "The office is closed for the day."

The hairs on the back of Liberty's neck prickled. "That's odd."

"Find his home phone for me."

She didn't have it, so she tried the church and got shuttled to a message system. But Vivian, thankfully, was cruising around with a client and had the number in her PDA.

Jack punched it in and waited. She heard the tinny answer, "Mowbray residence."

"This is the Rev. J. Hartley Ford," Jack began. He'd told Liberty he only used his title when it would help.

"Are you calling about the funeral?" Liberty heard.

"The funeral? May I have details?" Jack looked at Liberty, eyebrows raised.

She shook her head. He said a few more words and closed the phone, face grim. "Duff died this morning."

A chill slid down her back. She shut her eyes, sick at heart, confused and stunned. "I can't believe it. The other day, he looked fine. Slim, tanned, lots of energy."

Jack drummed on the table. "They'll do an autopsy on someone his age with no prior health problems. He's the senior warden, you said?"

She nodded.

"First the rector, then the senior warden. Think we ought to tell the junior warden to watch his back?"

"Jack. I can't bear a joke right now."

"Sorry." He extracted a paper napkin from the holder on the table and clicked his silver ballpoint. He wrote numbers one through three. "Two deaths—same church—within two weeks. Coincidence, or were the two related? Did Duff know something he shouldn't have about Sam Maginnes?"

"He's on the Shadrach House board, remember?"

Jack wrote by number one: *coincidence.* Suppose there was no connection whatsoever." By number two, he wrote: *silence.* "Suppose Duff knew something about Sam's murder and was killed to shut him up."

"But—"

By number three he wrote: *eliminate obstacles.* "They both were in someone's way."

"Jack, let's not get ahead of ourselves. It might have been a heart attack or something."

"Okay. But I'll keep this in mind while we investigate." Jack sipped the last of his coffee and stared into the empty mug. Then he said, "Oh, by the way, I did talk to Foley about calling the NIMBYs. But now I'm going to my appointment and then visit Alicia. I don't think I've given her my condolences."

Liberty felt tears rising in her throat. Duff had been a good, decent man, great to work with. "I've got to go," she said, reaching for her sweater.

They both rose, and Jack held the cardigan for her. "Just to put your mind at ease, Liberty, can you find out what your husband was doing before he came home that day?"

She pushed up her sleeves. "What? He didn't even know Duff."

Was the man she'd counted on to help her proving to be a complete lunatic?

Chapter Nineteen

Friday evening, Dallas had returned her squeaky-clean, newly detailed SUV. "How about that, babe? Thanks for helping me."

She'd clenched her fists, bit her lip, and reminded herself that right now, she was going for an Oscar. "How sweet of you," she said, docile as Melanie Wilkes. "Did you see an envelope in there?"

He shrugged. "There wasn't anything you needed, was there? All I saw was junk mail, and I told them to throw out all the trash."

Because of that remark, she hadn't slept much last night. If that envelope had contained her missing material, it was gone forever.

Today, Saturday, she planned to arrive at Shadrach House early in the afternoon, as Foley was going to have the boys clean and paint the interior that morning and then feed them lunch. She'd already bought Christmas presents for their party next week: socks and toiletries and hand-held games.

Emmy would go with her friend Caitlin to the mall to have her picture made with Santa. She figured Dallas would do as he usually did—sleep late, watch some football game on TV, and go to the office to catch up with work. She wondered if he was coming down to breakfast. She poured herself a second cup of coffee, picked up the newspaper from the table, and turned to the Jumble. She began to mentally unscramble the letters FNEKI, and just when she'd figured out the answer, she was grabbed from behind, a hairy arm encircling her waist. Half expecting a KNIFE to be held to her throat, she screamed.

"Hush, babe, you'll scare the kid." Dallas laughed and let her go. "Really got you good, didn't I?"

She wheeled around, fuming. "That wasn't funny."

"If you could have seen the look on your face . . ."

She brushed the hair away from her cheeks and calmed herself. Best to ignore his stupid prank. "What are you doing up? I thought you'd sleep all morning."

He yawned and stretched. "Thought it was time I was up and about. A bright new day in my un-hung-over life. How about going for a hike?"

"A hike?" she squeaked. "Today?"

"Sure, it's a beautiful day."

"It's foggy. It's fifty-six degrees out there."

"It'll burn off and warm up, Florida girl."

"Do you feel all right?"

"Are you kidding? I'm completely over that bug," he said. "I enjoyed the attention, though."

Her mind raced with excuses not to go hiking, and all she could manage was, "You haven't wanted to hike in ages." She walked over to the stove and lifted the lid off a pot she'd forgotten to wash the night before. "What do you want for breakfast?"

He smiled. "Granola will be fine. I'm serious about changing my habits. You keep saying we never do anything together on the weekend. So I'm proposing something. Let's walk that trail by the river."

She was speechless. Should she go to the woods with the man Jack hadn't ruled out as a suspect? Or was Jack crazy? Or didn't she trust her husband? He'd let her down so many times, it was hard to pull the trust out of the bucketful of disappointment.

The doorbell rang. Jen Hollywell, Caitlin's mother, had come to pick up Emmy.

Liberty opened the door and Caitlin, a pretty girl who'd suffered brain damage as a toddler when a tiny marble lodged in her airway, bounced into the kitchen, her Victorian sausage curls springing like Slinkies.

Emmy clattered down the stairs in her green velvet dress. She burst into the kitchen trailing hair ribbons and her ballerina bear, Twinkle. Liberty finished buckling Emmy's shoes, tied the sash on her dress, and gave Jen money for the Santa photo. The girls giggled all the way out the door, happy to be together. After they'd gone, the house felt huge and empty.

"See?" said Dallas. "Now we have a whole day." He slipped an arm around her waist. He kissed the back of her neck and rubbed against her. She could feel him bowed against her backside, insistent. Once upon a time she would have melted.

"I thought we were going hiking," she said.

"We've got lots of time, baby." He nuzzled her neck.

His hands squeezed her waist, then crept under her sweatshirt up to her breasts. Just as he'd managed to cup one, the back door burst open, and Emmy rushed back in, Caitlin on her heels. Dallas dropped his hands and ducked into the den, and Liberty let out a grateful breath.

"Well, girls, what is it?"

"I forgot!" Emmy jumped up and down. "Hurry!"

"What did you forget . . ." Liberty began, and then realized it was the play clothes she'd forgotten to pack. Dallas strolled in, smoothing his hair. Liberty escaped upstairs and, not thinking, tossed the purple warm-up Emmy had worn to Florida into a tote bag along with her socks and sneakers. She ran back downstairs and handed Emmy the bag. "See you this afternoon, sweetie."

Emmy peered into the bag, as she was getting particular about her clothes. She looked up innocently. "What happened to that man?"

"What man?" Dallas looked from her to his wife.

She froze, thinking of Sam. "Man?" Her heart thumped in her throat, and she prayed her daughter wouldn't say anything more.

Caitlin's mom tooted the horn. "We'll talk about that later," she said. "Off with you."

She ushered the girls out the door and into the car, helping Emmy to buckle up. When she came back, Dallas was waiting. "What man?" he said.

"Oh," she said quickly, "some jogger down in Maysville who'd fallen on the road." Words kept spilling out. She was afraid he was dead. But really, it was—"

"Joggers?" Dallas interrupted. "In Maysville, the back of beyond?"

She stuck out her tongue. "Don't put down my town, buster. They're getting new retirees now—the houses are cheaper. The old man was all right, it turned out. Just a dizzy spell."

Dallas walked over and casually poured himself a cup of coffee. "Why'd you rush her out of here?"

"Well, for heaven's sake." Jen was honking the horn. "They need to get to the mall and get a place in line early."

"Okay," he said. "I'm ready to get you into the woods." He gave her a wicked, teasing look.

To the woods? To the cliff above the river? "Dallas. I have a lot of chores to do this morning, and then I have to go to Shadrach House this afternoon."

He faced Liberty then and put both hands on her shoulders, smiling in that patient, dreamy way he'd had when they'd first met. "Honey, you've been acting mighty peculiar these last few days. I know I haven't been the best husband, but, heck, give me a chance. Haven't I stayed sober?"

"Three weeks," she said carefully. "That's a good start. I'm very glad. Still, I don't know what you do when you're out of town." Should she mention the liquor under the seat of his car? Then he would know she'd been snooping, and a fight would start. She was so tired of fighting.

As if reading her thoughts, he said, "You've got to have a little faith in me."

Her faith in him had died some time ago. Could it be restored? If she told the truth about how she felt, they'd start on the road to divorce, and Emmy would be without a family. She couldn't make that kind of decision while she was looking into Sam's death. She did love Dallas once. Maybe she would just let things ride for now and face those hard questions when her grief had lessened and she had found out the truth about Sam.

"All right. Let me get my hiking boots." She thought about the gun she had brought in from the car and hidden among her sweaters. Should she bring it along? No. She ought to act as if she still trusted Dallas. Sometimes when you acted the part long enough, it became part of you. She left the gun wrapped in black wool.

It had rained the day before, and the trail was muddy. On the steep single-file descent from the parking lot, she slipped and slid, catching branches to steady herself. She didn't want to ask Dallas to hold or catch her, and anyway, he insisted on going in front. For her safety, he said.

The problem was that his maroon plaid flannel shirt was in front of her, and that shirt made her sick. She could almost feel the bile rising in her throat. Why did she hate that shirt so? Could it be because he liked to wear it on weekends, and weekends were when he usually went on a bender and passed out in the hideous marshmallow chair, after they'd had a doozy of a fight, of course, with plenty of vile name-calling.

Maybe he hadn't been wearing it the night he'd hit her, but there had been so many other times he'd been cruel in that shirt. Maybe she could simply misplace the thing one day, or pour bleach on it by accident, or—

"Hey. Come up here and talk to me."

"Sure." At least if she was walking beside him, she wouldn't have to look at that shirt.

The trail broadened and smoothed, taking them to relatively level ground with a layer of late leaves. They scuffed along side by side, and Liberty breathed in the fresh smell, reaching up to touch a dogwood branch, smiling at the tiny birds flitting in and out to eat the red berries.

"You're not saying much," Dallas grumbled.

"I was just thinking how nice it is out here," she said. "How lucky we are to have this mild December day." After the horror she'd been through, she was taking all the small pleasures that came her way. The cool, damp breeze ruffled her hair, and the chill she'd felt at first had disappeared.

"You never talk to me any more," said Dallas.

Surprised, she stumbled over a root and caught herself just in time to keep from falling into his arms. "What do you mean? I talk to you all the time."

He walked along, looking at the trail. "You talk *at* me, not *to* me. You talk about Emmy and the house, about that volunteer job of yours, but not about anything that matters. I don't know what goes on in that curly head of yours."

"Hey, Dallas," she joked. "That's supposed to be my line." So he'd actually noticed a change in her? When had she quit talking to him? Maybe when she'd quit trusting him to keep his word about the alcohol.

He looked over at her slantwise. "Just like you to make fun of it."

"Well, sorry for being myself!"

Now they had reached the river and they walked alongside it, hands staying warm in pockets. On the opposite bank a fisherman cast his rod into the shallows. A runner padded by with steady footfalls, gliding gracefully along the uneven path. How he could keep his footing on this root-rich trail she'd never know. The ripples and sun flashes of the broad rushing river distracted her for a lovely moment, but the plaid flannel shirt wouldn't go away.

"I sometimes wonder where the Libby I married went to."

"What? Who did you marry, Dallas?"

"The sweet, funny girl who thought I was the greatest."

She was wrong was on the tip of her tongue. But he wouldn't understand her sadness, her confusion, her feeling of helplessness. She couldn't say anything to him now about what was in her heart. Her mistrust. He turned away from the river then, starting on a trail back to the forest. Now they were climbing, pulling, and she stopped to catch her breath, a good excuse for being quiet. She didn't want to play the drinking card, bring up all those times he'd come home and disappeared after dinner into his home office, the place where he hid the bottles, and then came up to watch TV in the hideous marshmallow chair.

Once upon a time, they'd snuggled on the sofa and watched together.

She could almost feel his jaw clenching. They climbed up, up, and her heart was beating fast—not only from the exertion, but in anticipation of what he'd say next. Hikers going the opposite way came by, a whole gaggle of them— mother, dad, and teenagers shambling along, the latter not really wanting to be there, wanting to be back with their iPods and Blackberrys and Nintendos.

Dallas stopped at the top of the highest cliff, and Liberty gazed through the trees at the steep bank toward the river. *If he tries to push me, I'll kick his knees out the way Papaw showed me.*

He put his arm around her, clutching her shoulder, and gave her a squeeze. "It's a long way down."

She held her breath, tensing all her muscles. "Hey, you're all knotted up." He began to massage her shoulder muscles. Easy for his hands to creep up on her neck—

"Hey. Relax."

Yes, she was being silly. But he did hit her once . . . but he did apologize . . .

What if he was waiting, waiting, for all the people to be gone, to not be able to hear any sound, no crackle of twigs, no shouts in the air, no piping children? The river glittered below the descending rocks, steep rocks that could batter a person's skull if they fell.

Well, officer, she must have slipped, and I tried to catch her—

She felt his hands around her waist.

He squeezed. Hard. With a cry she broke free and raced along the path. But just as she gained distance, she tripped over a root and went sprawling, her shoulder hitting the ground first. She burst into tears just as Dallas jogged up.

"What in hell got into you, Libby?"

"It's my shoulder," she gasped. "I might have pulled a muscle." He bent down and very gently lifted her under her arms to her feet. He probed the area with caution.

"I'm taking you to a doctor," he said.

Chapter Twenty

"So he didn't push you off a cliff." Liberty stirred her coffee, not meeting Jack's eyes. "It's partly your fault, scaring me, telling me that he might be a killer. And then he squeezed me too hard. No wonder I bolted. I feel like a fool."

"It was your active imagination." That's what Jack was saying, but all Liberty could see was the red tie he wore. Printed on it was the image of a man with a floppy forelock and the slogan HERMAN TALMADGE FOR GOVERNOR. The Monday morning coffee shop hummed and rattled around them, pungent with the smell of roasted beans.

She wanted to talk about something else. "Excuse me, but who is that on your tie?"

"You like my tie?" He fingered the neckwear and gazed at it fondly. "I found it in an old chest of drawers in the room I rent. The landlady begged me to take it, along with some of her late husband's things. I have golf sweaters from the most exclusive clubs. This guy on the tie was governor back in the Truman years. How's your shoulder?"

"Dallas took me to a doc-in-the-box," she said. "I had to get an X-ray. It was partly dislocated. They put it back and gave me a pain pill."

"Ouch. You'd better hope you don't have to sock him."

"Don't you have any other suspects?"

He waved her question aside. "Did you get to interview the boys?"

"As a matter of fact, I did. Even though Dallas insisted on driving me there. Honestly."

She told Jack that when Dallas dropped her off at Shadrach House—for the present, a storefront in a half-empty strip mall—she saw a gray Toyota parked next to a small yellow sports car from the sixties: a real antique, patched and faded. Melvin had mentioned seeing an MG over at Sam's. She caught her breath and walked over to look. The car wasn't an MG, but an Austin-Healey. Melvin had said "maybe" an MG.

The gray Toyota belonged to one of the volunteers, but she'd never seen the Healey before. One of the boys, Jesse Everly, lived for cars and had once bragged he could steal most anything with wheels. He'd know about the yellow car.

She walked into the largest of the rooms that made up the center and scanned the billiard table, ping-pong table, and foosball table. Jesse's thin frame leaned over the pool table, his elbow cocked to take a shot.

Another two boys were playing games in front of the TV, and another one was microwaving a snack in the small corner kitchen. Cedric Martin was hunched over the computer in the study room, and in the office, a boy she didn't know was talking to a volunteer from St. Chad's.

A couple of the boys waved in greeting, and she stood for a moment and watched them. Jesse's ball caromed off the side and hit the 14-ball smartly, which rolled into the side pocket.

She walked over to him. "Jesse?"

He looked up and gave her a dimpled smile, his light brown hair flopping over his forehead. He flipped it back. "Hi, Office Lady."

"Hi, Office Lady," echoed a tall, dark-skinned boy she didn't know.

"Some people call me Mrs. Chase," she told Jesse. "Can you spare me a few minutes?"

He frowned. "I'm not in trouble, am I?"

"Of course not. Didn't Father Foley mention I wanted to talk to you?"

His features relaxed. "Yeah. Can I finish this game?"

"Sure." She walked over to the study room, furnished with desks and two donated computers. Cedric, who'd also been at the funeral, sat engrossed in a game of Grand Theft Auto. He zapped and zoomed; lights and explosions and screeching filled the screen. What was *this* thing doing on the computer?

"I didn't know we had that game," Liberty said mildly.

"We didn't," Cedric said. "I just loaded it."

"Did anyone okay it?"

He looked sheepish, but she didn't lecture him. Foley could do that. She looked back at Jesse; he was racking his cue. He sauntered over, the tough-boy grin on his face. "Good game."

"Yours or that one?"

He shrugged. "What can I do for you, Ms. Chase?"

"I want to talk about Father Sam."

"Whatever." He looked at the floor, and she could tell he was uncomfortable.

She pointed to the shabby gold sofa on the far wall. "Let's sit down. Coke?"

"Sure."

She pulled some quarters from her bag and handed them to him. "Diet, please?"

"You got it." He walked over to the machine and came back with one red can and one white one.

He sat beside her, elbows on knees, studying her out of the corner of his eye. Why wouldn't he look at her directly?

"First," she said, "that old Healey—where'd it come from?" She fished a notebook out of her bag and laid it on her knees.

He cracked his knuckles and studied the splits in the brown vinyl flooring. "Sam didn't tell you?"

"Should he have?"

Jesse shrugged. "I thought you knew everything that went on here. One of the church people giv'it to him. I was going to fix it up and we'd sell it. I'd get my cut, and the place would get the rest. That was the deal. Now what's going to happen?" He cracked another knuckle.

She swallowed the lump in her throat. "Is it drivable now?"

"Just barely. I can swap work with a guy I know who owns a body shop once I get it running good. I been looking for parts. Sam and me was going to go junking before he—" Jesse let the word tail off and looked away.

"That project will go on," she said. "I'll talk to Foley about money for parts." She thought for a minute. "Who took you to Sam's house to get the car?"

"Well, that's the funny part. He was going to pick me up here after he left the hospital, then take me to his house, and then I'd drive the car back here. Then he changed the plans, called here and left a message that he couldn't come and get me. Said he had to meet with somebody, it was real important."

"You did get the car that day?"

"Yeah. Foley got some guy to drop us by there, it wa'n't too far out of his way. Cedric and me, that is. He wanted to come, and I needed him 'cause he knew the way back. He's got maps to everywhere in his head."

"And Sam?"

"We picked up the car and came on over. Sam wa'n't home yet."

She looked over to the room where Cedric was playing his game.

"He's smart, isn't he?"

Jesse nodded. "He's one bad dude with a computer. Sam says—*said*—if Cedric'd get back in school and study hard, he'd help him get into Tech one day. Cedric just seen his future gone down the shithole, excuse me, ma'am." He glanced over at her notebook. "Why're you asking all these questions?"

She had to be careful. "I'm finishing a book Sam started, about his life story and helping you guys. I just wanted to know how the guys felt about him."

He leaned back in his chair with a smirk. "Could have fooled me. You sound like a cop."

She told herself to breathe steadily. "Well, maybe you could tell me a little of your story—how you came to be here, what Sam did to help you. Would you?"

"Sure, why not," said Jesse. He turned up his Coke and finished it, then set the can on the floor. "The worst thing in life is to feel you're worthless. That nobody wants you or needs you. That you're just rat shit. That's what my old man thought of me. And when he started beating my mama, I grabbed his shotgun and like to have shot his head off. Good thing I didn't, or I wouldn't be here now."

"Oh." Her pencil slid out of her hand and dropped to the floor.

Jesse scooped it up for her and shrugged. "I missed his head, but I put his beating arm out of commission. Soon's he got better he started beating her with the other one. I was the guest of Juvie by then, but she'd gone out and got an iron poker, and she used it. Now he's in a coma and she's up in Hardwick doing time, hoping he don't die."

"I see."

He took a long swallow of his drink and looked off somewhere, somewhere Liberty couldn't see. "When I got paroled DFACS wanted to send me to a foster home, but I didn't want to go. Seventeen's a crappy age. I wanted to stay at the house, work at a job, pay the rent, so Mama'd have a place to go when she got out.

"Sam found a seminary student to live with me and the court said that was okay. Sam told me to be the kind of guy my mama could depend on. She ain't a bad woman, Ms. Chase. She just couldn't take no more."

It was a few minutes before Liberty could speak. "I understand, Jesse, believe me, I do."

He looked at her, then, and this time he was all there. "What's going to happen to this place?"

Liberty knew she had to be encouraging. "Sam would have wanted it to go on, and I'm going to help see that it does."

"Ms. Chase," he said, "I sure hope it does. Look over yonder." She looked. In front of the TV, the feathery-haired boy she'd seen earlier was playing a game. He looked hardly older than twelve. "They picked him up turning tricks," said Jesse.

She felt sick. Since she'd been working with Sam, she'd found out all sorts of things people living in suburbs tend to block out. They lived their comfortable lives, not wanting to see what went on in those mean streets on the other side of town.

"Tell me, Jesse," she said. "Was there anyone here who was angry with Sam?"

"No, ma'am," he said. "They all liked him. Even Rico."

She felt a pang at the thought of that night. "Why did you say 'even Rico'? I thought he was Sam's right-hand man." He had become Sam's loyal sidekick after the thwarted robbery, after Sam had gotten him through drug treatment and found him a job at a grocery store.

"You mean Sam didn't tell you about the fight?"

She bit her lip. "No, he didn't."

He stretched and cracked his knuckles again, looking mighty uncomfortable. "Maybe you'd better get Rico to tell you."

She kept her seat. "I want you to tell me."

A truck rumbled to a stop out front, and a volunteer came out of the office. He motioned to Jesse and the boy at the pool table, and Jesse looked at Liberty apologetically. "I gotta go help unload this truck. I hope it's the load of food Apostles is sending us for Christmas. Nice talking to you, Ms. Chase."

"And that's all I could get out of Jesse," Liberty told Jack. She took a sip of coffee, but it was cold. "Wait a sec. I really need coffee." She got up and went for a refill, then settled back in the booth. Cradling the cup in both hands, she sipped, grateful for the warmth and the buzz.

Jack nodded. "It doesn't seem that Jesse had any grudge against Sam."

"No. And I didn't find Rico at the store where he worked. He was off today, and Sunday he was out sick."

"Okay," Jack said. "Did Jesse indicate how bad the fight was? Was Rico a violent type?"

She shook her head. "Rico does have some anger control problems. I can't see him poisoning anybody. If he wanted to kill somebody, he'd go for a knife. And I can't see him going to Sam's house. He doesn't have a car, for one thing."

"It's unlikely, but not impossible. You're planning to follow that up, I hope?"

"I'll go back to the store for Rico tomorrow. Have you found out anything?"

He wore a smug look. "What if I told you I'd had luck with the widow?"

Chapter Twenty-One

LUCK

"What kind of luck?"

Liberty raised her eyebrows and gazed at the politician from another age on Jack's tie. Had this quirky guy worn some normal clothes to meet Alicia?

Jack took a sip of coffee. "That's beneath you, Liberty. I paid her a condolence call. I told her Sam and I were childhood friends. She seemed surprised, said he'd never talked about his childhood. I said I didn't talk much about mine, either. Her curiosity was aroused, and before long she was offering me a drink, hoping I'd talk."

"Jack! What did you say?" Liberty leaned toward him, catching her breath.

He shrugged. "Let me get there. First, I asked for gin and tonic. She brought out a bottle of Bombay Sapphire, about a quarter full. 'I guess someone gave this to Sam,' she said. 'He usually buys Beefeaters.'"

Liberty now was on edge, waiting. "What next?"

"I asked for a twist of lime, calling her *pretty lady,* and she smiled at me almost coquettishly. Maybe she's a little starved for appreciation. While she was in the kitchen getting the lime, I poured a slug of the gin into a vial and slipped it in my pocket. Then I asked her to dinner. She accepted, of course."

"You were sure she'd go?"

"Why wouldn't she? With an old friend of Sam's to talk to about him? I took her to Grille Louis. You ever been there? Great '40s atmosphere, dark red walls, booths big enough to hide Julia Child, and while I enjoyed the *escalopes de veau Marengo* I plied her with a bottle of *côtes du rhône.* Soon I had *her* talking."

"Thank you, Mr. Hercule Poirot. And?"

"Alicia is truly grieving. She feels guilty because Sam knew he wasn't making her happy. I've got a pretty good nose for who's lying, and I don't think she was giving me BS. She's trying to hold it together, but Sam's death hit her hard."

"So she really loved him?"

"Yes, I believe so. But she hadn't realized how little of Sam she was going to get. It was hard sharing him with all those people, and helping all those people was what floated his boat.

"She did what a lot of women do. She turned away, angry at what he wasn't giving her, angry for what she'd left behind for him. My guess is that it was a pretty lonely marriage. And then you came along to fill the gap for him."

"That's *not* how it was, Jack," Liberty said, miffed. "We just worked together. And had conversations." A thought nagged at her. "Do you think Alicia minded that?"

Jack gave her a quizzical, serious look. "Maybe. If he didn't talk to Alicia."

She rose from her chair and swished her sweater off the seat. "You don't need to make me feel any worse. He wanted a friend. Friends are the people who don't judge you." She tried to struggle into her sweater but couldn't reach the arms.

Jack stood and gently took the sweater from her and smoothed it. "Liberty, Liberty. Good old psycho-Nazi Doctor Jack, tromping all over butterflies in my hobnailed boots. Sit down. I haven't told you the rest."

She managed a weak smile and sat down.

"Alicia told me she hated St. Chad's. She missed the church they'd left, where she'd made friends that were more like the type she'd grown up with. She couldn't adjust to Shadrach House, to all those boys with problems. She felt she couldn't complain, because he told her he was finally doing the Lord's work, the work he was meant to do. She knew he was right. She was trapped."

Finally, Liberty met Jack's eyes: golden eyes, looking at her with the compassion she'd thought he didn't have.

"It would have taken a saint to live with him," Jack said. "People with missions make very poor partners, whether that mission is from God, the devil, or almighty commerce."

"I think it would take a saint to live with my husband," Liberty said. "And all I wanted was a happy family."

"I know this is hard for you," said Jack. "Do you want me to finish, or shall we call it a day?"

She felt wrung out and hung up to dry while an F5 tornado was heading for the clothesline. "Finish. Please."

"Alicia told me all she knew of his last day."

She forced herself to stop stroking her coffee cup. "Please tell me."

"Wednesday morning, school was out, and she packed for the trip to Charleston. Around ten Sam called her from the church to tell her to leave the keys in the old Austin-Healey so the boys could get it. He told her he was going to see a couple of people in the hospital that afternoon. He wished her a good trip. That's all."

"Jack! He didn't mention meeting the woman Jesse told me he said he was meeting? The reason he couldn't come by and pick him up?"

"No. I don't know if that means anything."

Liberty took a deep breath. "He knew that morning he wasn't going to meet Jesse that afternoon, and he didn't tell Alicia?"

Jack shrugged. "It may not mean anything. Maybe somebody called him after ten, after she'd already left."

Liberty considered this. "He called me sometime that day and left a message to call him, but I didn't check my phone messages until that night."

"He didn't say why?"

"He said something happened that might be . . . troublesome. I thought it might have to do with Shad House. That's why I felt I had to see him." A thought struck her. "Do you suppose Duff Mowbray knew who he was meeting?"

"That's immaterial," said Jack, "since Duff can't tell us. Are you going to his funeral?"

That hadn't occurred to Liberty. "Should I? What do you think happened to him?"

"Heart problem, septic condition? It happens to people in their sixties. They'll do an autopsy, I think. You should go, make an appearance, scope out the crowd."

She could do that, hoping desperately that there wouldn't be any more funerals for a long while. "What will you do next?"

"Get the gin analyzed," he said. "On the QT. It happens that a friend who's a chemistry professor at Tech is going to run the sample and see if we have a match for penicillin."

"How will he do it?"

"She. Mass spectrometer. It breaks the compound into a pattern of ions. Each substance fragments in a unique way. The molecular weight of the ions."

"Okay. How do you know a chemistry professor?"

"She needed my help a couple of years back, much as you do now. Her talents helped her solve her own case."

Liberty sighed with frustration. "Mine won't. A knowledge of the dramatic arts doesn't solve murders."

"I dunno. Shakespeare was a canny old dude."

Liberty's mind was back on the chemistry professor. "How soon do you think she'll have the results?" She wondered about that relationship. Jack seemed very sure of his chemistry.

"Tomorrow, the next day. Honey, you never can tell when some little scrap of knowledge will help you solve a case. Don't ever apologize for doing what you love. Learning is always useful."

"Well, all right, and don't call me honey," she said.

He made a mock-sad face, like a French clown. "I was hoping you liked me a little," he said, "because I want you to invite me over for dinner, so I can check out your husband."

She closed her eyes in disbelief. "You're barking up the wrong tree. Don't you have some concerned citizens to interview?"

"Patience, my dear," he said.

As she got up to leave, something nagged at her. "Did you follow through with Alicia about your boyhood friendship with Sam?"

Jack gave her a smile. "Somehow, she never got around to asking."

Chapter Twenty-Two

A Visit to Josie

Counting lesson: "One, two, three knives. One, two, three forks. One, two, three . . ."

"Spoons," Emmy finished, taking them from Liberty to lay the table for dinner. Why did Jack seem so fixated on Dallas? Was he falling for her and wanted the culprit to be her husband? That was not professional, but people had done weird things when their emotions got involved.

But then again, maybe he was just concerned for her, after all she'd been through, and she liked him. A lot. They could be good friends, she hoped.

She walked over to the stove and stirred the simmering pot of homemade vegetable soup before she reached up into the cabinet for three bowls. Just as she had them in hand, the phone rang. Startled out of her thought, she lost her grip on the bowls and they crashed to the tile below, littering the floor with fractious fragments.

Emmy surveyed the scene. "Way to go, Mommy."

Liberty headed to the pantry for a broom and dustpan, dodging white shards. "Get that phone, sweetie."

Emmy sashayed over to answer the telephone with a superior look, then called, "A lady."

Liberty fetched a paper grocery bag. "I'll be right there."

"Mommy smash the dishes," Emmy said into the phone.

Red-faced, Liberty handed Emmy the broom and took the phone. "Are you all right?" Josie Robillard said, concern in her voice, maybe for Emmy's mother's sanity. Liberty explained what had just happened.

The sounds of sweeping and her second-best china clinking in the background, Liberty listened as Josie apologized for not returning the call sooner. She'd been up to her ears in parish matters, especially Duff Mowbray's funeral, planned for four o'clock the next day, Tuesday. She could see Liberty to talk about Sam on Wednesday morning at nine-thirty. Liberty told her that was fine and she'd also see her at the funeral.

Emmy gave the full dustpan to her mother, who emptied the soup bowl fragments into the bag. "Who Jack?" Emmy asked.

Liberty turned to see Emmy reading the note by the phone with Jack's name and number. Who *was* Jack? Liberty would really like to know what made him tick. "Someone I work with, sweetie."

"Fm," Emmy said, the expression that meant she didn't like the answer. If it wasn't good enough for her, it wasn't going to be good enough for Dallas. Liberty scooped up the paper and slid it in her pocket.

After Emmy had been tucked in bed and Dallas had disappeared into his basement home office, Liberty assembled the manuscript pages into four stacks: those Sam had finished, those Gracelyn had finished, those Liberty had completed, and the raw notes, all in chronological order.

She re-read the material line by line, heart in her throat, to see if she'd missed anything. What she wanted to find was any clue which might shed light on Sam's senseless death, any thread from his past. Was there a mysterious woman who'd come looking for him with murder in her heart? A man? Someone with a grudge, or with mental problems?

The clue she longed for wasn't there. Also missing was his early life in New York, the event that finally made him leave home and catch that bus to Florida. She had a hunch that story was the key to the book.

Had he committed it to paper before he died?

"I've got to tell my story," he'd said to her once.

"Tell it to me," she'd offered.

"Not now," was his reply. "In the fullness of time." The slow turning of the seasons, the leaves dying and falling, the earth lying fallow, waiting for the sun: that was the fullness of time, and for him, it was gone.

Trembling, she laid her head on the pages. After a time she pulled herself up. She couldn't give in to regret and longing. If he'd written the missing material, she was going to find it.

If it was at the church, either Gracelyn was hiding it or Sam hadn't given it to her. Gracelyn would have no obvious reason to hide it. Alicia had given Liberty all she had. So she'd said.

So where was it? Not at Shadrach House, for Liberty did most of the filing. And there were no secret compartments there, but maybe she hadn't looked carefully enough.

First she had Duff's funeral to get through. She picked up the phone and arranged for Emmy to go home with Caitlin, indenturing herself for extra carpool duty, and she felt wracked with guilt because Emmy was beginning to notice her absences.

She thought about her mother out in Los Angeles, about how she'd withdrawn from her only child after her husband died, and how that child hadn't understood being deserted. Maybe Paloma had loved her husband so much that looking at Liberty reminded her of him, of that that awful day when a man in a dark suit had come to the door. Liberty knew she looked more like her father than her mother, more's the pity for her success as an actress. She was attractive, sure, but not head-turning like her mother.

Wearing her nondescript gray suit, hair slicked back into a bun, Liberty arrived at the church early. She slid into a back pew, planting herself in an aisle seat for a good view of the congregation. Men in suits and women in dark dresses filed in and found their places; the dim light from the overcast sky dulled the colorful stained glass. The church, fragrant with incense and lilies, fell into a hush during the silent funeral procession, the muffled, eerie footfalls echoing in the gloom.

As Josie Robillard took her place, Gracelyn Rodgers, wearing the same black-and-white tweed coat she'd worn to Sam's funeral, slipped into the pew in front of Liberty. A young man with black, spiky hair and two earrings in one ear, handsome in a punk-rocker way, slid in beside her. Gracelyn patted his shoulder maternally, and Liberty noted their similar profiles.

Gracelyn and her son intrigued Liberty throughout the service. After a few dabs with her handkerchief at the beginning of the service, Gracelyn remained dry-eyed, as she had for Sam's funeral. The young man, whose shifting body language telegraphed that he was bored and angry, most likely had been coerced into accompanying his mother.

The service ended with Communion. Gracelyn and her son slipped out after going to the altar, much to Liberty's frustration. She'd hoped to catch the secretary after the service and question her about the missing information, as well as what she may have seen at Sam's house that awful night.

Liberty joined the crowd heading to the church parlor where Duff's widow, Elise, and her grown son and daughter were receiving people. Gracelyn wasn't there. Liberty joined the group waiting to speak to Elise, whose trim figure was draped in a black dress and shawl.

A black wide-brimmed hat shaded the widow's eyes, blocking Liberty from reading her expression when she took her hand. "I worked with Mr. Mowbray on the Shadrach House project," Liberty told her. "It was a pleasure to know him, and I'm so sorry."

"Thank you." Elise Mowbray's voice was husky, throaty, like a forties movie actress. As Liberty walked away, she felt that the widow was watching her.

Was this paranoia? Elise had surely overheard Duff talking to Liberty, agreeing to meet. Was she the jealous type? Since Vivian hadn't attended the funeral, Liberty had no one to ask. It was time to leave.

DECEMBER 13

The next morning, Liberty was at Josie's office ten minutes before the appointed time, waiting in a dove-gray side chair within sight of Gracelyn's vacant desk.

Josie opened her office door, her face drawn and tired. "I've been working fourteen-hour days since all this happened," she said. "I hope we get some help soon. The bishop's sending a deacon. Poor Duff."

Liberty rose. "He was a good man." She wished she didn't have to vex Josie further and followed the young priest into her office.

"Duff was the proverbial church pillar," Josie said, closing the door. "He kept this place together between rectors. Shadrach House needed his talent."

Liberty took the seat she was offered. "Yes. Sam may have been the driver of the project, but Duff was the mechanic. He's the one who got us the Joshua grant. And for that grant, we need church financial statements. He'd planned to bring them to the meeting."

"We never got the chance to pull them." Josie settled in her chair. "We close out the books at the end of January, and since they want this material by December 31, we thought we'd do a year-to-date summary and add last year's balance sheet. Shadrach House was one of our major projects, but we'd only budgeted for the seed money and a small yearly support fund. You know as well as I do that sponsors and grants are the only way this shelter can remain open for the long term. This church is too small to carry it."

"I don't understand the holdup," Liberty said. "Surely all the data is on the computer."

Josie looked at her visitor over her glasses and sighed. "Actually, Gracelyn's dragging her feet about learning our accounting software. She's set in her ways, and she's done the job alone too long. Sam hired a young woman, Kelsey

Bales, to take over the accounting part. Kelsey's been trying like mad to get all the kinks worked out and everything ready for the audit at the end of January."

"How long has it been since you had an audit?"

"Oh, some time. You don't realize how short of funds we were, Liberty. Father Landring, bless him, was such an idealist—wanted to give more and more to the poor, which was a fine idea, but he didn't want to spend money on computers, and audits cost a lot of money." She gave a sad smile. "Gracelyn was a little miffed when we hired Kelsey and asked if we thought she hadn't been doing her job."

"A little protective of her turf?" Liberty raised a skeptical eyebrow.

Josie shrugged. "One person shouldn't handle everything. St. Chad's is her life, but change comes to us all." Josie had had her share of life's changes. Sam had mentioned the broken engagement, the addicted sister when telling Liberty why he'd hired Josie to take some of his load. Her resilience had impressed him.

Liberty nodded. "Gracelyn will have to get used to a new way of doing things. We all have to, God knows." She herself had been running on denial, and now she found herself wishing once again she could talk this whole matter over with Sam. He'd know what to do. Tears stung her eyes, and she forced herself to take a deep breath.

"You're wondering why Sam? Why now?" Josie, tired and serene, clasped her hands.

Liberty nodded, glad to know that good people like Josie existed.

Maybe—just maybe—Josie could be trusted. Maybe she could fill Liberty in on some necessary information.

Liberty leaned forward. "Josie . . . it's so strange how Sam died. So suddenly. That's what throws me for a loop. Did he ever speak to you of his asthma?"

Josie shook her head. "He didn't talk about it, but we all knew it. He kept an inhaler here. I had no idea the asthma was so severe."

Liberty swallowed. "I didn't either. And I had no idea Duff might be in bad health."

"That surprised me," said Josie. "The man was such a health promoter—organic foods and all." She smiled ruefully. "Wheatgrass smoothies. I didn't see how he drank them. Coffee's my fuel."

"Mine too." Liberty yearned for a cup of coffee right then but plowed on. "Maybe Duff wasn't well, and that's why he was so gung-ho for health. But what I really want to know is, did Duff or Sam mention any threats to them personally? I mean because of Shadrach House? Not just bluster and hot air from the NIMBYs?"

"No, they didn't." Her eyes narrowed. "Liberty, you're not suggesting these deaths are related, are you?"

Her tone was so incredulous it shook Liberty, but she pressed on. "It was something I considered." She leaned forward. "Two untimely deaths from St. Chad's."

Josie clasped her hands on her desk then. "Liberty, we're all overwrought," she said. "What a thing to happen in Advent. This is a season of watching and waiting, and that's what I suggest we do. Watch and wait."

No, Liberty wanted to scream. *We have to hurry! There's no time to watch, no time to wait!* In Josie's soft brown eyes, despite her words and her tone, there was something—*something*—that made Liberty feel the young priest had thought about the possibility those deaths might not be an accident. But what evidence was there? Only a disembodied footstep, a light that had gone off, and the death of the last man who'd talked to him.

"I'm sure you're right, Josie." Liberty opened her notebook. "One more thing. Alicia has given me Sam's memoir to finish."

Josie had missed her calling. She ought to compete in the World Series of Poker with that face. Had Alicia mentioned it to her? Liberty went on, "There seems to be some material missing. Had Sam given you any to read?"

She shook her head. "Not right away. He asked me to look it over when he finished, before he sent it in."

"May I ask what he told you about himself?"

"Of course." As Josie talked about things Liberty already knew, Liberty reflected that Sam was a master of smoke and mirrors, hiding himself, giving the impression he was revealing, but actually concealing. Why hadn't she seen this?

"I suppose that's all," Josie said. "Oh, my goodness, look at the time."

Liberty heard the cue to leave. She reluctantly rose and gathered her things. "Did you, by any chance, meet with Sam late that afternoon? Did something come up?"

Josie, standing behind her desk, looked almost stricken. "I wish I had. Maybe it would have changed the outcome. Why?"

"Something one of the boys told me. That Sam couldn't pick them up as planned because he had to meet with a woman."

She shook her head and eyed Liberty keenly. "Not me. You could check his appointment book." She paused, thinking. "After he left for hospital rounds, he didn't come back. We closed the office early, in fact."

Liberty thanked Josie for her time, put away notebook and pen, and turned to go. When she opened Josie's office door, Gracelyn stepped back so fast she almost stumbled. "I was about to knock."

"And I was about to come see you." Liberty clutched her notebook to her chest, trying to muffle the pounding in her chest. "Can we talk?"

"Certainly, Liberty," she said, friendly tone at odds with her narrowed eyes. Her tongue slid across her lips. "As soon as I speak with Josie."

Liberty walked out into the open foyer and waited in another dove-gray chair. Gracelyn didn't keep her waiting long. Wearing her customary pleasant face, the secretary strolled back to her desk, and Liberty gave her a most pleasant smile in return. "Do you have those printouts for me?"

Gracelyn lifted a file folder from a plastic sorter. "Right here. I'm sorry I haven't mailed them. It was such a shock about Duff, you know, and—"

Nodding her understanding, Liberty reached out and took the folder. She leafed through the chapters—of course, the ones she'd stolen earlier. She didn't see any further material. After a moment she looked up, radiating innocence and perplexity. "Gracelyn, are you sure these are all here? Sam didn't have any more chapters, perhaps, that he hadn't given you? That he might have kept in his office?"

Gracelyn shook her head and said, with tightness lacing her professional pleasantry, "Alicia took all his personal files home. Now, if you'll excuse me . . ." The secretary reached for a folder on her desk.

"Just a minute, please. What about files on his computer?"

Gracelyn pretended to study the folder. "Oh, I hardly think so. He wrote in longhand. Said it helped his thinking, the connection of the hand to the page. He was quite mystical about it. Then he had me type up the material."

Liberty gazed toward Sam's office, toward the open door, toward the boxes of books stacked inside. The computer stood on the desk. "Do you think I could look anyhow?"

She jerked her head up sharply. "Out of the question. There might be sensitive information."

"I'd let you monitor my search."

"I wouldn't want to be responsible. It's out of the question," she repeated.

Liberty said in a reasonable voice, "Well, then, would you look for the material?"

Gracelyn's fingers drummed on the desk. "Really, Liberty. I have so much to do. You're on the wrong track. I gave you all there was."

"I have reason to think there's more." Liberty dealt out the words like cards. "I think he was working on another section, a part he found hard to write. A part he hadn't given you yet."

"That's pure speculation." She frowned and tried to swish back her elegant silver hair, but the coiffure still didn't move. She coughed. "If such a thing exists, it's not here. Maybe you'd better ask Alicia."

The phone rang. From the speed at which she snatched up the receiver, smiling, she made it clear she had nothing more to say.

Liberty stubbornly stayed put while Gracelyn routed the call to Josie. When she hung up, Liberty said, "I need to know one thing more. Did anyone meet with Sam late that afternoon?"

"What does that have to do with anything?" Gracelyn was scowling now.

"It might have to do with the missing material." Liberty felt her lie was for a good cause. "Josie told me I could consult Sam's appointment book if I needed to."

"Alicia has his personal book."

"But surely you keep one, too? On the computer?"

"I don't care for computers." She glared at Liberty, drew a red book out of a drawer, and turned the pages. "He had no appointments after three." She slapped the book shut, looked up at Liberty, and smiled. "So that's that." *And will you please go away now?* was left politely unspoken.

Liberty had the feeling that the "meeting with a woman" was something Sam hadn't written down. Unless Gracelyn was lying. And why would she lie?

Chapter Twenty-Three

A Poisonous Thought
December 14

L iberty knew it was going to be a bad day.

Things had been going too well, and Liberty feared some sort of reverse karma. Her husband seemed to be trying out for Poster Dad of Suburbia, not even complaining when she'd served soup and sandwiches—again—for dinner the night before and blamed her lack of culinary production on Christmas shopping. He came down to breakfast cheerful, bantering with Emmy, listening to her halting story of her visit to Santa.

Then he dawdled over his newspaper. Why couldn't he be grumpy and hurry off to the office the way he usually did? She needed to call Alicia while she was sure of finding the widow home, and she didn't want him listening in.

If she took the cell phone outdoors or upstairs to make a call, it would be obvious. At his request, she made another pot of coffee, then while he drank it, she rinsed each dish, loaded the dishwasher, and moseyed around picking up clutter.

Then he offered to bring the laundry down. How could she refuse? He set the basket beside the washer, and then he finally left, pecking Liberty on the cheek. How long since he'd done that?

After she heard the car leave the driveway she hurried to the telephone, feeling just like a rat.

"Liberty? What is it now?" To say that Alicia didn't sound happy to hear from her was an Olympic understatement.

Liberty explained the obstacle to accessing Sam's church computer. "Gracelyn's being difficult. Would you be willing to go to the office and look for the missing material?" She hadn't yet figured out the best way to ask for Sam's appointment book. It had nothing to do with the memoir.

"Oh, Liberty," Alicia said with exasperation, "I just don't have time to deal with it. I'm putting the house on the market. I was just on my way out. I'm taking some things to the woman in charge of the church rummage sale."

"You're going to *leave*?" Liberty's words rushed out.

Alicia sounded almost amused. "There's nothing to keep me in this city. I'm moving home to Charleston."

Moving! And Sam barely in the ground! What things was she taking to the sale? Sam's things? How could she?

"Frankly, I don't know much about computers," Alicia was saying. "E-mail and eBay are about all I can manage."

"What about his papers?" Liberty asked. "What are you going to do with them?"

Alicia was quiet for a moment, and when she spoke her words were edged with irony. "I have Sam's papers packed in boxes for the children someday. If you like, you can go through them. I don't think you'll find anything new."

She was tossing Liberty a bone, but the actress playing detective was ready to gnaw. Perhaps the boxes would yield a draft, or at least some notes.

That afternoon, after she picked up Emmy from school, Liberty headed out to Alicia's house, down the highway she'd traveled in the rain the night Sam died. Her companions then had been fear and horror; now it was a dull constant ache.

"Mommy?" Emmy said.

"What is it, sweetheart?" Liberty didn't have her full attention on the child as she was merging for the exit, avoiding a red pickup truck hell-bent on swerving in front of her.

"You look sad, Mommy."

"I'm just thinking."

"Fm."

Obviously, Emmy didn't approve, and Emmy's hair would have gotten a ruffle if Liberty'd had a free hand. The

Waffle House sign flashed by, the symbol, once so friendly, making her wince. Emmy was sunk in her own little world as the car navigated the streets, but when they rolled up to Sam's driveway she looked up in alarm. "I don' like it here."

Liberty turned in, halted the car, and looked at her baby, hating the fear she'd caused. "I'm sorry, honey," she soothed. "We won't be long." She reluctantly switched off the engine and opened the car door.

Emmy tugged at her sleeve. "Mommy."

The back door swung open; Alicia must have been watching for them. Emmy began to sob. Her mother gave her a comforting pat and slid out of the car before Alicia could notice the child's tears.

Liberty hated having to bring her.

Alicia looked taut and jangly, as if strings and pins were holding her together. She stood aside as Andrew, arms wrapped around a cardboard box of his father's words, came around to the back hatch of the car. Liberty sprang it open and he shoved the box in. He told her there was another box and plunged back into the house.

As he stuffed the second box into the cargo space, Sam's son looked curiously at Liberty's frightened daughter. Tall and darkhaired like his father, Andrew was losing his childhood early. She thanked him and told him she'd return the boxes as soon as she'd finished, but he just shrugged, went inside, and closed the door behind him.

Driving out, she glanced over at Melvin Milton's house. How did he fit in here?

She cursed silently. Melvin was waving to her from his front yard, flagging her down, walking her way. Maybe she could just floor it; screech out before he got up to the car, but it was too late. She lowered her window as he approached her door. He grinned and waggled his fat fingers at Emmy. "Hiya, little lady." Emmy responded by shrinking back in her seat.

"I got a question for you, sweetheart." Melvin gave Liberty a broad, knowing wink.

"If I can answer it, I'll be glad to." She welcomed the cold air on her face, but not his hot breath.

"What's a pretty lady like you doing diving through trash bags? You not some kind of identity thief, are you?" A gold-edged tooth gleamed.

Her body jolted as though she'd just had a shot of the Bombay Sapphire, but she forced herself to look him directly in the eye. She'd play the part he expected and see what happened. "I was looking for a . . . a memento, and I didn't want to ask Alicia." She smiled weakly. "I'm sure you can understand."

He raised his eyebrows. "A memento? Something to remember the plaster saint by?" She could tell he didn't believe her.

"Yes," she said. "And why are you so interested? Do you plan to tell her?"

He pulled a sad-looking face and shook his head slowly. She shivered in her wool pea jacket. "That lady and me, we don't get along," he went on. He gazed at Vivian's

Homeworth Realty sign on the front lawn and leaned into Liberty's window, blocking the cold but dousing her with beer breath. "So she's selling."

"There's no reason for her to stay," Liberty said. "If that's all, Mr. Milton, I've got to be going."

"Didn't I tell you to call me Melvin?" he said with mock indignation. He jerked his head back toward the house. "She talk to you?"

"Of course," Liberty said carefully. "You know I'm working on that memoir book of Sam's."

"A pretty motley crew came by that day," he said, and now his eyes took on a shrewd expression. "You think somebody did him in?"

She bit her lip to keep from reacting. Melvin knew something, but he wasn't telling. Why? "It was asthma," she said. "You know that."

"I don't know that."

"Well, that's what killed him," Liberty said.

He looked as if something was slowly dawning. "No damn body ever told me what it was."

It was a chink in his manner, but she could use it. "You can help me with something, Melvin," she said. "Did anyone come to see him late that afternoon? A woman?"

He looked at Liberty knowingly. "Nope. After the guys left in the sports car, nobody came until he got home and then just those folks I told you about."

"Thanks," she said. "I've got to be going." She indicated Emmy, who shrank back, keeping an eye on Melvin. Kids bicycled by on the street, oblivious.

Finally he stepped back from the window. "Hey," he said. "Let me know if I can help you again."

She still felt he knew more than he was telling. "Goodbye, Mr. Milton." She shoved the car in gear.

"I'm in the phone book," he called as she drove away.

When she got home, she gave Emmy a snack and settled her by the TV, and then she brought in the boxes and set them on the dining room table. When she opened the first one, she caught her breath. Lying on top of all the papers was Sam's personal appointment book, apparently tossed in as an afterthought, perhaps of interest to the children one day.

She felt guilty going through it, but it held nothing he'd have kept secret. The only thing he'd written for that afternoon was *meet S,* underlined twice. She didn't know if "S" was a woman. All she had was Jesse's word, and that was hearsay.

She spent the next hour going through Sam's writings— sermons, prayers, quotes he enjoyed, notes for Sunday school classes, lesson plans, long-ago fund-raising speeches to civic clubs, copies of handouts. He hadn't kept rough drafts, but there were a few notes scribbled on yellow paper.

When she finished, the boxes were filled with folders to be returned. She took only two scanty pages of handwritten notes that related to the manuscript, and they just served to flesh out the chapters she already had.

The only place where the missing material could possibly be, she reasoned, if it existed, was on Sam's computer in the church office. Would Gracelyn have had time to search it and delete anything she didn't like? Or was it protected with a password?

Or, horror of horrors, was the missing material in the envelope that the car wash crew threw out?

Chapter Twenty-Four

"**D**id you get the name of the girl?"

Jack Ford didn't waste any time with a preamble. They'd just begun walking the trail in the park near her house, certain of not being overheard. She had forty-five minutes before she had to pick up Emmy from her last day of school before the winter holidays.

A glistening jogger chugged heavily by. Two young mothers, ponytails swinging in unison, hustled their industrial-strength strollers toward them, giving Jack and Liberty a sideways glance as they passed.

The two must have seemed an incongruous pair. Liberty wore a blue fleece jacket, Calvin Klein jeans, and Reeboks, while Jack had chosen a lime-green sport shirt, ragged jeans, and orange jacket with TENNESSEE lettered on the back. Liberty waited until the ponytails had passed before she answered.

"Did I get the name of what girl?"

"The new bookkeeper. Don't wait for Josie. Ask her directly for the financials."

"Go over Josie's head?"

"Why not? Get one of your board members to ask. It's strange that such a simple thing's been held up. Is there a reason?"

She stopped and gave him a worried frown. "Josie said it was because Gracelyn was slow about learning the software, but you think it's something more?"

Jack gave her a searching look. "I'm detecting a rat. First audit in years? Maybe somebody's buying time to cover their tracks."

Liberty wasn't convinced. "Jack, do you really think somebody could have gotten any financial hoodoo by Sam?"

"Sam was a heart-and-soul guy. Finance was not his strong suit." Jack, hands in pockets, ambled along.

Liberty picked up the pace. "Duff was the man for figures. Wouldn't he have noticed?"

"Money can be siphoned out, little by little." Jack stopped now and gazed at her. "Over time it adds up. And if somebody is trusted absolutely—"

Liberty shook her head. "I can't believe it. Gracelyn's been working there for years and years . . . ." And then, remembering Gracelyn's expensive handbag, her stylish clothes, she felt a little sick.

Their path led by a public golf course, and the *thwack* of balls seemed comforting somehow—that life was going on, people were playing games, despite her inner turmoil, despite death.

Jack continued, "You say Foley asked you to be on the board of Shadrach House? That gives you all the authority you need to ask this girl for information."

"I haven't agreed yet to be on the board."

"Why not?"

She put one stubborn foot after the other. "I don't want to upset Dallas."

"Whoa." Jack gripped her arm, not hard.

She stopped, perplexed. "What is it?"

He looked directly at Liberty, his topaz gaze unflinching. "You've got courage and you've got brains. All you need is a life of your own."

She turned angrily, shook him off, and kept walking. "Reverend Ford, I've got all the life I can handle. I have a lovely home, a child who needs me, a fulfilling volunteer job, a husband who's a good provider . . ."

Tears slid down her cheeks and she patted her face with her hood, embarrassed to be crying within sight of the golf course.

"You want more advice?" Jack whipped out a handkerchief and pressed it into her hand.

She mopped her face and shook her head. "Your advice is upsetting."

"It's meant to be."

"Let's not talk about me." She gave a long sniff, blotted, and folded the handkerchief. She gave it back to him. "Let's focus on the case."

He nudged her cheek with his knuckle. "I haven't given you my bulletin of the day."

"What's that?"

"There was nothing in the gin."

Now they were descending a slope under trees, out of sight of the golfers. Jack's words jolted her. "Nothing?"

"Nothing but booze."

She sighed. "So much for our plot."

"Yes. I did pick up one other fact from Alicia. Tell me again how you found Sam."

"Do I have to? I keep trying to forget."

"It's important, honey."

They'd stopped by the creek, cool in the shade of the overhanging trees, the rushing water soothing. She closed her eyes and imagined that Sam was near, telling her to go on, and she calmed. "I tripped over his shoe. I saw that he was on the floor, face turned to the side, and his mouth was open, and one arm was stretched out in front of him . . . as though . . . as though . . . he was reaching for something." Her knees deserted her, then, and she took a few shaky steps to the bridge, propping herself on the rail.

Jack came to her side. "Alicia said he must have been trying to get to the desk. He kept an adrenaline injector there."

"That makes sense," she said, her throat thick. She gazed down at the whorls of water, muddy after the recent rains, as if the answer lay somewhere underneath.

Jack leaned on the bridge rail beside her and gazed out at the trees. "He leaves the church, makes hospital rounds, and meets some woman, we don't know who, late that afternoon."

Liberty continued, "Then he comes home with supper in a takeout bag from the deli for himself and Duff. Duff comes over and they have a couple of drinks and sandwiches. Melvin sees Duff's car. While they're there, Gracelyn Rodgers comes and leaves off the manuscript."

"Duff goes home and Sam starts working on what the secretary brought—proofing, adding notes—am I right?"

"That tallies with what I saw."

Liberty, emotionally exhausted, sank to a bench and waited for two joggers to pass by. Jack sat beside her and continued, "Melvin had left his house with his girlfriend by then, and we don't know if anyone came during that time . . . except the killer, if there was a killer. You got there at ten-thirty. From what you told me about the temperature of the body, he was dead at least two hours before that. Now tell me why you're so sure Sam's death wasn't an accident."

Liberty took a deep breath and closed her eyes. "Because someone was upstairs, someone listening to him gasping for breath. Somebody turned off that light. I didn't imagine *that*. Nobody . . . nobody could be that evil, Jack!" She choked on all her held-back tears.

"Easy, Liberty." Jack's soothing hand rested on her back.

"It's just weird!" She shook her head. "If the footsteps belonged to a killer, it doesn't make sense. If somebody killed him two hours or so before I got there, why did I hear someone after ten?"

Jack took her arm. "Come on, girl, let's walk and think." Liberty made herself leave the bench, and they plunged deeper into the wooded area to a shaded leafy path dappled with light. Walking did make her feel better.

"Let me throw this out for you," Jack said. "Let's assume Sam was poisoned somehow or given something that would trigger an attack. Maybe whoever it was came back later to see if it had worked. And remember, you found the back door open. Someone left in a hurry and didn't lock up after himself, or herself."

"Because he—or she—didn't have a key?"

"Which means Sam let him in."

"Or her."

"Or her," Jack agreed.

They were coming out of the woods now, the sun boring through a cool, cloudy sky, and above, a few stubborn leaves waved in the breeze.

"What do you really think?" Liberty asked.

"Either he ran across an asthma trigger accidentally, or some killer set out do him in."

"Are they going to test for poison in that autopsy? Isn't it obvious if a person's been poisoned?"

"Not if you're not looking for poison," said Jack. "Cyanide would be obvious to a doctor, but arsenic has been missed before. And would they test for penicillin without good cause?"

She shook her head. "You can quit suspecting Dallas. He's no poisoner, and he didn't know about the asthma. And he was out drinking when the murder was committed."

"So you think," said Jack. "But just to rule him out, I'd like to meet him. You can learn a lot by little movements. It's not hard to tell when someone's lying, if you know what to look for."

"Dallas is about as subtle as a bull," she said, "and I don't want him to know I'm sleuthing—for lots of reasons." She didn't want to talk about Dallas. Should she ask Jack if he had an ulterior motive? For instance, herself? But that would be embarrassing, especially if it wasn't true. To change the subject, she told him about finding Sam's appointment book, and the notation he was to meet someone with the initial S. "What should we do?"

"You want to start calling all the S people in the phone book."

"Quit it, Jack. He met somebody, somewhere. Not at the church. Not at his house."

"He was going to make hospital visits. Maybe somewhere near there?"

"Good idea, but who was it? Someone out of his past?"

"Maybe someone who wanted to kill him?"

Liberty was stunned into silence. Then she told him about the missing section of Sam's memoir, the section that described what had happened to make him get on the bus for Florida. She told him Sam's story about Isabel, and he nodded slowly, understanding more about the friend he knew. "Maybe there was a secret he was finally going to reveal in this spiritual journey. Maybe he was a drug user. Maybe he was abused."

Jack listened without comment, and they walked for a few more moments before he spoke. "I don't know of any memoir authors who've made anyone mad enough to kill them. Maybe shunned by the family, but that's it. How many people knew he was writing it?"

Liberty's shoulders slumped. "All I know for sure are Alicia and Gracelyn."

"Alicia claims she didn't know what he was writing. What about Gracelyn?"

"She claims she's given me all she typed. If she's telling the truth, maybe he didn't give that material to her. I have a feeling he wrote it on his computer at church and it's still there."

"It's possible," said Jack. "So how do we get at this material? Do we confess our suspicions to Josie Robillard and ask to see the computer?"

"Every time I try to suggest that Sam's death might not have been an accident, Josie's uncomfortable," she said. "And Josie's already had to deal with Gracelyn's ruffled feelings when Sam hired a bookkeeper. I don't want to make an enemy of Gracelyn—not yet, anyhow. We might need her cooperation later."

They were nearing the end of the trail, and the parking lot lay ahead. "Well," said Jack, "we'll just have to access the computer without telling anyone."

Liberty whirled to face him, her eyes wide. "What! Break into the church? We can't do that!"

He smiled at her. "No, ma'am, we can't. But I might be able to talk Josie out of a key if there was a good reason I needed to go by after hours. Maybe some reason having to do with Shadrach House?"

"Well . . ." she said slowly, letting out a breath. "Do you suppose you could pose as the temporary director?"

"You know, I don't want to lie to Josie," Jack said. "And I don't want the job."

"God will forgive us for a white lie."

Jack clapped a hand on her shoulder. "But will anybody else?"

Chapter Twenty-Five

S aturday morning, Dallas obliged by sleeping in, exhausted, after arriving late the night before from a trip to Miami. Liberty scooped up the shorts, T-shirt, and socks he'd left on the floor and shoved them quickly into the hamper before she went downstairs.

She was going to play the part of Perfect Wife this morning. She started the coffee, set out cereal for Emmy, and fried link sausage in a skillet. Then she cracked open a can of biscuits to bake. Unfortunately, since Mama Jean had climbed onto the oatmeal bandwagon long before it was cool, she'd never taught Liberty how to make biscuits from scratch.

She set out eggs to fry and was rummaging in the freezer for a blueberry bagel when the phone rang. She didn't recognize the number, and figuring it was for Dallas, she picked it up.

"Hello, Lady."

"Jack!" She bit her lip, hoping Dallas hadn't heard her.

"How are you this morning?"

"Wondering why you sound so amused."

"We're okay with Josie," he said.

"What? Okay with Josie how?"

"I mean we've got permission to go to St. Chad's to pick up some extra chairs for Shadrach House. I found out that Sam had ordered some new stacking chairs for the Sunday school rooms and never told Josie what to do with the old beat-up wooden ones. I convinced her he'd meant to give them to the center. She said we could have as many as we could haul away."

"So she believed that you're going to be the temporary director?"

"Why shouldn't she? I'm so sincere."

"I don't suppose you'd really do it, Jack." Liberty let herself hope.

"Sorry. My plate runneth over."

"Couldn't you have found something less heavy? I'll bet those chairs are oak."

"Hey. The Lord provides. Do not question."

"Hope you're in good shape."

"We'll take that boy you mentioned. He can help us with the computer. I'll borrow my landlady's minivan and I'll pick him up. She likes to garden, and she's got it fitted out for hauling plants."

"Jack, Cedric isn't one of the big guys, and he's a geek."

"Do you want my help or not?"

"Sorry. I'll look up Cedric's address for you." Liberty heard the timer for the biscuits ring and told Jack she had to go.

After Dallas had eaten his big breakfast and gone to the office to catch up on work, Liberty checked the church calendar on the new St. Chad's web site. Nothing was scheduled past 7:30 p.m. Monday night. She wondered how the construction was coming along. She hoped there wouldn't be any trouble in getting in.

Tonight she and Dallas were invited to a neighborhood holiday party, and she dreaded it. Alcohol would flow freely, but there was no question of not going. She had gone to great pains to make friends with the neighbors, because that's what happy families did.

Now the problem was Cedric, and if he could go. She'd go by Shadrach House this afternoon and see if she could find him. She thought belatedly that Jack hadn't mentioned what he'd found out about the NIMBYs.

DECEMBER 18

Monday arrived with hope. Dallas had behaved at the Friday night party, and she'd found Cedric at the House on Saturday. He was gung-ho to go with them on the after-dark adventure.

She took Emmy out to the park playground to make sure the child would be good and tired that evening and not give her father any trouble about bedtime. While Emmy was on the swings, the blustery wind made her squeal about cold ears, but Liberty hadn't brought a wooly hat for her. Still, Emmy wasn't ready to leave, and nervous as Liberty was about the upcoming stealth operation, Emmy was allowed to stay.

During dinner Liberty thought about telling Dallas the truth, or at least the half-truth—that she was going to pick up chairs for Shadrach House. But no. Then there would be questions and complaints. She would have to concoct a story, even though she hated to lie, but she couldn't risk interference with the plan.

She told him that she'd been invited to Vivian's book group, and he seemed okay with it, not asking why they were meeting so close to Christmas. Then she called Vivian to give her a heads-up, but all she got was voice mail on both telephones. She left messages, confident that Vivian would check. Vivian always checked. It might be a client.

"Don't be late." Dallas hardly looked up from a basket-ball game when Liberty left.

When she drove up to the parking lot of Cheshire Cups & Books, she saw Cedric's serious face, with his slim square eyeglasses, framed in the window of a slightly beat-up maroon Voyager with Jack at the wheel.

When she opened the door of the Plymouth, she burst out in nervous giggles. All three of them were decked out in black.

"So tell me again what I'm supposed to do?" asked Cedric, when they hit the expressway. Towers, hotels, offices, neon signs all raced by, and cars, buses, and 18-wheelers droned. Planes winked in the dark sky, a train clacked on an overpass, and skyscraper windows shone in tree-shaped patterns. Liberty handed Cedric her flash drive and a list of keywords she'd devised. "You're looking for some files. We need to download them."

"Piece of cake. Why's this on the down low? Man, I don't need more trouble."

Liberty cleared her throat. "Cedric, Father Sam wanted us to have this material. But for some reason that lady at church won't give it to us. Keeps saying she's too busy. So we just thought we'd save her a little time."

"Uh-huh. I hear you."

"It's to help Shadrach House, you know that."

"Yes, ma'am."

She knew they were skating on thin ice bringing Cedric. She had a hunch Sam wouldn't have approved. But if they ran into any problems getting into the computer, they'd need him. And as for the chairs, she hoped Cedric was stronger than he looked.

The front door of the church, built a hundred years before when churchgoers walked to church or rode in leather-topped buggies, faced the sidewalk, and Jack had to turn down a side street to reach the rear entrance and parking lot.

Jack pulled in and lurched to a stop before he got very far. "Whoa."

Liberty didn't understand. The parking lot was deserted except for a bus used for preschool. Then she saw it: a cream-colored Avalon parked directly in front of the back entrance.

"You know who that belongs to?" Jack asked.

Melvin had mentioned a "lady's car," maybe an Avalon. "It looks familiar. What do we do now?"

Jack peered into the cone of light. "Let's wait in the shadows and see if anyone comes out. It's almost nine. Can't believe anybody would stay at this hour."

"Wait? Here?" Liberty's heart raced like a swollen river. She wasn't sure if she could endure the suspense. What if someone saw them?

"A lot of PI work is waiting," he said. "Waiting and watching."

"Like Advent," Liberty said softly. "I'm no good at waiting. I'd never make a PI." She thought, then, of her father. How many hours must he have spent waiting and watching on a stakeout?

Jack pulled the mini-van underneath overhanging trees at the edge of the lot, away from the tall sodium vapor lamps, where he had a good line of sight but wouldn't be easily spotted.

The damp odor of the woods stole into the musty earthiness of the van. As Liberty's eyes adjusted to the darkness, the lights inside the building became brighter, as if someone had switched on more. Something about the scene struck her as wrong. Gazing at the church, she tried to figure out what it was.

She *had* seen that car before. Parked there. She tried to picture the time she'd come to see Josie. In the distance, mall lights pinkened the night sky; a few clouds drifted by. A truck rumbled down the street. Headlamps cut into the side street and disappeared. Blood throbbed in her throat and damp patches formed under her arms.

"Aunt May says I've got to be back by eleven." Cedric's words knifed the silence.

"Not to worry," said Jack.

"Maybe it's burglars in there," said Cedric.

Jack frowned. "Burglars in an Avalon? More likely an Altar Guild lady picking up the fair linen."

Then it struck Liberty what was odd. "Jack, why would anyone be on the upper floor where they're building?"

"Building what?"

"Another of Sam's projects. Converting the attic space into two rooms. And they drive a van, not a peach-colored Avalon!" The light upstairs went out. A few minutes later, a figure hurried from the building—a tall, slim woman carrying a bag, a woman whose silvery hair shone in the lamplight. Liberty knew that hair.

Jack gave her a gentle push. "Get down!" Liberty slid forward, hunkering in her seat. An engine started and the Avalon roared past, squealing tires as it left the parking lot.

"Okay," said Jack.

Liberty unfolded. Her teeth chattered, although she was bundled in sweater and jacket. "Are we really going in now?"

"Why not?"

"I swear, that looked like Gracelyn Rodgers. What if she comes back?"

"So what? We have a reason to be here." He cranked up the van and drove to a spot as close as possible to the back entrance to the Sunday school wing, where they'd find the old chairs in one of the classrooms. They quietly let themselves out of the van. Jack gave Cedric a flashlight and then he unlocked the doors. They walked into the cool, dark, concrete-smelling hallway, where a security light burned dimly in the distance. Liberty's eyes tried to adjust, and she reached for a light switch.

Jack covered her hand with his. "Don't turn on any lights."

"Why not?"

"When we're ready to load the chairs, we'll turn them on. If the woman does come back, I don't want her to see anywhere else in the building lit up."

Their steps creaked along the soft vinyl tiles of the corridor, while Cedric bobbled his flashlight over the ceiling and into corners. When they reached the office area, Liberty walked over to Sam's door and found it locked. Jack took out a credit card. "Let me," said Cedric.

"You any good at this?" said Jack.

Cedric looked down modestly. "The best."

Jack gave him the card and the boy got to work on the thumb latch. The door fit well against the frame and it wasn't easy.

While he was occupied, Liberty glanced across the reception area, where Josie Robillard's office door stood slightly ajar. That surprised her. Why hadn't Gracelyn closed it?

She walked over to Josie's door and peered into the dimness, some light leaking in from the outdoor floods. Everything looked all right, as far as she could see. Then she heard a scuffling noise above her head—rats, mice? She froze.

"Jack?" She laid her hand on his arm. "Up above?"

Jack stood still and listened. The sound wasn't scuffling— it rustled and crackled, and it was right on top of them. Then she smelled the smoke.

Cedric's head whipped around. "This f–ing place is on fire."

"Come on!" said Jack. He grabbed Liberty's wrist. "Cedric!"

"Don't need to tell me twice," Cedric said. The three clattered down the hall and burst out into the cold night. They looked up, where a plume of smoke was roiling out of the vent in the attic.

Jack unpocketed his cellphone and called 911, then Josie. "We came here to get the chairs," he told her, "and found a fire."

"I'm coming right away," Josie told him. "I'll call the Junior Warden too." Liberty could hear the fright in her voice.

Jack snapped the cellphone shut and turned to the others, frowning. "We can still get the chairs. The fire may not reach this wing."

"No, please, Jack." Liberty's knees buckled, and she grasped his arm for support. "Don't go back in there. We can get them another time."

The fire trucks roared up five minutes later, and after they'd told them what they could, they felt they ought to take Cedric home. Josie rang Jack and said she was on the way. He told her that the fire brigade had arrived and he had to take a boy home, but he'd be available if she needed him.

"Somebody is trying to destroy this church," Liberty sobbed. "Sam, and Duff, and now this." They drove past the mall, its lights flashing by, and then they passed the Waffle House.

"It could have been an accident," Jack said.

By this time Liberty was trembling. "And pigs can soar like Superman. You'd better tell Josie about the Avalon. I know that was Gracelyn Rodgers. Did she set the fire?"

No one said anything. Liberty glanced over at Cedric. "Are you okay?"

Cedric frowned. "Do I still get my ten bucks?"

She glanced at Jack and saw the corner of his mouth twitch up. When they reached a light he pulled a twenty out of his wallet and gave it to the boy. "It wasn't your fault we didn't get the information." He paused. "But listen, Cedric. I'll expect you to keep quiet about this. If that fire was set, we don't need to tip anyone off that we might have seen them."

"You got it," Cedric said, putting the twenty in his pocket.

Jack dropped Liberty at her car, and they made arrangements to meet the following day. She drove home, drained and jittery. She hoped Emmy had gone to bed early and slept well.

When she opened the door, Dallas growled, "Where the hell have you been?"

Chapter Twenty-Six

THE BOOK CLUB
DECEMBER 19

"At the book club, of course." Liberty, quaking inside, projected boredom.

Dallas gave Liberty his King Kong expression. He wasn't buying it. Why? Her fingers tightened on the strap of her shoulder bag. Time to act innocent. She shrugged out of her parka and dropped the bag on the kitchen table.

"Like hell you were. You didn't answer your phone." He stalked toward her like the gorilla inside his husband outfit. He told her that Emmy had come down with an earache. He blasted out the description of pitiful howls from a mother-deprived daughter, absent in the time of need, unreachable by cell phone. He'd called Vivian's house to ask her husband to give him Viv's cell number, and Vivian herself had answered the house phone.

And after he'd asked Vivian what the hell she was doing home and not at the book club with Liberty, Vivian told him she'd had to cancel at the last minute— a client, a contract. She'd told Liberty to go ahead without her. He told Vivian about the earache.

Liberty let out a silent breath. Vivian, no dummy, was always quick on the uptake.

Vivian had advised Dallas to give Emmy three children's Tylenol.

Dallas told Liberty that he'd gotten the medication into Emmy and had practically demolished the floor by pacing until his wife had finally decided to come home. "Where was this book club?" he demanded.

"Over by the University. Another faculty wife, and you know it was a long drive. They were discussing a book I loved. And we're supposed to turn off the phones while we're discussing. Now I've got to go see about Emmy." She left the room and rushed upstairs, wondering if Dallas believed her.

Emmy whimpered on seeing Mommy, and Liberty gathered her up and gave her a long hug. The child was weepy and teary and afraid of missing Christmas. Liberty fluffed the little girl's pillows, gave her some decongestant, and dripped warm olive oil into her ears. She rocked in the chair by Emmy's bedside long after the child had drifted off, thankful for her deep and regular breathing. Outside, a gibbous moon hung in the clear frosty sky. The slow rocking cleared her mind, and bits of the puzzle about Sam's death came together, pulled apart, seemed to mesh, and then did not fit. She needed more pieces.

She mulled over the conversation she'd had with Rico at Frank's Fine Foods the previous Tuesday.

Wheeling the groceries out to her car, he'd denied there had been any kind of disagreement with Sam. But when she told him what Jesse had said, he stiffened. He loaded the groceries into the back before he spoke.

"Me and Rudy Chavez got into a fight in the parking lot—hell, Ms. Chase, he hit on my girl! But Sam and some of the guys grab me, break up the fight. Sam take my knife, mad as a devil. Said this time he turn me in. That I not keep my word."

Rico looked up to the sky. "What can I do? Already I am in trouble. I tell him if he go to the cops I tell the whole church a secret." He couldn't look at Liberty and was reddening. "So, you see. That was the fight."

She felt her throat go dry, but she couldn't leave it. "Tell me the rest of it."

He shook his head, turned away. "It is not a good idea."

"I need to know, Rico."

He started to walk off, but she grabbed the back of his collar. It might have something to do with Sam's death. "Tell me!"

He wheeled, a look of anguish on his face. "I wish I never sayed it. I told him I know about—about you and him."

"You mean Sam? Me and Sam?" Liberty managed to say, stiff as a zombie.

He shook his head and spread his hands. "You know."

"How'd you get such an idea?" she demanded.

Rico studied his shoes for a long moment. "The guys were saying."

"Guys will say things like that. And what did Sam do when you told him what you thought you knew?

"He haul back like he going to punch me out—the other guys, they still hold me—but then he drop his hands and say, 'No violence here. Not by me.'"

"And then what did you do?" Outside, the traffic zoomed by and in the distance a siren wailed. People were coming and going with their groceries, looking our way.

"I leave Shad House. What else? He kick me out. But when I hear Sam is dead, I come back and beg Foley take me to the funeral."

"I see," Liberty said, feeling limp and teary.

She gave him a generous tip and wished him a merry Christmas.

Jack Ford didn't answer his phone.

Dallas had left for work, and Liberty was anxious to know what Jack had found out about the fire.

She left a message and fretted and got Emmy ready to take to the doctor.

The pediatrician's office was thick with runny noses, and at the pharmacy, she stood in line behind old folks waiting for their blood pressure and arthritis pills. Emmy, regressed to thumb sucking, clung to her side until they arrived home.

She'd just gotten Emmy in bed with a tray of Chicken and Stars soup and cherry Jell-O, quivering in its instant container, when the phone rang.

"Okay if I come in?"

She looked out the window. Jack's old green MG sat at the curb. Her heart lifted, then sank again. "What if Dallas decides to come home?"

"All the better. I'll get a chance to meet him without your having to cook."

"But he might have the wrong idea." She was still upset by what Rico had told her.

"What can he say? I'm the temporary director of Shadrach House, remember? Does he come home often in the middle of the day?"

"No." Liberty gave a rueful little laugh, realizing how many firsts had happened to her in the last month.

She stood by the window and watched Jack park in the driveway. He strolled up the front walk, wearing his tweed jacket, this time over a red sweater. Red socks flashed beneath his trousers.

She flung open the door before he rang the bell. They hugged briefly—it seemed natural, after what had happened at the church. It felt good. She needed a hug. "I tried to call but didn't get an answer," he said. "I thought I'd better check and see if everything was all right."

"We were at the pediatrician's. I clicked my cell phone off inside and forgot to turn it back on." She filled him in on what had happened the night before. "You know how it is with kids."

A gust of cool wind skittered leaves across the walkway. "No, I don't know how it is," he said. "I never had any kids." He came in and shrugged out of his heavy tweed jacket.

She hung the jacket in the hall closet. "You said you were married?"

"Yep, once," he said. "Just as well we didn't have any."

That mysterious shadowed look again. She led him back to the kitchen, fragrant with chicken soup, warm bread, and coffee. "Have you had lunch?"

"I don't need anything, thanks. Well, maybe. That coffee smells good." He seemed to relax a little, and Liberty wondered if he missed having a wife.

Perhaps thinking of her own impulsiveness, she said, "You know, Jack, you're a careful man."

He shrugged. "Carelessness has unpleasant consequences."

She took two mugs down from the cupboard. Beneath his casual exterior, his odd clothing, she could see that he was not the type to take an uncalculated step. She had a feeling the mismatched gear was a deliberate move to throw people off the track. What had gone wrong with his marriage? she wondered. Surely, unlike her, he would have looked twice before tying the knot.

She poured a mug of strong brew from the percolator and set it on the table in front of him. The cheerful red of his crewneck sweater reminded her of how drab she looked and felt. She glanced down at her rumpled tan corduroys and lavender turtleneck—sexless Mommy clothes.

She hadn't bought clothes for fun in a long time.

A wail came from upstairs. "Mommy! I'm thill hungry!"

She glanced toward the stairs. "If Emmy's calling about food, she must be feeling better. Just a minute, Jack."

He waved her away. "Give the little lady some dessert."

Liberty went upstairs, carrying a napkin folded over two of the Christmas cookies that their neighbor Netta Robinson had brought over. When she set them on Emmy's bed tray, Emmy gave her mother a challenging frown. "Who that man? Father Sam?"

A couple of times Sam had come over to bring some papers for Liberty to work on, but only when he was going to be on her side of town anyhow. But Emmy remembered.

Liberty smoothed the child's hair. "Oh, honey. I'm afraid Father Sam has gone to be with Jesus. Can we have a talk about that later?"

She shook her head. "He ith dead." She lay back against the sheets. "I don't like 'at man."

Liberty licked her dry lips. What should she call him to Emmy? "Now, now. Dr. Jack is helping me with a project."

She crossed her arms. "I don' like him."

Right now Emmy wouldn't like anybody. "Don't worry, honey," Liberty said. "He's a nice man. He's not the kind of doctor that gives shots. If you need me, call and I'll come." She gave her daughter a kiss. "I'll come up and read to you the minute he leaves." Emmy quieted then. The medication was making her sleepy, and she lay back against the pillows. After patting Emmy's cheek, Liberty went down to the kitchen.

Jack gave her a freighted look. "Girl, it's hitting the fan."

"You've found out something." Liberty poured her own coffee and took a chair across from him.

He shook his head. "There's a hell of a mess over at St. Chad's. Police are investigating for arson. The contractor is mighty upset. They're calling it malicious vandalism."

"What about Gracelyn?"

"That's the funny thing. She admits she was there. But she says she didn't see or hear anything. She claims she just ran in to collect her forgotten phone."

"Bull. She was in that building longer than that. And there was a light upstairs."

"That's the second light upstairs, kid. You saw one at Sam's."

"What can it mean?"

"Look. Let the police handle this one. When we need to tell what we saw, we will. But until then, it wouldn't hurt to talk to that new bookkeeper. Nothing like burning the church down to eliminate embarrassing evidence."

"Gracelyn's life is that church, Jack. Would she have set fire to it?"

"If she had something to hide. If she was desperate. To keep you from seeing that computer?"

"Whatever was on it can't be that important to her, could it? What will I say to that new bookkeeper?"

"You'll think of something." He checked his watch. "I only meant to stay a minute. I've got a client to see."

"One more question. Have you made any progress on Sam's mystery woman?"

"I've checked a few cafés and coffee shops near the hospital," he said. "No one remembers seeing Sam that afternoon." He lifted Liberty's hand and kissed it. "Au revoir, girl. By the way, I'm talking to the head of the neighborhood group that's against Shadrach House tomorrow morning."

Liberty walked him to the door and let him out. Then, dumbfounded, she stared at her hand. And then it came to her. Had he checked the Cheshire Cups & Books? It wasn't near the hospital, but Sam liked to meet people there.

She ran back to the door, flung it open. "Jack!"

He turned and smiled. The smile faded as she told him her idea.

Vivian knew all about the bookkeeper. Kelsey Bales, a young woman in her twenties, daughter of a longtime church member, had been laid off from a prestigious firm when upgraded computers had taken her job, and took the church job as a stopgap. "Why do you want to know?" asked Vivian. "Or should I even ask?"

"I need a year-to-date church financial report for the grant. And Gracelyn Rodgers seems to be, well, obstructive. I don't want to ask her for anything else if I don't have to."

I could almost hear the wheels turning in Vivian's head. "If I do this, you promise you'll tell me sometime what this is all really about?"

"Vivian. You're an angel."

Her friend sighed. She didn't have Kelsey's home number, but she gave Liberty the number for Kelsey's mother.

Charity Bales supplied the daughter's address and cell phone number and wished Liberty luck in contacting her. "She spends too much time with that boyfriend."

Liberty tried the cell number but it didn't answer, and she left a message for Kelsey to call her back. If Kelsey was working at the church, Liberty didn't want to give Gracelyn a heads-up by calling the new bookkeeper on the church line.

She checked on Emmy, still sleeping, and then went back downstairs and picked up Sam's manuscript from the coffee table. The Christmas ornaments shimmered in the afternoon sun, scattering patterns of light over the manuscript. Liberty read over the first few pages again. She flipped through the chapters, focusing on the missing material—the time between Sam's awful childhood and when he got on that bus heading to Florida.

Could Gracelyn have taken it on herself to excise that part from the manuscript after his death? Or was Liberty reading too much into the secretary's noncooperation? And what about that missing envelope? It was addressed to Sam from elsewhere, though. Anything might have been in it, and now it was gone for good.

Could there have been anyone at all who knew what happened? Had Sam told the truth to his sister Isabel? She'd been at the funeral. Maybe they'd remained close. If she was someone he'd trusted, Liberty wanted to talk to her.

Alicia answered her call with a tone approaching the temperature of absolute zero. "Liberty? People are coming over to see the house."

"Please, Alicia. I'd like to talk to Sam's sister. Do you have her number?"

"Isabel or Nan? Nan's off in Africa in mission work, and Bel won't talk to you. Don't waste your time."

Nan? Another thing Sam never talked about—his other sister, Nan. "But why won't Isabel talk to me?"

"Listen, I've got to run. Try Aubrey Maginnes, Sam's father. He's in the phone book. Still lives in St. Augustine."

"Thanks." The phone clicked dead.

On the telephone in his study in St. Augustine, Aubrey Maginnes sounded tired, resigned, and very interested to know what Sam had written in his memoir. "Sam had secrets," said Father Maginnes. "I never knew what they were."

"He never told you about his early life?" Liberty held her breath and waited.

"I knew the story he gave me was full of holes," the older man said. "But I never succeeded in getting the truth. Perhaps I should have been more" —he paused— "insistent. Wounds have to be exposed to air before they can heal, but he did a good job of covering them over. I was afraid if I probed too deeply, he'd leave again. And I wanted him to stay. Perhaps Hazel and I were selfish that way. We loved the boy. He had a good heart."

"Did you know he wrote about Isabel?" she said, as a way of getting around to her real objective. "About the time they got in trouble at your house?"

Father Maginnes chuckled softly. "Did he write that she became a fine young woman? She's a social worker. Married a Cuban refugee. They have two lovely children."

"I believe he would have written about her success if he'd had the chance," Liberty said. "Father Maginnes, I have to ask you: will this story embarrass you and your wife?"

"Well, Mrs. Chase, let me say this. When Sam, or Richie as he called himself then, first came to us, he was very much into self-preservation. But I could tell that a good soul lurked beneath the toughness and wariness, a soul that desperately wanted to be loved and accepted. I wanted to see if a little nurturing would make that seed grow. Apparently, it did. I can't see how telling his past would hurt, as long as he wrote it in a respectful way."

The good man sounded so kind, so understanding, Liberty nearly wept. "Sam did," she told him. "He said his real name was Tony. Tony what, I don't know. He told you a complete fable about his early life?"

"Oh, yes. I knew he hadn't grown up on a farm. He had street smarts. He was a city kid."

"The manuscript said he came from New York."

"That sounds about right. I've got a pretty good ear for accents. I never told him my suspicions. I figured if God had sent him to me, it wasn't my business to send him back."

Liberty paused, unsure about the next question. "And Isabel? Would she mind if her story was published?"

He was quiet for a minute while he thought. "If he told about Isabel's life, he must have asked her permission."

"Do you suppose she'd talk to me?"

He hesitated for an agonizingly long time before he said, "You could try. She's taken his death very hard." He told Liberty where she could reach Isabel, and they said their goodbyes.

Liberty had her finger poised above the telephone to make the next call when Dallas walked in the door.

"Hi, babe," he said. "Thought I'd get home a little early. I'll get some take-out for us, and then you can go to the mall and finish your Christmas shopping."

The tree in the living room had so few gifts underneath, it looked like an old lady stepping over a puddle with her skirts lifted. Liberty looked down at the note pad on which the Florida number was written. She slid it into the drawer and pasted a sincere smile on her face. She hoped she looked grateful.

Chapter Twenty-Seven

NUMBERS GAME
DECEMBER 20

Wednesday morning, Liberty was on edge. She'd placed a call to Sam's sister Isabel, but got a machine, and left her number without much hope that Isabel would return the call. It was the holidays, and Liberty herself hadn't managed to get all her shopping done the previous night.

Working quickly, she arranged to drop Emmy at Caitlin's house for the morning with a promise to take Caitlin for the afternoon so Jen could do her own Christmas errands. And off she went, headed for the biggest mall near their house, hoping to find three more good gifts.

That afternoon, to the tune of happy giggles from Emmy and Caitlin playing upstairs, she surveyed her shopping finds on the dining room table. The scent of orange and apple peels simmering with cinnamon and clove wafted in as she measured out holly-printed paper for the gardening book she'd chosen for Mama Jean. She stared at the picture on the front, a popular TV plant wizard, and imagined Mama Jean cracking a joke about how handsome he was. Impulsively, Liberty went to the phone and called her.

"You still doing okay up there?" her grandmother asked.

"Fine, Mama Jean."

"That skunk treating you right?"

"He's trying."

"And the other?"

I knew she was talking about Sam's murder. "I'm working on it. I've got a helper. A friend of Sam's."

"I worry about you, Liberty Jean."

She had always worried. After losing a son, it was understandable, and Liberty wished she were here to hug. "Please, can't you come for Christmas? I'd be so happy, and Emmy would love it. I know Papaw hates the drive, but—"

Mama Jean chuckled. "I have a surprise for you, honey. I booked airline tickets for the twenty-fourth right after you left to go back to that fool. I felt you might need us. I've been meaning to call, but I didn't want to put any pressure on you."

"Oh, Mama Jean!" Liberty knew that her grandmother hoped a divorce was in the offing and Liberty would return to Florida, but it was just like her to back off gracefully. Now Liberty felt about ten pounds lighter. Mama Jean and Papaw being with them would make Christmas a little more jolly.

The older woman lowered her voice. "What did you do with that thing I gave you?"

She was talking about the gun. "It's under the sweaters on the top shelf of my closet."

Mama Jean snorted. "If you need it in a hurry, you're going to have a problem."

"But what if Dallas found it? What would I tell him?"

Her grandmother didn't have an answer for that and made a sound of disgust. Liberty decided it was time to say goodbye and avoid any more lectures about Dallas.

Before Liberty had left the kitchen to go back to the wrapping, the phone rang again. Heart hammering, she picked it up. Kelsey Bales was on the line: uncertain, curious. "Mrs. Chase? I was returning your call?"

Disappointed it wasn't Isabel, Liberty told Kelsey the usual story—that she was working on Sam's memoir and she wanted to ask her a few questions about him.

The young woman's words tumbled out in a torrent, quick and breathy. "Oh. It was horrible, Mrs. Chase. Just horrible. We're going to miss him so much. I don't know what I could tell you that you don't already know. I hadn't worked there very long, but he was great to work for. Such a caring man."

"Are you at the church now?"

"Yes, but I leave at five."

"Kelsey, may I come to see you at home?" Liberty felt the young woman would be more likely to give out information where she was comfortable than if they'd met somewhere.

"That's cool. When?"

Liberty made a quick calculation. "After supper? Seven-thirty or eight? My husband will be here to look after my daughter."

"Not a problem."

"Where do you live?"

She told Liberty. It was near Westbury Mall, a long drive.

"Do you live alone?" Privacy was important.

She laughed. "My boyfriend's there a lot, but we don't live together."

Liberty could deal with the boyfriend if she had to.

After she'd given Dallas a good chicken tetrazzini dinner, oozing with cream and Parmesan cheese, she told him that she had to run out for about an hour.

"What for?"

"I need to do an interview for the book."

"It can't wait?"

"Do you need me for something?" she asked, sweetly but firmly, daring him to try and stop her. "I'll be back in time to read Emmy her bedtime story."

He gave her a long, hard, look before he answered that he could do that very well. She told Emmy to mind Daddy, and she left.

Once again she found herself driving that road she had driven so many times lately. Going toward where Sam used to live and work. Going toward the strip mall where Shadrach House served boys who needed him. And now, without Sam to advise her, she felt like a butterfly in a net, hopelessly beating fragile wings. She had to become stronger, for what she needed to do.

He had come close to telling her about the memoir just once.

It had been a day when Emmy was in school and Liberty was spending the day at the center, trying to sort out the paperwork for the latest grant they'd applied for. Sam dropped in and poured them both a cup of coffee. She'd brought blueberry muffins to share with the boys, and they drank coffee and ate muffins in the quiet space before the boys arrived. He found some classical music on the radio, and they started to talk. He asked her about her background, and she told him about her father dying and her mother going away and Mama Jean and Papaw raising her. Then she didn't want to talk about them any more and asked him what his coming-of-age story might be. He smiled and said he would tell all in the fullness of time. Then he said, "I haven't been a saint."

Liberty had laughed. "Nobody expected you to be a saint."

"You'd be surprised," he said and changed the subject.

She'd never given it a single thought until now.

The tiny parking lot of Kelsey's apartment building, a three-story walkup on an oak-shaded street near the University, held no space for visitors. Liberty squeezed into a slot at the curb, wishing she drove a Mini Cooper. As she snugged the SUV's wheels to the curb, a door on the ground floor swung open. A spike-haired supercool type, clad in black leather jacket and tight jeans, sauntered her way.

The young man she'd seen at Duff's funeral. Gracelyn Rodgers' son.

His gold earrings glinted in the lamplight. His hooded eyes and dark eyebrows and sinuous walk gave him animal appeal. He reached the curb and melted into his low-slung red ZX, and then he roared away. Liberty finally slid out of her clunky SUV.

Kelsey waited by the open door. "I thought that might be you," she said. "That timing worked out pretty well."

"It did." Kelsey's wholesomeness, the well-cut chestnut hair, guileless look, and makeup-free complexion didn't seem to jibe with the type of young man Liberty had just seen.

Inside, Kelsey took Liberty's coat and motioned to a blocky reddish-orange sofa. "Have a seat. Of course, it looked better in my other apartment," she said.

"Other apartment?"

"Rent got too high. I miss my white loft," she sighed. "But this is better than moving back home."

That recent visitor might have been the reason she didn't want to live at home. Liberty lowered herself onto the cushy sofa and glanced around the room. Kelsey's high-tech look didn't fit this apartment's genteel shabbiness. A glass-topped table held a variety of DVDs and computer games, but no books or magazines. She wasn't a reader. "Would you like a Coke?" Kelsey asked. "Afraid there's not much else. I've been working all day and I haven't had time to go shopping."

"I'm fine, thanks." Liberty took out her notebook.

Smiling thinly, Kelsey perched on the seat of an uncomfortable-looking chair, looking for all the world like a bird preparing for takeoff. "What can I help you with?"

"Quick question. Was that your boyfriend I saw coming in?"

Her face lit up. "Actually, we're engaged," she said. "We've been looking at rings."

"Really? He doesn't look like the type to settle down," Liberty said, and immediately regretted it when Kelsey's smile disappeared.

"I hope that was a joke," she said. Maybe she'd heard similar remarks from her parents.

"Stupid attempt at one. Sorry. He's so good-looking, is all." Liberty hated to see the girl make the same mistake she'd made: being sensible, except for a weakness for bad boys.

Kelsey shrugged. "So what did you want to know about Father Sam?"

The usual questions were duly asked: what Sam was like as a boss, what were the duties he gave her, what she liked best about his style in the pulpit. The answers were good and thoughtful, and Liberty dutifully wrote them all down, leading up to the most important question.

"One more thing. I'm a member of the Shadrach House board, and I'm helping to write the grant. We need a church financial statement, up-to-date. Did anyone mention it to you?"

She shook her head. "No."

The "no" seemed truthful. "Sam was planning to ask you. I understand you're transferring all the data to the new program. Would you pull one for us as soon as possible? Would that be a problem?"

Her eyebrows drew together. "I can get you what we have. But if it's important, it would be better to wait until after the audit in January."

"Why is that?"

Emotions—concern, alarm, worry—flitted across her face and settled behind a mask of caution. "I'm not sure I'm supposed to talk about it."

Whoa. Full alert. Liberty forced herself to be positive and upbeat. "I'm sure it will be all right," she said encouragingly. "Josie Robillard's given me the go-ahead to get what I need."

Kelsey slid back in her chair and knotted her hands, still not sure whether to trust her questioner.

"Our grant application must be postmarked by December 31," Liberty went on. "I'll hold everything you tell me in confidence."

Kelsey shifted in her chair, tapped her fingers, and when her eyebrows relaxed, Liberty could tell that she'd decided to risk it. "You know the new construction? There were a couple of hefty checks made out to R&S Painting, and I thought it was odd. We hadn't had any painting done, and it's not the custom to put so much money down before-hand. You know the usual—one-third up front, one-third when half done, one-third when completed. I went to check the estimates and invoices and couldn't find any for R & S Painting."

"No?"

"I asked Father Sam if the procedure for paying con-tractors had been changed. He said no, that one-third was the norm. I asked about the painters and he said to ask Mr. Mowbray, who was dealing with the contractor, and Gracelyn, who'd been keeping the books before I got there. Gracelyn told me that the invoices must have been misplaced, and that she'd look for them."

"What about Mr. Mowbray?"

"He said he didn't hire any painters, that the renovation company was going to subcontract, and that he'd look into it."

Liberty froze to her seat. "Did you go to Mr. Mowbray's funeral?"

"No," she said. "I didn't really know him that well. I think Van went. My boyfriend," she added.

"Oh, yes. He's the young man I saw with Gracelyn Rodgers. She's his mother?"

Kelsey nodded, and her eyes grew misty. "I liked Mr. Mowbray. He wasn't that old. Mrs. Rodgers said it was a heart attack."

Liberty's own heart sped up, and she tried hard to keep her voice even. People assumed both deaths had been natural, because it was inconceivable they could not have been. "It's a blow to our shelter."

Kelsey bit her lip. "That project was such a good idea. Poor Father Sam. So much on him. No wonder he was under stress. What with the renovations, and the project, and the church always being short of money. Mom says the stress is what brought on his asthma attack."

Liberty let that pass. Something was nagging at her mind, perhaps the way she'd said *Mrs.* Rodgers. "Do you and Gracelyn get along?"

Kelsey examined her short, well-groomed nails. "We have to work together, and she's my boyfriend's mother. I can't talk about her behind her back." She glanced meaningfully toward a canvas laundry bag on the floor. "Look, Mrs. Chase, I've got to get that laundry done tonight."

Liberty followed her gaze. "You do your boyfriend's laundry?"

"Why shouldn't I?" she said, pushing out of her chair. "Mrs. Rodgers doesn't have time, and it's really none of your business."

The amateur detective rose and picked up her bag. She needed to smooth over her *faux pas.* "You're right. Sorry.

You just seem so in love. It reminds me of when I was dating my husband."

Kelsey relaxed a little, and Liberty knew she'd hit the right note. The girl's smile crept out again. "I had a crush on Van when we were teenagers," she said, "but he never noticed me. We got to know each other better after I came to work at the church, and things just happened." She smiled again, validated at last.

"I'm glad you're happy. I'll be going now. Sorry if my questions upset you."

She shook her head. "It's all right. I know things are a little weird. I'm sure Father Sam would've gotten all that business straightened out, and I'll get you a statement."

"I appreciate it," Liberty said. "Thank you for your help, Kelsey." Liberty slipped her notebook back into her bag, took her leave, and walked to the car as fast as she decently could. Her hand was trembling as she opened the car door. When she reached a stoplight well away from her apartment, she punched in Jack Ford's number on her cell phone.

He didn't answer.

"Some woman called you," growled Dallas, when Liberty finally got home. "She left a number."

He'd scrawled Isabel's number on a yellow Post-it on the wall, and Liberty punched the numbers so hurriedly that she missed it twice before she got it right.

Isabel's voice—her cool, thick, and rich voice—came on the line. "Hello."

Liberty introduced herself and said that Alicia had asked her to finish Sam's memoir.

"I suppose you've read what he wrote about me."

"Yes, I have. Did he let you see the manuscript?"

Her voice betrayed no emotion. "Of course he did. He sent me chapters. My early life was nothing to be proud of, but I was very confused back then." She paused. "Having boys and men want me gave me my only feeling of power." She was quiet again, as though wondering just how much to tell. She finally said, "Lots of people had hard beginnings. I tell the kids that the only shame is if you don't overcome them."

"Isabel," Liberty said, "That's wonderful, and I understand. But there's one thing I don't know. Did he tell you what happened to him back in New York to make him leave?"

She was silent. Liberty heard her breathing.

Desperately, Liberty blurted, "I can't find the material, Isabel. I'm sure he wanted to put it into the book. Did he send it to you to read? If so, please send it back so I can include it. It's an important part of the story."

She sounded thoughtful. "I sent it back some time ago. He might have changed his mind about including it."

"I don't think he did, Isabel. He wanted to tell everything." She recited the opening paragraphs, which she now knew by heart.

"I'm sorry, Mrs. Chase," she said haltingly. "I don't have the pages any more. I didn't make a copy. I'm really glad you're finishing it for him." The last words were choked, full of tears. "Excuse me," she said. "I'd better go now." She hung up the phone.

December 21

Liberty and Jack Ford sat in Raoul's Deli the next afternoon, Thursday, after she'd left Emmy at Netta Roberts'. It was no wonder Miss Marple and Lord Peter Wimsey solved all those crimes, Liberty concluded. They didn't have children, and those detectives could tell people what they were doing.

Today, Jack looked subdued in the tweed jacket and a dark green golf shirt embroidered with HCC. She wondered which golf club it had come from. He'd ordered pastrami on rye with extra pickles and chips. "I forgot to eat lunch," he said.

"Remind me to stay away from you and those garlicky pickles." Liberty picked up her coffee and regarded her Napoleon. Maybe caffeine and sugar would jump-start her foggy brain.

"What do you think I should do about Isabel?" she asked. "Try to convince her to tell me what he said? The problem is that it's painful for her."

"Did you tell her you suspected Sam was murdered?"

"Should I have?"

"Maybe," Jack said. "Maybe she'd have been more cooperative. I would've wanted to see how she'd react."

"Well, she certainly didn't kill him."

"She could have reasons for never letting that manuscript see the light of day, no matter what she told you."

Liberty took a sip of coffee. "She told me she gave Sam permission to use her story."

"And he never told you about her, never told you about that part of his life?"

She shook her head. "He didn't really tell me all that much about his life."

"That was part of his shadow," Jack said, almost under his breath. "He had a dark side."

"Did he trust you with that side of him?"

"No." He frowned. "Maybe no one—not even Alicia—until now, and now it's too late."

They had much to think about, but a pressing matter was at hand. "Jack. Remember Kelsey, the bookkeeper? She found something irregular about some checks." Liberty repeated Kelsey's story.

Jack stroked his chin. "I won't call that a smoking gun, but it looks suspicious, especially with that fire. I have a pal in the cop shop, but I can't get anything out of him about the arson investigation."

"What was that fire meant to destroy, Jack? Sam's memoir, or the financial records?"

"Interesting question. What if Gracelyn Rodgers was embezzling? Or Sam himself, with Gracelyn covering up for him?" Jack said.

"Do you honestly think Sam would do anything like that?"

His eyes told Liberty before his words. "I don't. I'm playing devil's advocate. Some people might think he was so intent on getting money for the project, he'd stoop to a little borrowing."

"That would be cutting off his nose to spite his face."

Jack crunched on his pickle. "Nobody ever thinks they'll get caught. It's hubris. By the way, Josie called me to find out when I was going to pick up those chairs."

"Oh, my God," Liberty said.

"It's not that earth-shattering."

"I was thinking of Cedric. His fingerprints are on the door."

"I wiped it down," said Jack.

Of course. He was a PI. Liberty grimaced. "I'll call Foley and Bill and see if a volunteer can take some boys to get the chairs this weekend."

"This weekend, sugar," he reminded her, "is Christmas."

She slumped on her chair and took a bite of the Napoleon. She'd lost track of time completely. "We'll deal with it," she sighed. "Here's something else. Kelsey is madly in love with Gracelyn's son."

Jack smacked the table. "What is this, an investigation or a soap opera?"

"Listen. He just doesn't seem like the kind of guy she ought to be involved with. She's so wholesome, and he's so . . ."

"Why are you blushing?" Jack rubbed his chin. "Fancy him yourself?"

She gave him a laser look. "I don't fancy that stud muffin. I liked Kelsey. I tried to warn her, but I she didn't appreciate it."

Jack returned a sad smile, one she'd seen before. "Nope. Remember what I told you about love?"

"Did you tell me anything about love?"

"Maybe we didn't get that philosophical."

Once again, she saw the shadow of pain and just as quickly it passed. For some reason she didn't want him to make a joke right then.

"What's our next move, Jack?" she asked.

"Can you find out any gossip about Gracelyn?" Jack asked. "I want to know if she's got any bodies in the basement."

"Madame Pillar of the Church?"

"You never know," he said. "I've got a theory, and I'm still working out the details. But make those calls, OK?" He looked at his watch.

"Go ahead, if you need to go," she said. "I think I'll warm up my coffee and eat the rest of the Napoleon."

She glanced over at his plate and saw that he had eaten perhaps half of his sandwich and the rest lay in ruins, as if a small tornado had passed by. "Is something wrong?" she asked.

"Liberty . . ." he said. Their eyes met, and for an instant she felt numb. And breathless.

"I need to go," he said. "I'll pay the tab." He picked up her hand and kissed it.

She watched him go. That strange emptiness fell on her when the front door closed behind him.

She asked for a box to take the Napoleon home to Emmy.

Chapter Twenty-Eight

Gathering her courage, Liberty set Dallas's bacon, eggs, and grits along with biscuits in front of him, glad that Emmy was still asleep.

She took three steps back from the table and announced that Mama Jean and Papaw would be spending Christmas with them. "Your folks will be away on that cruise," she said. They hadn't been invited to go with Dallas's parents, a small mercy to be thankful for.

Dallas gazed at his plate as if the eggs were threatening to rise up and smack him in the face.

Liberty decided to escape from the line of fire. She picked up a bag of garbage and walked outside, straight into a raw blustery day. She jammed the bag into the big green curbie and hurried back into the kitchen, hugging her blue fleece robe around her.

Tiny needles of sleet pinged against the bay window. Dallas picked at the grits on his plate. He lifted a half-eaten biscuit, smeared with grape jelly, and put it back down. He looked at her. "Libby," he said.

Here it came. Men didn't say *we need to talk* to alert you that something alarming was coming down the pike. They just came out with it.

"Yes?" She held her breath.

"It's okay with me if Jean and Charley come." His gaze nailed her like a police searchlight.

"And?"

"Are you seeing someone else?"

Her mouth dropped open then, and the sound she made was maybe a laugh, maybe a cry. Dallas hadn't cared when she'd been all wrapped up in Sam's project; he'd been doing his own thing, his drinks and his dinners and his nightspots on the expense account, and for all she knew, the strippers to go with it as well.

Liberty was conducting a perfectly innocent investigation with a guy she hardly knew, but she couldn't admit what she was doing. "What makes you think that?"

"You've been cold to me," he said. "Ever since the day we went hiking. You don't have any interest in being with me."

He meant sex, of course. She swallowed and stalled for time. "You haven't exactly been Romeo."

"I've been waiting to see what you'd do," he said.

She picked up a wooden spoon and plunged it into a pan of water to soften its coat of grits. "You weren't well."

"I'm okay now." He paused for a long moment. The sleet pattered the panes, the pale light outside like sheet steel. She poured herself more coffee and sipped it, holding the mug with both hands to warm her fingers.

"Libby," he said, "I'm staying sober. Where's the appreciation?" He waited for an explanation.

An explanation! She didn't owe him one. "Look here. I left because you struck me, Dallas. Some people call that abuse. Some people call the cops. Some people get restraining orders."

"Christ. It was one time. I swore I wouldn't do it again." He gestured dismissively, as if wife abuse might be a concept he didn't believe in, like the tooth fairy or national health insurance. "Where are you? I call home during the day, think maybe we can meet for lunch, maybe I have a question, maybe I want to tell you to pick up the frickin' cleaning. You're not here. You're not shopping. What the hell are you up to?"

Her hands froze on the back of the chair. After what seemed to be a very long time, she took the coffee pot and filled his cup.

Did he really care? She thought about the time when she had been giddy with love for the golden boy. Could she find that love again? Was there a wizard at the end of the yellow brick road who could change things, or would she find a con man behind a silly green curtain?

She fitted the carafe back into the machine and doled her words out like cards. "The youth project, Shadrach House, was in jeopardy after Sam's death. The grant we were applying for needed Sam to shepherd it through. Sam died, and then the chairman of the committee died too. It's fallen on me, Dallas. I need to finish up the application by December 31." She plunged ahead. "Remember what else I told you? Sam's wife, Alicia, asked me to finish the memoir he was writing."

"So you drop everything else for this dead guy's pet project? Me, Emmy, Christmas?" Liberty could feel his scowl at her back.

She wheeled to face him. "He'd signed a contract; he'd spent the advance on the boys. It's the least I can do for his memory, Dallas."

He rose from his chair, his stony gaze unyielding. "You're a busy girl. We've got a marriage to work on. What say we leave all this mess behind, send Emmy to your folks and cruise to the Bahamas, just the two of us?"

She couldn't control her incredulous look. *So you can throw me over the side of the ship?* was the first thought that came to her. She was getting paranoid, maybe, but there had been two murders.

"You act like I was planning to drown you," he said.

His mind reading unnerved her. "We *can't* leave Emmy at Christmas. You know how she loves it."

"Does the whole world revolve around that child?"

Liberty shook her head. This was a lot to take in. "Give me time, Dallas."

"Okay," he said. After a moment, he came over to embrace her, kissing her lightly on the lips. Then he let her go and picked up his coat. But she had one more hard thing to put in front of him.

"Dallas, please. I've invited the temporary director for Shadrach House over tonight. I'll cook from scratch, the way I used to. I want you to get to know him. Maybe then you'll be supportive of what we're doing."

"Anything to improve what's been passing for food here lately," he said.

As soon as the roar of the Audi dopplered to a hum, she called Jack Ford. He was free for a quick lunch at the deli.

Having dropped Emmy at Caitlin's house, Liberty went to meet Jack. The scene with Dallas had left her nerves raw, and it felt comfortable to be having lunch with Jack— maybe because, with him, she didn't have to *act*. Life with Dallas had long since become her most challenging role. There was an authentic Liberty under all her confusion and despair, although right now she wasn't sure who it was.

Why did she think she could trust Jack? Maybe it was because they were trying to find out what happened to someone they both loved. That was, she told herself, the reason he was a safe harbor. Without that, he'd just be a guy in funny clothes. She told herself that they had to stay on a professional level. That old bugaboo, Duty, kept rearing its head.

Today he was wearing a gray sweater with gray suede panels in a checkered pattern, the sort of thing her mother in Hollywood might have given him.

"One of your landlady's gifts?" she asked, touching the monogrammed sleeve. The initials weren't Jack's.

Jack stroked the wool. "English wool. She was going to toss it out. It had a few holes in it. But I know a clever Asian lady who fixes things for me. I'd tracked her son down, got him out of a cult, and persuaded him to come back to the family business."

"I see." She wondered if the Asian lady was attractive and single, and how good a friend she was, and then she told herself Jack's private life was none of her concern. Had to be none of her concern.

The counter girl called their number. Jack went to pick up their soups and sandwiches, refusing her perfectly good cash. He threaded his way back between the tables as gracefully as a lynx, just as unconscious of his grace, and just as mysterious. She wasn't used to hidden depths in a man. She couldn't afford to be too curious about Jack. Her life was complicated enough.

He set the tray on the table. The bacon and lentil soup smelled homey and enticing. The sandwich looked fresh and appealing with ruffled lettuce and slices of mozzarella cheese. Jack passed her a paper napkin. "What have you got?"

"Got?"

He looked at her curiously. "Your assignment. To find out anything you could about Gracelyn, stories that people could tell you. Her past. The kind of woman she is. Gossip, don't'cha know?"

She grimaced with dismay. "I'm still trying to find the right person to ask, Jack."

He raised one eyebrow. "Got it," he said. "Let's review. Sam's dead. Duff's dead. A fire may or may not have been set at the church on the night Gracelyn was there. Did this have anything to do with Shadrach House? You've talked to boys at Shadrach House. I've been by there, too, doing *my* homework. I had a talk with Foley. I can't believe the boys had anything to do with it."

"Nor can I," Liberty said. "But weren't you going to meet with what's-his-name from Hollydale Hills? The head of the NIMBYs?"

Jack nodded. "I did. Sam's death and Duff's death have rattled those folks. They're afraid they're going to be suspected of having something to do with one or both deaths, especially since I told them I was a private investigator working for the families. And as for the shelter, I told them that one of their sons or grandsons might need a place like that someday. All it takes is a parent's bad divorce, addiction leading to crime, and the kid is stealing from the parents, acting out, and they want him out of the house. I don't get the impression those folks would've done anything more than make noise."

Liberty sighed, guilty about not checking up on any gossip about Gracelyn. "You've done so much. I've had to deal with family matters."

"And tonight I'm going to meet your husband. Has he been threatening?"

"Threatening to take me on a cruise."

"But you say he didn't get home until after nine the night Sam was killed."

She noted that he'd said *killed* instead of *died*. He was definitely thinking homicide now. She recounted to Jack the morning's conversation with Dallas, and Jack made a few notes on his pad.

"I can't believe Dallas would murder," she said.

"That's why I've got to meet the man. I don't want emotion to cloud my reason."

"Emotion? But—" She knew what he was telling her, and her cheeks warmed. *"Don't,* Jack. We have to be professional if this is going to work."

He shook his head slowly. "Forget I said anything. I'll let you know my conclusions after tonight."

She smiled then. "You'll get to see me at work. Remember, Jack, I was trained as an actress."

"I have never forgotten that." His gaze was hard. Her fingers were resting on her notebook, and he reached over and took her hand in his. He turned it palm up, examining it. "What does the future hold, Liberty?"

"I don't know, Jack." She looked down, her cheeks warm, unwilling to meet his eyes.

He lowered her hand gently to the table and, as if it were a gerbil, patted it. "We've got a murder to solve. I'm going to do that. And then I'm going to be out of your life."

"Can't we—" She realized that she didn't want to lose him. As a friend, of course. "Must you?"

"Believe me, honey. It's gotta be that way."

She opened her mouth to object but closed it again.

"Donovan Rodgers," he said, "has a record. Here's the story."

Van, as they called him, had been a brilliant but lazy computer science major, and the collegiate party scene had fitted him like a pair of biker pants. After he'd flunked out, he'd been arrested for cocaine possession. With the influence of a church member—some thought it was Duff Mowbray—he'd been given probation and eventually allowed back in school. That time he'd tried to make a go of it.

He wasn't cut out for the classroom. He'd dropped out after another year to take a job with a dot-com company, which, because of the demand for computer experts, was hiring without looking too closely into backgrounds. Then he got laid off, and because of that blot on his record, he'd remained unemployed.

"No one knows if Sam was involved in helping him," Jack said.

"Well, if Sam helped him, the boy surely wouldn't have wanted to kill him. Did you talk to Gracelyn about any of this?"

He held up a cautionary finger. "Remember, doll, we're investigating on the QT."

She thought back to the flashy car she'd seen in front of Kelsey's apartment building. "I'd like to know where he got the money for that car. His arrest must have cost Gracelyn a bundle for the lawyers."

"Unless your pal Duff worked pro bono."

"That's not his field. He's more corporate."

Jack's cell phone bleeped "Ode to Joy." He glanced at it. "Excuse me." He answered, listened for a moment, then walked outside, phone to his ear. The more Liberty thought about Donovan Rodgers and his expensive tastes, the more it bothered her. But there was no proof any money was missing—yet.

Irregularities, missing invoices, sloppy bookkeeping—this from a woman with organizational skills to envy. Some people, she reminded herself, would go to any lengths for their children.

Had Donovan managed to get his mother to take money? And, to cover it up, was he capable of killing a man who'd helped him?

Jack returned and slid into his seat, his face betraying nothing. While they finished their sandwiches, they discussed how to find out more about Van Rodgers and his saintly, chilly mother. "I'm going to see if I can talk to Doyle Landring," Jack said, "You know, the rector of St. Chad's before Sam. He'd have known Gracelyn better than anyone. She worked for him for fifteen years. And now, sweetheart, I've got to be going." He downed his last sip of coffee. "Duty calls."

Liberty smiled, but regretfully. "I'm sorry for not completing my assignment. It's almost Christmas, and my grandparents will be coming day after tomorrow." She took his hand and squeezed a goodbye. "I promise you a good dinner tonight."

A broad smile spread across his creased face. "Honey, I'll wear my tweeds. I'll even wear my monocle." He winked at her and was gone.

Chapter Twenty-Nine

ADVICE FROM VIVIAN

How could Liberty rule out Dallas as Sam's killer?

It wasn't something she wanted to believe. He'd never do such a thing when sober—but drunk? In his Mr. Hyde personality? She hoped Jack's visit would make things clear. As she cruised the aisles of the supermarket, filling her basket with food she could prepare quickly, she thought about how she could get through dinner without letting Dallas know what they were doing.

Into the basket went mahi-mahi fillets and crumbly apple tarts from the bakery. She could whip up a potato-and-cheese casserole, and green beans dressed with butter and almonds would do. She bought a package of slaw mix, a baguette, and some vanilla Häagen-Dazs to top the tarts.

On the way home, she picked up Emmy from Caitlin's house. She settled Emmy and went to the kitchen, where she squeezed lemon into olive oil and herbs to marinate the fish. When the casserole was assembled, ready for the oven, she called Vivian. Her friend sounded as if her mouth was full. "You caught me right in the middle of lunch!"

"Late lunch, girl."

"I was showing a house. My stomach refuses to cooperate with real estate hours. What's happening, Libs? Can you believe the church caught on fire right here before Christmas? Thank goodness they got it before any real damage was done. Just a bunch of smoke, but that's bad enough. The cleaning has been going on all week. Did you find what you needed from Kelsey?"

"She was very helpful," Liberty said, but decided to stop there. She could almost hear Vivian's antennae click forward.

"I've been meaning to call," Vivian said. "Life has been so damned busy. I think all these people who suddenly decided they're in the market for a house just want to see people's Christmas decorations."

Liberty cleared her throat. "I need one more favor from you, Vivian, but if this is a bad time to talk . . ."

"Any time is a bad time these days. Did you ever see Hartley Ford?"

"He goes by Jack, by the way."

"First name basis? I'm impressed."

"Vivian, be serious. I didn't think Sam's death was an accident, and Jack agrees with me."

"My God, this *is* serious. Tell me more."

Keeping what she'd discovered from Vivian was one of the hardest things Liberty had ever done. "Viv, I swear I'll tell you the whole story when we get it all sorted out. Right now please tell me anything you know about Gracelyn Rodgers and her son."

"Gracelyn Rodgers?"

"I'm not one of her favorite people, it seems." Liberty glanced through the window at the sun breaking through the overcast sky and heard Emmy giggling, watching a video in the neat and tidy house. But Liberty's heart was pounding as if she'd run a five-mile race.

"Gracelyn has her ways," Vivian said. "Don't take her coolness personally. She was always protective toward Sam."

"Protective?"

"It goes with being the gatekeeper. She's had that job for eighteen years, ever since she was widowed, and I don't think she ever considered marrying again. After Wick died, she lived for her son, Van—Donovan—whatever. Spoiled rotten."

Liberty wasn't surprised. That went with the swagger, the car, the attitude. "Yes, I've seen him. I figured it was something like that. He thinks a lot of himself, doesn't he?"

"Oh, Libby. Girls swooned over him as a teenager. He was the acolyte from central casting, heavenly looking in those white robes! *Everybody* wanted him to serve at weddings."

Now Liberty was surprised. "The young man I saw was no altar boy. Does he still come to church?"

Vivian gave a short, ironic laugh. "Not for ages."

"I wonder how he hooked up with Kelsey Bales."

"*Kelsey*? Are they *dating*? He'll break her heart. Oh, my goodness, there goes my other phone. I've got to go, dear. Keep me posted."

And Vivian was gone, leaving Liberty to consider a young man without a father, spoiled by his mother, attractive to young women, with a taste for expensive cars—and into drugs.

She carried a basket of Bratz dolls in tiny bits of skimpy garb upstairs, pondering Kelsey and Van. The phone rang, startling her. Jack? But it was Dallas, sounding combative. "I might be late tonight," he said.

"You can't." Her fury began to rise. How could he! After all her work! She tried to sound firm. Not hysterical. "What's so important?"

He cleared his throat. "A customer."

"Look. We're having company," Liberty said patiently. "I've already bought the food. It's almost Christmas, for heaven's sake."

"Who's coming?"

"The temporary director of Shadrach House."

"Another one of those freaking priests?" He bellowed. "I'm not giving up this dinner meeting for that. It's important."

"Dallas, please."

He hung up the phone.

O-kay. Not for the first time did Liberty wonder if he was really meeting with a customer. In the past, after those business dinners he nearly always came home looped. She forced the thought out of her mind. She'd have to call Jack, but she wanted to have some progress to report on Gracelyn.

She closed her eyes and recalled Sam's funeral, trying to remember the remarks she'd heard about the longtime secretary. *So calm. So collected,* they'd said. *She's so wonderful. Such a pillar of strength. She'll help Josie get through it all.*

The church is lucky to have her. And then something Vivian had said made her think again. *She's a widow.*

She called Vivian back.

"Libs? I'm on the way to a client," she said when she answered.

"Sorry, Viv," I said. "Quickly. Can you tell me anything about Gracelyn's husband?"

The phone hissed and crackled in Liberty's ear. "Not really. When I came to St. Chad's, she'd been a widow awhile. You might ask Ruby Drake. She's been there forever."

Liberty licked her lips. Ruby was the woman who'd come in while she was sitting at Gracelyn's desk pretending to be helping out. "But Vivian . . ."

Vivian paid no attention. "Wait. Wait. I just thought of someone better. Elise Mowbray. You've met her."

Elise Mowbray. Duff's widow. Just about as bad a choice as Ruby. Before Liberty could object, Vivian continued, "Libs, I've got to go. I'm here, and there's my client."

Liberty thanked her and rang off, racking her mind for another choice, and then realizing there was no choice. She still had the Mowbrays' home number, and she tapped it in.

Elise herself answered. Liberty apologized for disturbing her and asked if she could pay her a visit, to talk about Sam. She'd get the conversation around to Gracelyn somehow.

"Darling, I *need* to talk to people." Prepared for a rebuff, Liberty was surprised. Elise's throaty purr sounded as if she might be a little drunk—in the middle of the afternoon— but Liberty didn't blame her. She was still grieving.

Elise went on, "I'm leaving town day after tomorrow to be with friends over the holidays. I wish I'd gotten to know you, my dear. I understand you worked closely with Sam, and we just loved him." Did Elise remember her from Duff's funeral?

Just as Liberty braced for the sluff-off, Elise said, "Come over for a drink tomorrow night. I'll be ready then."

Ready? For what? Anything is allowed for grief—eating too much or too little, drinking too much or drying out, acting up or shutting down. But when one is not allowed to grieve, one does what one can. Solves mysteries or becomes one.

"All right," Liberty said.

Elise asked her to come at eight.

Liberty finally got in touch with Jack late that afternoon and told him Dallas wasn't going to be home and the dinner had to be canceled.

Jack replied that he'd decided that Dallas was a long shot as a suspect, anyhow. Liberty said it was all right. She and Emmy would have a nice fish dinner and Dallas could have the leftovers tomorrow night. He wouldn't dare complain.

Chapter Thirty

C ourage . . .

Liberty dreaded having to talk with someone else recently widowed, and told herself that she might be uncomfortable, but justice for Sam came first. She busied herself with a flurry of Christmas housecleaning and decorating, and that evening she placated Dallas with the delicious food she'd planned for dinner with Jack the night before. When she placed a tart with ice cream before him, she mentioned casually that she had to visit a recently widowed friend that evening.

He snorted his disapproval but forgot it while spooning up the dessert. Afterwards, he retired to the TV, demanding that she get Emmy ready for bed before she left.

She slipped out after tucking Emmy in and reading her a Christmas story about elves. Emmy loved elves.

She drove past the middle-class neighborhoods surrounding St. Chad's, a few of the houses artistically built or renovated in a Craftsman style. The area was near a university, after all, where many residents had more taste than means to indulge in art. She finally arrived at the rolling acres where earlier Mowbrays had farmed a hundred years ago.

Duff had sold some of the surrounding land for subdivisions and had built himself a grand house in place of the old family farmhouse. At the end of a winding driveway the house faced her, a soaring fusion of European stucco and cathedral windows, through which a faceted chandelier cast pinpoints of light into the December darkness.

Elise Mowbray greeted her at the door, a red embroidered caftan swirling around her ankles, a glass of white wine already in her hand. Her short salt-and-pepper hair had been freshly coiffed, and makeup freshly applied: lashes mascaraed and cheeks rosy with blush. Still, makeup couldn't hide the caverns of grief.

She greeted Liberty with a wry smile, and Liberty felt Elise was trying to make her guest comfortable. "We can talk in the back." Liberty followed Elise through a pale ivory-and-beige living room, glancing at a creamy marble fireplace, above which hung a giant flower in the style of Georgia O'Keeffe.

They arrived at a spacious garden room at the rear of the house, and Elise murmured with a pain-thickened voice, "We loved to entertain here."

Liberty took in the lofted ceiling, the polished ceiling fans, the painted wicker furniture, the pastel dhurrie rugs underfoot, the tropical palms hunched like exotic beasts in the corners. "It's lovely."

Elise slipped behind a marble-topped bar at least six feet long. "What would you like to drink?"

"Wine?"

"Of course." From a small refrigerator, Elise drew out a bottle of chilled Chardonnay, already open, and set it beside an open bottle of Merlot.

"Red or white?"

"Red, please." Wondering how many glasses Elise had already downed, Liberty was handed a balloon wineglass filled nearly to the top.

"Thank you." Liberty took the Merlot and picked a cocktail napkin from a stack on the bar. Elise refilled her own glass with Chardonnay, nodded, and floated over to a wicker sofa. She lowered herself into nubby coral cushions and beckoned Liberty to a love seat across from an abstract painting blazing with corals and reds and greens.

"Prosit." Elise sipped her wine.

Liberty nodded. "Prosit."

Elise extracted a cigarette from a box on the table. She flourished a small porcelain lighter and lit the tobacco, smoke curling and disappearing into the heights. "Forgive, me, please," she said. "I quit two years ago. But after Duff was gone, I couldn't bear it. I'm like a boat without a rudder." Stiffening with resolution, she turned and faced Liberty squarely. "All right, my dear," she said, "What can I help you with?"

Liberty knew she'd have to be calm and patient. "Thank you for seeing me. I know it must be hard for you." She explained about the memoir, leaned back, and took a tentative sip of wine, waiting.

Elise nodded and took a long draft of her cigarette. "We hadn't known Sam very long, but we were truly fond of him."

Liberty took another sip of the heavenly wine and, trying to look comfortable, nudged her derrière to the back of the sofa. This wasn't going to be easy. "Yes. Mr. Mowbray had planned to talk with me. He told me he'd been the last one to see Sam alive, and he hinted that he had something to tell me that might have been important. But—" She took a deep breath, trying to calm her racing heart.

Elise, still and watchful, smoke drifting, waited for Liberty to continue. Had she known what Duff planned to talk to Sam about?

"I never got to talk to him. Did he mention anything to you, Mrs. Mowbray?"

Elise narrowed her eyes and fixed her gaze on Liberty as though wondering what this might have to do with any memoir, then sat back, tight-lipped. "It was church business."

Evidently, she thought it was no business of her visitor. "All right," Liberty said softly, clocking it to tell Jack. "What I really needed to ask you about was Gracelyn Rodgers."

Elise's eyes widened and her nostrils flared, but she took control of herself. "And what do you need to know?"

Liberty didn't miss the reaction. She had to tread carefully. Only the truth would gain her cooperation. She cleared her throat. "A part of the manuscript is missing, and Gracelyn is being, well, obstructive. She says she doesn't have it, but I think she might be keeping it from me. The question is why? If I knew more about her, maybe it would make sense."

"And why did you come to me?" The widow's words were cool as sharp steel.

Liberty took a larger sip of wine for courage, welcoming the warmth. "Vivian Clark said you'd been in the parish for ages, so you must have known her a long time."

Elise puffed on her cigarette for a moment, then let the smoke stream out. "Yes, I seem to have a reputation for knowing where the bodies are buried." She looked far away, through a painting of peonies that echoed the colors of the abstract. "Odd expression," she said, then stubbed the cigarette angrily in the ashtray, snapping the butt in two. "I have got to stop." She fidgeted and took a long sip of her drink, and then turned the wineglass in her hands. Back and forth, back and forth she turned it.

"Gracelyn Rodgers," she said.

A range of emotions crossed Elise's face just then: alarm, anger, disgust, hope, resignation. "Oh, hell. What can it hurt? Duff's dead. I need to talk. He liked your dedication to the cause. I know you won't tell."

Liberty bit her lip and told herself to remain calm. Focused. Elise planted her glass firmly on the table, leaned forward, and said, "About twenty years ago, Wickerson and Gracelyn Rodgers moved into one of the Meadows subdivisions—that's land Duff sold. We met them at church, and they had that little boy, Donovan. Van, they called him. They talked about wanting another child. Our Amelia was three and Claire was on the way, so we had a lot in common with them.

"Wick and Duff became friends. Duff put Wick up for membership in the golf club, and they played together. We socialized a lot with them—drinks, parties, you know. Wick was a stockbroker, much older than Gracelyn, and liked to tell people he was working on his second fortune for his second family. I wondered what had happened to the first fortune, the first family, but I never found out."

Elise leaned forward. "Wick was a mover and shaker, always trying to get Duff to invest in high-risk offerings, but Duff was always cautious about investments. To be fair, Wick was loads of fun to have around. He and I were the big talkers, always had a lot to say, knew a lot of people in common. Duff and Gracelyn were the quiet ones. Too quiet, now that I look back on it. Stupid me. I didn't guess a thing. Next thing you know, Amelia, who was just a perfect chameleon—blending into the background—one day giggled and told me she'd seen Daddy kissing Mrs. Rodgers out on the patio.

"Oh! Duff and I had such a fight then. I found out that the affair had been going on for months. I thought about leaving him. When he found me making a list of the furniture I wanted to keep, he said he'd end it, and I believed him. I was angry, but I knew it wasn't serious. It was just a midlife thing."

She seemed to be trying to convince herself.

Liberty looked around the stylish, comfortable room, and wondered if Elise's love for her husband went deep. There was no way to know, Liberty concluded, in this echelon of society. There were too many other factors to consider. Elise liked the good life, and her good taste showed in this house, in its quality and comfort. Even so, Liberty could tell how hurt Elise had been, and was hurting even now.

Her hostess lit another cigarette. "More wine? No? You won't mind if I have another." Walking to the bar to fill her glass, she almost toppled from her French-heeled mules. She reached out to the bar to steady herself. "Gah, I'd better watch it or that sister of mine will come in and give me hell. She's a sweetie pie but she does get, well, cross with me sometimes. Keeps telling me to pull myself together. Hell, I don't want to pull myself together. I have a perfect right to come apart and that's just what I intend to do."

Acutely embarrassed, Liberty sipped her wine and sank further into the nubby coral love seat. She couldn't have taken a note if her life had depended on it. She'd remember every detail of this conversation.

Elise pointed the neck of the wine bottle in Liberty's direction and Liberty shook her head. Elise brought her glass back to her chair and settled in. "Duff would never have left me for Gracelyn. I know he wouldn't. Odd to say, but he did love me. Anyhow, he needed me—needed someone like me for his career."

Elise swayed slightly as she leaned in Liberty's direction. "Of course, he didn't love her. Couldn't have. She was a cold fish underneath all the fake emotion. Did she love him? Hmph. She didn't love anyone but that boy."

Liberty wasn't concentrating on what Elise said next. Something kept niggling at her. Was Elise's pain making her aware of her own guilt, what might have happened with Sam if they'd allowed it? Yes, but there was something more. "Are you listening, love?" Elise said. "I'm getting to the good part."

Liberty blushed down to her painted toenails. "Sorry. Yes. I'm listening."

Elise took another sip of wine. "Wick was fun, but he didn't have any depth. He was all flash and dash, and she was beautiful and ambitious. Duff couldn't have loved that trollop. Oh, maybe I shouldn't go on. Maybe I'm telling you too much. Why do you want to know all this?"

She was thinking out loud and repeating herself. Liberty knew too well about becoming lost in an alcoholic haze. She had to cut through it. "How did he die?"

"Who?" She took a long drink of wine, reached for another cigarette, and flared the table lighter, missing the cylinder of tobacco three times.

"Wick Rodgers."

Elise faced Liberty with her red-rimmed eyes. "Terrible thing." She stopped again, apparently considering whether to go on.

"What happened?" Liberty asked softly.

Elise sighed. "Wick liked his toys. He'd just bought a new boat and was talking about buying a house on the lake. . . . Lake Altamaha, I mean. At least he was before Duff and Gracelyn . . ." She gazed out into the dark night at the ghost of a moon rising above the trees. Then she sighed. "I can only say it was very odd."

Liberty gripped the cushions of the love seat. "What was odd?"

Elise flicked ash off her cigarette. "Wick and Gracelyn were out in the boat. Nobody's sure exactly what happened, but she claims she dropped her Birkin bag in the water while searching for her cigarettes. Said she didn't want to leave it in the car because there had been break-ins in the parking lot. She said that Wick jumped in the water to retrieve it."

"She took that kind of bag on a boat?" The Gracelyn that Liberty had seen didn't seem that careless.

"It was insane to take that bag on a boat—I have an L.L. Bean canvas boat tote; they are very good. Can't remember why he went into the water after that thing."

"Was there a lot of money, credit cards?" Liberty prompted.

"Oh, honey, do you know how much those things cost? Five or six thou, these days. Just the bag would have been enough. But she claimed she'd put her diamond rings in there to keep them from slipping off into the lake. Family heirlooms and all that. Well, to make a long story short, he went over after the bag and he drowned."

Elise looked at Liberty then with a strange alcoholic smile, waiting for a reaction. Liberty didn't have to act horrified; she felt sick to her stomach and short of breath.

Elise snickered. "Gracelyn had a big surprise when the dust cleared from the estate. Of course he'd left everything to her and the boy. But wouldn't you know, it turned out Wick had a little Ponzi scheme going. Duff lost some money, but it wasn't all that much. As I said, he was a careful investor."

"Ponzi scheme?" Liberty reminded, noticing that Elise was swaying and her eyes had lowered to half-mast.

"Oh, yes. Gracelyn sold the boat and the house, but there were some hefty debts. She would've been out on the street if Father Landring hadn't felt sorry for her and given her a job at the church. She claimed insurance for the jewelry." She looked at Liberty slyly. "Just as well. You never get back what you spend for that, if you sell it."

Liberty felt as limp as a boneless chicken. "How awful for that boy."

Elise waved her hand. "She spoiled him rotten. I'm sure she thought the church job was beneath her, but she took it to give herself some respectability. Don't think gossip didn't get around. And let me tell you this. You never saw a more pious woman after that."

Liberty let out a breath. "They say she's a rock. Steady."

"Rocks are cold and hard," Elise said. "I forgave her, of course. It was the Christian thing to do. Some nasty minds thought she had a thing with Father Landring but he was just being kind. He was a very unworldly man."

"Why would anyone think she was involved with him, if he was so unworldly?"

"She was possessive. Guarding his time, she called it, not wanting people to waste it with their silly problems. Well, look, dear. Time was the main thing he had to give."

Liberty swallowed hard. "Did she act that way with Sam?"

Elise Mowbray shrugged. "Of course she did. But I can't imagine why she'd hide his—his—papers? Papers. No. No clue to that at all."

Duff's widow sighed, laid her head against the back of the chair, closed her eyes, and in a moment a small snore escaped her lips. Liberty snatched the burning cigarette from her fingers and stubbed it out in the ashtray. She rose from her chair, went into the front hall, and called "Hello? Hello?" since Elise had mentioned a sister.

A taller, thinner, version of Elise, hair cut in a Dutch bob, reading glasses dangling from a chain around her neck, materialized from another room. "Oh, hello," she said. "I was getting worried. I always get worried when the talking stops."

"She just lay back," Liberty said. "And now she's asleep."

"Poor thing," said the woman. "I'm Daphne."

"Liberty Chase," she said. "I hope I didn't upset her."

"She's beyond upsetting. It did her good to talk."

"Are you from here?" Liberty had caught a slight New York accent.

"My home is in New York," said Daphne. "But I'm here for however long she needs me."

New York? "Have you always lived there?"

"Very nearly—thirty years. My husband's family business is there, and we married straight from college."

Liberty's mind was whirring. She had a fleeting notion to ask Daphne questions about a boy named Tony, but that would have made no sense. Why would she have known anything about a boy on the wrong side of the tracks?

Still, she could try. "This may sound crazy," she said. "But did you ever hear of any crime or anything involving a teenage boy named Tony? A long time ago?"

"There's so much crime," Daphne said. "It would have to be really sordid to catch anyone's attention."

"Of course," Liberty said. "It was just a wild thought. I'll retrieve my things and let myself out."

She followed Daphne back to the sitting room and picked up her bag and notepad. She glanced at the sleeping Elise. "Tell Elise goodbye for me."

"Thank you for coming," Daphne said. "I think it did her good."

Liberty nodded and walked to the front door and let herself out. Elise had looked peaceful.

Liberty felt anything but peaceful.

Chapter Thirty-One

L iberty shuddered to a stop at the first red light on the way home. She punched Jack's number into her cell phone. This time he answered.

"Liberty! Sorry I haven't been in contact. I'm on the way back from a trip to the mountains to see Doyle Landring."

Relief flooded through her. "I've just seen Elise Mowbray."

"Great. Let me tell you about Landring."

"But, but . . ." Liberty's vision of Elise passed out on the sofa, the burning cigarette in her fingers, demanded to be told, demanded that Liberty tell the story of the drowned husband and the unfaithful one.

Jack, hopped up on information, rushed on. "He's become sort of a hermit," he said. "Got himself a peaceful cabin on the lake, lives simply."

"Wasn't he married?" Liberty snapped. *Listen to me*, she wanted to say.

Jack picked up her terseness. "You'll get your turn," he said. "Patience."

Ooh, she wanted to strangle Jack. But she listened.

"Landring's wife died six months ago. He's adjusted remarkably well. He says he likes being a monk, there with his books and his writing. He's a very spiritual man. Thin, ascetic, hawk nosed. He cooks himself a chop and tosses a salad, drinks no hard stuff at all. He offered me tea and English biscuits."

Liberty just couldn't hold it. "Jack! I've got something to tell you about Gracelyn Rodgers!" All the frustration that she'd felt toward the woman crowded in—the way she'd brushed Liberty off, the way she'd been listening outside Josie's door.

"Simmer down, girl. So have I, if you'd let me finish!"

"Don't patronize me. Did the good father tell you how her first husband died?"

Jack went on. "What he told me was that he hired her because she was widowed, broke, needed a job. He told me she was efficient and hard-working and he couldn't have run the church without her. He said he had no interest in administrative details."

"Did he tell you her husband drowned?"

"*What?*"

"In Lake Altamaha. The story was that he jumped off the boat to retrieve a designer bag with some jewelry. Elise hinted it wasn't an accident."

Jack gave a long, low whistle. "That's gossip, Liberty."

Liberty let out a long, slow breath. "Gossip was what you wanted."

He paused a minute, then said slowly, "You might have something. I know what her salary looks like, and the clothes she wears don't come from a budget shop, nor do the shoes and haircut. I can see her on a yacht, in yachting clothes."

Jack had a point. Whenever Liberty had seen her, Gracelyn was appropriately dressed. Her boating outfit would most likely be navy and white and boat shoes. So would she have gone boating with a six-thousand-dollar bag that didn't go with her outfit?

"Elise told me Gracelyn worked at church for the respectability after Wick died," she told Jack. "She'd been having an affair with . . ."

At that moment the cell connection sputtered and failed. A few minutes later Liberty pulled into her driveway.

She found Dallas leaning back in the hideous marshmallow chair, beer in hand. Beer obviously didn't count as alcohol. "You got what you needed?" he asked.

"That and more." Liberty took off her jacket and hung it in the hall closet, then laid her car keys on the entrance hall table.

"Come watch basketball with me." In a good mood and ready to be chummy, he was trying to re-establish a connection. But Liberty didn't feel like watching basketball and regretted her efforts at becoming a sports fan when they were dating.

"Maybe later," she said. "I need to check on Mama Jean's flight number, and then I need to work on the manuscript." He snorted with annoyance, but she went into the kitchen and picked up the phone, feeling guilty for avoiding him. Wasn't she interested in repairing their marriage?

She thanked God for her grandparents. They were the only normal beings in her whole bizarre life, and she wasn't sure she could get through a family Christmas without their steady presence. She calmed down when Mama Jean's voice came on the line, telling her they'd arrive around 11:30 the next morning, December 24. Liberty took down the flight number.

Afterward, she slipped out to the garage with her cell phone and called Jack.

"Who did she have an affair with?" he asked, as if they hadn't been disconnected.

"Duff," Liberty whispered.

"My God," he said.

"Jack, suppose Duff's death wasn't natural."

"I suppose they'll do an autopsy."

"Will they do toxicology?"

"I've got to go," he said. "I'll call you back."

"Libby? What are you doing out there?" Dallas yelled. Oh jeez, she'd left the door cracked. How much had he heard?

"Freezing," Liberty yelled, and slammed the car door, pretending to be looking for something in the car, wondering once again about the envelope that had gone missing. Had Dallas thrown it away? Had he read it? Had it disappeared at the car wash? Back inside, she walked into the living room, where the manuscript lay on the coffee table. She wasn't ready to face it; she needed some busy work. She walked back to the hall closet and took out a bag of gifts to wrap.

On the dining room table she cut and taped and folded, twisted ribbon into scarlet and golden bows, thinking about a husband—older, maybe not in good shape—who'd gone into cold lake water to retrieve some valuables for his wife. Had he gone for love? To rescue his investment? To keep the peace? And then he'd lost his life.

Had he suspected her affair? How good a swimmer had he been? What had he been wearing? Did he go willingly? Did he try to climb back in the boat and she pushed him? Too many questions.

Liberty placed the wrapped gifts under the twinkling tree to the usual Sunday background of shouts, cheers, and whistles from the den. She gazed over at the manuscript and steeled herself. It was time to work.

She found a blue pen and a pencil and took the manuscript to the dining room table, the windows behind her casting moonlight on the page, and began to correct spelling, sharpen phrases, and reword clumsy sentences, of which there weren't many. How much had Gracelyn done for Sam? She imagined him at his own table that night, looking over the work Gracelyn had brought.

Suppose Gracelyn had come back to the house after Duff had left—and done what? Had she come back a third time and hid upstairs? If so, where was her car? It didn't work as a theory.

Liberty picked up a completed page, and found it was stuck to the one below. She wetted her finger and separated the pages, then a shiver went up her spine: Sam used to do that. A harmless quirk. Such a small thing, a personal habit, but it brought him into focus as if he were there. Liberty shuddered with pain, reminded that he would never again touch a sheet of paper, or the people he loved.

She shoved that thought into a pit and covered it, and then worked steadily for another hour despite the basketball noise blaring from the den. Then she sighed, stacked the pages neatly, and told Dallas she was going to bed. He just nodded, never looking up from the screen.

She peeked in on Emmy, still sleeping, and then took a hot bath. When she emerged from the bathroom, relaxed and ready for bed, she heard the TV click off. She slipped under the covers and closed her eyes, and was drifting into a safe, fuzzy, half-sleep when she heard the faint tinny bleep of a cell phone ringing.

Her eyes blinked open; she catapulted out of bed and raced downstairs, passing Dallas on the way up. He grasped her arm. "Where're you going in such a hurry?"

She shook herself loose. "My cell phone!"

"I didn't hear anything."

Had she dreamed it?

Dallas called to her back, "Who the hell could it be at this time of night?"

Her handbag was in the living room, and the phone was still bleeping. She grabbed it out of a side pocket. "Hello?"

The voice was gruff, apologetic. "Sorry to call so late."

Her heart flipped like a gymnast. "What am I going to tell Dallas?" she murmured under her breath. "Jack . . ."

"Look, Liberty. Why do you stay with this guy?"

Liberty felt the heat rush to her face. "Who are you to ask me such a question?" It wasn't fair. She was doing her best to keep it professional and he was breaking the barriers. He was too involved in her case. He started out doing it for Sam, but now she suspected he was doing it for her. And she didn't need that, as confused as she was. Jack sounded calm. "I am trying like hell not to let my personal feelings interfere here."

She sank to the sofa, limp as a jellyfish. "You aren't supposed to. Let's keep to the case. Why did you call me?"

The phone crackled, a poor connection. "Suppose Gracelyn was embezzling, and Sam found out. Rather than go to the police, what if he confronted her and gave her a chance to return the money?"

"He would do that," Liberty said, perking up. "Suppose she denied everything, and he asked Duff over that night to discuss it. After all, Duff was a lawyer and senior warden."

"So Gracelyn knew about the meeting, realized she was in big trouble, and decided to kill him?"

"Why would she do such a thing?" Liberty gasped. "He wouldn't prosecute. He'd just ask her to pay back the money."

"He couldn't keep her on at the church. Her respectability would go down the drain. And what about that son? Maybe she was in a corner."

"So why hasn't she gotten the hell out of Dodge?"

"It would make her an obvious suspect, right? She almost got away with Sam's death. Natural causes! And we still can't prove anything. As for the embezzling charge, I've got a hunch she's been shredding documents right and left. She's probably been falsifying records on that computer, and that's why she didn't want you to see it."

Oh. Gosh. Liberty's head was reeling. "And Duff? I wonder if he told Sam about the affair after she came under suspicion. Maybe he wanted to get it off his chest."

Jack paused. "Until the autopsy reports come back, we won't know if he died a natural death. But I have a hunch she'll make a move soon. She'll get out of town before they grab her, and now is the time."

"Why?"

"Holiday travel. No one would question her taking a trip, and the church office will be closed. She'll take what money she has in the bank—maybe from collecting the insurance on those diamond rings, which I'll bet are *not* at the bottom of a lake, and leave the country."

"What can we do? Do we let her go?"

"I'm going to put a tail on her. Starting now."

"Oh, Jack. Be careful."

"You, too."

Liberty knew he was talking about Dallas. She laughed, but her heart wasn't in it. "My folks will be here tomorrow."

"All right. I'm going to be busy and you may not hear from me until I have something definite. Merry Christmas, Liberty."

"Merry Christmas, Jack."

She pressed the *Off* button and slipped the phone back into her handbag. She turned out all the lights and walked upstairs. The bedroom was dark, and only a thin stripe of light came from the slightly ajar bathroom door. Dallas's voice broke the silence. "Who was that? Your secret lover?"

She padded over to her side of the big bed and slipped in, as far away from him as possible. "Mama Jean. She wanted to be sure we'd be there at the airport."

"Why didn't she call you on the home phone?"

Liberty shrugged. "She has all her numbers on speed dial," she said. "Maybe she just hit the wrong one."

"You talked a damn long time," said Dallas.

She was ready with an excuse if he should ask her for sex. Thank God for Mother Nature. No arm reached out for her. Dallas snorted and turned away, taking most of the covers.

Chapter Thirty-Two

An Unexpected Gift
December 24

Sam touched her cheek and spoke to her. *Liberty, you have the answer.*

Liberty awoke with a start and sat up, disoriented. She wasn't in the office, she was in her own bed, and Sam was dead . . . .

Dallas shifted and let out a room-rattling snore. Shivering, she slipped out from the covers and snuggled her toes into fuzzy slippers, then wrapped her blue robe around her and went to nudge the thermostat higher. The clock read a few minutes past five, and she knew she wouldn't sleep again.

She padded into the kitchen, the night light guiding, while the furnace groaned and shuddered. A cup of coffee finally steaming in her hand, she walked into the empty living room and sat on the sofa, gazing at the quiet street beyond the shadowed Christmas tree. An early morning fog rolled and swirled under the streetlight.

Sam was a mysterious man she'd never really known. She accepted that he'd had a hard life, that he'd run away, that he'd told lies to his adoptive father. That his understanding father had seen through those lies and accepted him anyway.

She also accepted that he'd been intimate with his adoptive sister, and it had somehow come out all right in the end. She accepted that Isabel was fanatically loyal to him and knew all about his background, which she would not divulge to a stranger.

Sam had told no one else, including his wife, of his deception. Liberty suspected it wasn't just the fulfillment of a contract that made Alicia want this manuscript to see the light of day. She wanted to know about him for herself.

Liberty had talked to Sam about Dallas. Sam had told her that marriages take patience and understanding, but most of all, trust. And Sam hadn't trusted anyone with his secrets. Dallas had broken so many promises, he'd worn out Liberty's trust. Was he an alcoholic, sick and needing understanding, or just your garden variety drunk? Did it really matter? Whatever it was, when he drank, he lashed out at her. She fought back and said things she was sorry for. She was turning into someone she didn't like.

Then there was the mysterious Sam everyone had loved. Who was that woman he'd met on his last day? The woman with the initial S? Would the missing material reveal that woman—if it ever came to light?

Footsteps crunched upstairs, then the shower came on with a rush and whine and knock of pipes. Outside, wisps of fog were lifting, the sun painting pink in the sky above the trees. Liberty rose from the sofa, flipped on all the lights, and walked into the kitchen to make breakfast. It was the morning of Christmas Eve.

Around eleven, she and Emmy drove out to the airport. Dallas left for an office lunch party; she prayed that there wouldn't be alcohol. If it were offered, would he fall off the wagon again, as he'd done before? Would he consider his family, consider how Emmy would remember this Christmas?

People, cars, and rolling suitcases crammed the short-term parking lot. Young people under heavy backpacks hustled in for the holidays, vacationers carried skis. Liberty guided Emmy through the cheerful crowd to Baggage Claim, where the little girl stood on her tiptoes, unsuccessfully, to see past a group of tall men with gym bags.

Suitcases tumbled out from the conveyor belt onto the carousel, and Emmy, fascinated with watching them go around, almost didn't see her great-grandparents straggle through the arrival crowd, Mama Jean tanned and radiant, Papaw a skinny Santa without the beard, just a white mustache and merry eyes.

Liberty tugged Emmy over to greet them. Mama Jean kissed Liberty's cheek. "My lips feel like parchment paper. Flights dry me out."

"There's bottled water in the car."

"Good girl," she said, fishing around in her handbag. "Chapstick is in here somewhere."

"Mama Jean! Mama Jean!" Emmy begged for a hug. Mama Jean snapped the bag shut and opened her arms. "Come here, sweetheart. I'll find the Chapstick when we're settled."

Liberty took Mama Jean's carry-on while her grandmother took Emmy's hand, and Papaw dealt with the suitcases. When they reached the car, she opened the back gate of the SUV and helped Papaw load the bags. Emmy and Mama Jean settled in back, and Liberty passed water bottles to everybody. Leaving the airport, they all sang along with the radio: loud, off-key one-horse-open-sleighing. Papaw doodled with the radio and found Bing Crosby.

They were just getting into "White Christmas" when Liberty heard "Oh, shit!"

"Ooh-ooh, Mama Jean, bad word!" Emmy scolded.

"Sorry, dear," Mama Jean said. "Do as I say, not as I do."

"Too much bridge playing with those old gals," said Papaw. "The air turns blue."

"What's the matter, Mama Jean?" Liberty asked.

"I've dropped my Chapstick and can't find it."

"I got it." Emmy unclipped her seat belt and scrambled down to the floor before anybody could stop her. She rooted around under the seat and poked a chubby fist up. "Here!"

"Get back in your belt," Mama Jean commanded. She pomaded her lips.

Emmy, still fooling around under the seat, ignored the order.

"Get up, young lady," said her great-grandmother. "Santa's watching."

Paper crackled. Liberty's breath caught. Could it be? Could she have missed it in her certainty that it wasn't there? She willed herself to keep her eyes on the road. "Look, Mama Jean!" she heard. Paper crackled again.

"Liberty, have you been missing some mail? A big brown envelope?" Mama Jean asked,

Liberty's heart turned a flip, and she tried to sound happy without shrieking. "So that's where it got to." She casually took a sip of water to calm herself. "Some material for the book I'm working on." Thank God the car was too dark for Mama Jean to see that the packet wasn't addressed to Liberty.

"And I got my Chapstick too," her grandmother said. "A good thing."

Unfortunately, Mama Jean gave the envelope to Emmy to carry into the house, and Liberty, helping with the luggage, couldn't very well snatch it away. Emmy had laid the envelope on the kitchen table to get out of her coat, and now she was studying it.

"Fm," Emmy said. "Look, S-A-M Sam!

Liberty's stomach dropped. How she wished that Isabel had addressed it in cursive, which Emmy couldn't read.

Liberty took the envelope. Her grandparents were upstairs settling into the guest room, and she only had a few minutes until they returned. "It's to Father Sam." The puzzled child squinted at the letters, her brow furrowed. "But he'th in heaven."

"And the Post Office doesn't deliver to heaven," Liberty said, skirting any messy theology. "The only way to get a message to heaven is by praying." She kept her tone light and cheerful, but it wasn't easy.

Emmy still frowned.

"I'll have to give it to his kids," Liberty said. "How about that?

Now Emmy smiled. "OK."

Luckily, Mama Jean chose that moment to come downstairs loaded with presents. "Where's my favorite grandbaby?"

"Show Mama Jean the tree," Liberty said, relief flooding in as her daughter ran to meet her grandmother.

As soon as they'd left the kitchen, Liberty tore open the flap and drew out the typed sheets, with marginal comments scribbled in blue.

A sticky note in feminine handwriting was neatly stuck on the top left-hand corner, and Liberty instinctively shied her eyes away.

Curiosity got the better of her. All the note said was: *Be careful, Sam. Bel.* Underneath the note, she saw that this chapter may very well be the material she needed. She wanted privacy to read it, and the house was full of her nearest and dearest. All but her mother. She wondered if Paloma was enjoying her cruise.

Liberty tugged on her coat, scarf, and wooly cap, hollered that she was going for a walk before lunch, and slipped out of the back door before anyone could volunteer to come along.

Above her there was a brilliant cold sky, and her breath came in frosty puffs. She walked down the street to the lake, where the neighborhood clubhouse overlooked the water. She stepped out on the walkway and rounded the building to the other side, facing the dark water away from the street. She slowly sank to a wooden bench and lifted some paper from an envelope.

Chapter Thirty-Three

A Fight in the Park

I saw my friend Sonia walking home across the park near my apartment building. It was late afternoon on a dreary day in late March. She didn't see me. Not yet. I wish now I'd come up to walk her home. But I was hanging out with the guys.

The grass in that park had long been worn to dirt and the trees stood droopy and bedraggled, tortured and weary as our mothers. Fast-food wrappers tossed in the wind, landing against the dull gray diamonds of a chain-link fence; the sun struggled through the clouds with thin, cheerless light.

Sonia took a wide berth around a man in a ragged tweed coat staggering across the grass, pint bottle in hand, trying to keep clear of the mounted patrols. I knew he was living in the park under the radar, scavenging for lunch bag leftovers in the trash. I used to give him a sandwich the year before when I was a choirboy, in the days I wanted to be a priest when I grew up. I had grown up Catholic, and my ambition made my mother happy. That was before my brother died and she took to the drink, cursing God.

Neither she nor Sonia liked me hanging around with the gang. That day we boys had come to the park late—usually we came in the daytime to hang out, to shoot a little basketball, to smoke tobacco or pot, to get away from home.

Now night was beginning to fall, and the playground equipment threw long menacing shadows behind the broken, half-operational lights. The guys and I were loitering near the fence, where the scraggly shrubbery grew, smoking cigarettes, watching for what? I wasn't even sure. Yelling together in that macho-boy way we had. Up to now, we had been mostly swagger and posturing. Shoplifting was the limit of our crimes. That and fighting and staking out our turf.

But now the others spotted Sonia too, and she was approaching the bridge over a sluggish brown stream that smelled of sewers. She was one of the smart girls, and would help me in math sometimes, and wasn't a beauty but pretty enough, with dark hair and dark eyes and the most ample bosom many of us had ever seen. And her brother was what we called a fruit, in our politer moments.

"What say we have some fun with Sonia," said Vito, our ringleader. He took a drag on his cigarette then and blew a smoke ring and poked his finger through the ring. "Yeah," said Dolph, sometimes called "Clean" because he was clammy white and shaved his head. The other two guys agreed.

I froze then. "Hey. Leave her alone. She's all right."

"Whattaya mean?" said Vito. "She's stuck-up."

No she's not, I wanted to say, but the words froze on my tongue. I would get harassed out of the gang. Then they'd be after me.

"Come on!" Vito said. I followed them to the bridge. We stood in a pack not letting her pass. No one else was around, not even the old drunk scavenger.

"Look, guys," Sonia huffed. "Move."

"Why should we, Sugar Pop?" said Vito, preening. He knew he was good-looking, with girls clamoring for his attention. That's one reason I tagged along after him—to pick up his rejects. "Give us a feel. Get her hands, Dolpho."

I just stood there while Dolph grabbed her and pulled her, struggling, off the bridge and onto the dirt. Though she fought him, Vito and the other guys helped and they struggled with her all the way down to the creek bank, under the bridge.

"Now," said Vito. He slipped his hands down the front of her drooping purple tank top and groped. She kept struggling, squirming, swinging.

I wanted to make them stop. I looked from one face to the other, some worried, some eager. Me, I was afraid. I told myself that all he wanted was to cop a feel. And then when he pinned her arms, she reared up and sank her teeth into his shoulder. "My brother will get you for this," she yelled.

Vito laughed. "What, that little cocksucker?" He smacked her, laid the back of his hand across her cheek, and her eyes went wide. He forced her back down, his elbow across her throat. "Don't try anything," he said.

"He'll kill you." Her face was fierce.

"Vito," I croaked.

She spat at him. I saw the hatred in her eyes.

Growling, he ripped off her tank top and her breasts tumbled out, big and freckled. He unzipped his jeans.

And then she saw me standing there, looking on. "Not you, Tony." Her voice broke, full of tears. "Not you."

"Line up, dudes."

I couldn't move.

"Whassa matter with you, Tono?" The rasp of Vito's zipper was like the rasp of my breath.

"Vito, don't," I shouted.

"Me next." Dolph tightened his grip on her arm.

I saw Vito jump on her, saw him hump and thrust. I gritted my teeth but didn't turn away. That would have made me a coward in their eyes. When Vito was finished, he held her so Dolph could have a turn.

She looked at me. My mouth was open with horror but still I stood. She snarled with fury and broke one arm free. She struggled, she fought, and then they dragged her down into the water, her screaming all the while, and when she raked her nails across Dolph's face, he bellowed and shoved her face into the creek.

She pushed herself out and he shoved her in again. He forced her head under the water.

That was it. I yelled and jumped on Dolph and jerked him away from her.

"What do you think you're doing, man?" he roared.

"Leave her alone," I screamed. "You're going to kill her."

Sonia burst from the creek, choking and spluttering. Vito swung at me. I wheeled and swung back at him and knocked him flat. We were going round and round on the slippery bank, falling into the mud, and Dolph was shouting that the damned old drunk on the bridge had seen us. Finally, I gathered all my strength and shoved Vito away from me, tears running down my cheeks. He staggered backward and fell against the concrete culvert, his head connecting with a sickening thud before he sagged to the ground. Dolph gave me a savage look before he took off running.

I helped Sonia out of the creek. "Go! Get out! Now!"

She wrapped her wet and torn top across her breasts. "Tony?"

"Here." I yanked off my T-shirt and tossed it at her.

She grabbed it, jerked it over her head, and finally ran, not looking back. "Vito! Get up!" I pulled on his hand. I splashed water on his face. In the distance I heard sirens. I leaned close to him, and I wasn't sure he was breathing.

The sirens were getting louder.

I was in deep trouble. I ran all the way home bare-chested. I packed my worn duffel bag, stole enough money from my mom for a bus ticket—rationalizing that it might save her from one more bottle of booze—and got out of town.

I never knew what had happened until years later.

If I'd had one caring adult I could have gone to and spilled my guts to back then, I could have faced whatever was going to happen. Maybe I never would have even been in that park that day.

When I became a lawyer, I made some informal inquiries as to what had happened to my friends. Vito was dead, ten years after that day—died in a gangster war. Dolph was in prison for rape. And Sonia had disappeared from the face of the earth.

Sick at heart, Liberty laid the manuscript down without finishing the last page.

It was a horrific and moving story, and it explained a lot. And it was typed, so Gracelyn must have seen it.

Why on earth would she have erased it? She didn't know he'd sent it to Isabel; maybe after he died she wanted to stop the memoir.

Liberty could see now why he hadn't told Alicia. Would she have married a man with his background, one who might have killed someone—even if he was trying to save someone else?

No wonder he didn't want his adoptive father to know his story. Isabel, who'd been brought up on mean streets, was the only person he'd trusted to read it and not reject him.

But maybe he'd typed it himself, on that computer Liberty hadn't been able to see. She picked up the page again. *Every man wants to be a hero to his son,* she read.

It's in the blood. My own father was a thief, a drunkard, and growing up I despised him. Later I began to realize that in some ways it is difficult to escape one's milieu. It takes enormous reserves of strength and courage to break out of a life into which you have been thrust, and something in my father made it impossible for him to draw on those reserves. Something in him had been beaten down. Something had made him feel he was not worthy of a better life.

And he hated me, even as he loved me, because he could not be my hero.

I knew the only way I could be a hero to my own son was to help other boys grow to their full potential, and so I took the path that would lead me there.

I hope they will all understand. I'm telling this story to help others realize that redemption is possible. Sonia, if you are out there anywhere, I hope you have forgiven me. It's too late for Vito and Dolph. If only I'd had the courage to stop them sooner, things would have been different for all of us.

Liberty rolled the papers, thrust them in her pocket, and walked back to the house in a daze, cold tears running down her cheeks. Would he have been risking his career, his marriage, his relationship with his adoptive family, to publish this story?

She slipped in the back door, and warmth hit her like a blast. "Mommy!" Emmy and Mama Jean were pulling lunch makings out of the refrigerator. "Where have you been?"

Bread and mayo already stood on the counter. Mama Jean glanced at Liberty. "Awfully cold for a walk."

"It did me good." She fingered the pages in her pocket.

"You missed Daddy," Emmy said.

"He called," Mama Jean explained. "He's gone shopping."

"Good," Liberty said, her spirits lifting. Maybe he'd done all right at the party.

When she finally got a moment to call Jack Ford, he didn't answer.

Tomorrow, at least, would be calm.

Chapter Thirty-Four

MOTHER LOVE

Liberty read through the pages again, the pages that had shaken her so. Had Sam never quite believed that he was loved, no matter how much Aubrey and Hazel Maginnes let him know they cared? Perhaps she and Sam had had that in common. Her grandparents had brought her up lovingly, but could she really be so lovable if her father died and her mother abandoned her for a career?

Was that what had drawn her to Dallas? Was it the appearance of strength, a feeling that he could protect her? A feeling that he needed her? Or just plain physical attraction?

Her head was aching. She had to stop thinking about all this. She made a decision.

Liberty found her grandmother seated in the armchair in Emmy's room, mending the hem of the green velvet dress

Emmy had worn to see Santa. "After Christmas," Liberty told Mama Jean, "Dallas gets notice. My way—stop the drinking for good—or the highway."

Mama Jean tied off the thread and clipped it. "Don't make threats you're unwilling to carry out."

"I can make it on my own. I know that now."

Mama Jean laid the velvet aside and looked into Liberty's eyes. "You know, Liberty, one of the joys of my life has been your grandfather. I hope we pass from this earth at the same time, because neither one of us wants to live without the other." She brushed the hair away from her granddaughter's face. "With all my heart, I want that kind of love for you."

A big, soft wedge of pain lodged in Liberty's throat. "Mama Jean, you were lucky. I think I've been chasing illusions. I wanted a happy family so much."

Mama Jean misunderstood. "The plain truth," she said, "is that unless you and Dallas find some love for each other, your daughter is going to suffer."

"I don't think he really wants to change, Mama Jean. He's tried, but there's something that tells me he's just going through the motions. He needs to have counseling, but he refuses. I've read that addiction is nasty. One little drink, maybe to please a customer, and they're hooked again. They have to hit rock bottom, where they've lost everything, before they turn around. I don't want to think he's that far gone. I want to give him a chance, because of Emmy's security, because she loves her daddy, because I feel it's my duty. You know Dad was always talking about duty. But now—I'm so confused . . ."

"You give him that chance, then. Emmy's important. You were like a lost child when you first came to us, but I hope being with Papaw and me filled the empty places a little." Mama Jean took another stitch, tied off the thread, and snapped it off with the sewing scissors.

Liberty hugged her grandmother. "You did. You still do."

Jack called with the news that Gracelyn Rodgers had booked a flight for New York and Amsterdam at 10:30 p.m. This very night.

Liberty caught her breath. "How'd you find out?"

"Trade secret. I'm going to follow her, let her know she's being followed, and hope she does something foolish before she boards that plane."

"Follow her? Alone?"

"Told you I had a pal in the cop shop. My detective friend Hogan questioned her about the church fire. He was sure she was lying. He agrees she's a person of interest, and he's coming with me to the airport."

"You went to the cops? I guess Shadrach House can kiss that grant goodbye."

"Come on, Liberty. This is an arson investigation right now."

Liberty's heart felt squeezed in a vise. Was this woman Sam's killer? Or was she protecting her son? "I want to be there," she said. "Can I come?"

"Absolutely not. You belong with your family."

"Merry Christmas, J. Hartley Ford. Good luck." Liberty hung up and chewed on a nail, something she never did. How could she just sit back while a possible murderess got away? Maybe she just ought to leave it to Jack and enjoy Christmas.

Dallas called from the mall and said he'd be home by supper time. Liberty and Mama Jean started making ambrosia, grating coconut and sectioning the plump navel oranges brought from Florida, while Papaw played Hungry Hungry Hippos with a giggling Emmy.

Shortly before three o'clock, Liberty and her grandparents took a very aware angel, decked out in cardboard wings, a white chenille robe, and tinsel halo, for the Christmas Eve pageant and service. As they left the St. Nicholas party afterwards, they were greeted by a heavenly gift: great wet white flakes fell out of the sky, landing on noses, coats, and scarves, especially Emmy's red hooded coat. Christmas spirit floated Liberty high as a helium balloon.

There were carols in the car and laughter at home while they shucked wet coats and hung them to dry. Papaw stacked logs in the fireplace, Mama Jean dug out the Christmas CDs. Liberty heated hot cider and coffee, feeling warm and cozy and happy.

And then she checked her voice messages.

"Darling! I haven't seen you in so long. I'm at LAX now. I'll arrive tonight. Don't bother to meet me; I'll take a taxi." It was the unmistakable smooth Hollywood purr of Paloma Morgan—her mother.

What had happened to the cruise with Alan, or whoever was the man of the moment? "Mama Jean," she wailed, phone in hand. "Paloma's coming."

"Some nerve," huffed Mama Jean. "I never knew whether to hug that girl or strangle her. Where will we put her?"

Liberty let out a long sigh. "There's a daybed in Dallas's home office." Maybe she'd complain about being in the basement, but here she was, showing up at the last minute as usual. If Paloma didn't like it, she could get a room at the Ritz-Carlton or a Motel 6, depending on the state of her finances.

And then it came to Liberty how she could use Paloma's visit to her advantage.

Dallas arrived at quarter to six, laden with presents, and gave a hearty welcome to his in-laws, offering them drinks and taking only ginger ale himself.

Liberty remained cheerful over the family Christmas Eve supper, hot ham and cheese sandwiches and oyster stew that Mama Jean had made from Apalachicola Bay oysters.

After supper, after they'd tidied away the dishes and Emmy was bathed and dressed in her red flannel nightie and robe, the child was allowed to open one present. She picked the big box from Florida, and Liberty held her breath. She'd suggested to Mama Jean that Emmy might like another DVD, but Mama Jean had her own ideas. Emmy tore off the wrapping and found Liberty's old doll trunk, with the doll and all her clothes, and even a new tutu. She squealed with delight and Liberty shook her head. With kids you never could tell, could you?

Liberty didn't know if Emmy would sleep much tonight, but she knew that Emmy's mommy was going to pull an all-nighter, and it wouldn't be the first time. She closed her eyes and prayed the evening would turn out well for everyone. Everyone, that is, except for Sam's killer.

After she'd cleared away the wrapping paper and made sure Emmy was tucked up with her grandparents watching a Christmas special, she took an armful of sheets and blankets downstairs and found a sober Dallas, stretched out on the daybed with a Wall Street Journal. She cleared her throat.

"Dallas, my mother is coming tonight. I need to make the bed here."

"Hell of a time to tell me!"

"I just found out." Liberty took a breath and licked her lips. "I need to go to the airport to meet her." If, unfortunately, Paloma decided to take a taxi after Liberty had left, she'd just say they'd had a miscommunication. Now, if she got to the house *before* Liberty left, her plan was toast. She'd have to take that chance.

"Would you like to come too?" she asked Dallas, her heart in her throat.

He shook his head. "That lady and I don't have much to say to each other. What about Santa Claus?"

Liberty silently let out a breath. "I'll be back before midnight, if the plane's not late. The toys are in the back of our bedroom closet. The bicycle's in the storage closet. Papaw'll help put it together," she added.

"I can handle it," he said. "You've told your folks?"

"I'll tell them now. I'll ask Mama Jean to make the bed for Paloma." She hated to lie to them. Mama Jean would be skeptical, but what could she say?

"You be careful," he said.

"I won't spoil Emmy's Christmas." Liberty went upstairs, firmly telling herself that nothing was going to go wrong.

If ever there was a time for her father's gun, this was it. She slipped it out from underneath the pile of sweaters, loaded it, and slid it into her cheap designer knock-off handbag. Then she went downstairs, where everyone was watching TV, and told them she had to go meet Paloma at the airport, and she'd be back before they knew it.

Liberty wondered what her mother had meant when she said she'd arrive "late." It had been six hours since she'd called, so her plane might be arriving right now. Liberty was anxious to be off, and it tore her heart when Emmy came into the kitchen and asked if she really had to go, and why didn't she watch the Grinch steal Christmas with all of them?

Liberty told her that Po-ma was expecting her.

"Will she bwing Miss Piggy?" Paloma had once sent her an autographed picture of Miss Piggy and teased that she'd bring the famous Muppet home one day for dinner.

Liberty hugged her. "I can't promise Miss Piggy," she said. "But I'm sure she'll bring you something equally thrilling."

Liberty hit the expressway as she'd done a month, a lifetime, ago. Tonight there was no rain. The stars were high and bright, the air chill enough to frost breath, and a more perfect Christmas Eve couldn't be imagined. Here and there clumps of snow lay in shadowed corners. Somewhere choirs were singing; in some houses families gathered around fireplaces. In other places men patrolled wire fences and maybe thought of God.

And her mother was flying in from LA. She told people she'd been named after Paloma Picasso. That wasn't possible, given their respective ages, and anyhow, it wasn't the name she'd been born with. Now she was Paloma instead of Pamela, longtime "B" movie queen playing character parts. Her one starring role had been in a movie that had finished a two-week run and then disappeared from sight forever, not even given a video resurrection. And now she was on a TV show. Liberty hoped she was happy.

If Liberty's father had lived, would her mother have been content to stay in Florida? Would she have worked for the Mouse over in Orlando, or led a community theater, or taught drama like her daughter, who was not enough to make her stay?

The highway carried Liberty past the central city, its skyscrapers lit up, windows merry in tree shapes and colors. All was calm, all was bright. Still, trouble takes no holidays, and an ambulance passed by, lights flashing and siren screaming, veering down the rampway toward the public hospital, on the way to the trauma unit. A jolting dose of the real world.

Her mother was arriving to celebrate with her family. She didn't know about Liberty's flight to Florida, about her marital troubles, about anything. Maybe Paloma was counting on them to bring *her* some peace and stability.

"What would Jesus do?" Sam liked to bandy that buzz-phrase with the boys.

Jesus would forgive. It was his job to forgive. Must she forgive her mother?

Why should Liberty be the one to understand? Why was Paloma coming this night to distract her daughter from the business at hand? All Liberty knew was that Gracelyn Rodgers could not be allowed to leave town until they knew whether she had killed Sam. And Duff. And her husband.

Sometimes you just have to pray, and Liberty prayed.

Last Christmas she and Sam had been sitting in the coffee shop, where tinsel decorated the windows and wild-eyed shoppers thumbed through piles of novels with glossy covers. Questions about popular sold-out books filled the air.

Sam had bought a book as a present for her. He'd pointed out a passage with that eager way he had, leaning forward expectantly as he anticipated her pleasure in reading it, his pleasure in sharing something. She saw him then, in that habitual way he had, lick his finger as he turned the page.

Cold chills ran down her back. Now she got it. Gracelyn had been reading *The Name of the Rose*. It hadn't been anyone else's book.

She had to tell Jack. He'd be angry with her for coming to the airport, but she had to let him know. She reached for her cell phone right before she noticed the police cruiser flashing its blue lights behind her.

Chapter Thirty-Five

CAUGHT

“Liberty? What the hell?”

“I’m on my way to the airport.” She’d pulled over and was hyperventilating. “I’ve been stopped by the police. I’ve got to see you.”

“Keep calm,” Jack said. “Hogan’s here with me. Do what you’re supposed to and keep me on the line. I’m disappointed in you, Libby.”

Do not *ever* get involved with a psychologist, she told herself. Cussing her out would have been better. She grabbed for her bag and rooted in it for her driver’s license. She had it ready when the officer loomed in her window, dark, grim, and mustachioed.

“What did I do?” she croaked, handing him the license.

“Eighty-seven,” he answered, looking it over.

"It's an emergency, officer."

"Yeah, that plane's gonna take off without you."

"Let me talk to him," Jack said.

"Please, talk to this man," she begged the cop, holding up her phone. "He's a private investigator, and he has an officer with him."

The officer at the window shook his head. "It's Christmas Eve," Liberty pleaded. "My child is handicapped." He gave her a sideways look, took the phone, and stepped back from the car, listening, as planes roared and screamed overhead.

He leaned back into the window and handed her the phone. "I'll let you go with a warning," he said. "I understand that little girl's at home. Maybe you'd better get on back there."

"I need to be at that airport to pick up my mother. That child's grandmother."

"If I see you breaking the speed limit again, I won't be so nice. And stay off that cell phone," he said. "You don't want to spoil anyone's Christmas. Be careful."

Be careful.

"No, I mean yes. Thank you, officer." Liberty prayed thanks and merged back into the light airport traffic. She parked in the half-empty hourly lot, easily finding a convenient space.

The terminal was eerie with few passengers. Soldiers walked in groups. Women straggled along in puffy coats, holding children by the hand. She found the monitors announcing departing flights and spotted a Delta flight leaving at 10:30 for New York, nonstop, gate 12A. That had to be Gracelyn's flight.

Was Donovan leaving, too? Jack hadn't said. He could be driving to parts unknown in that fancy car, for all she knew, and she'd bet he wasn't taking starry-eyed Kelsey. Her stomach felt funny. Was Kelsey in any danger now?

She walked out into the big atrium and looked around. She didn't see Jack or his cop pal lurking about, but maybe he didn't want to be seen. If Gracelyn had already gone into the concourse, she couldn't follow. Could Jack and Hogan go? Did they have security clearance?

Not only did she have no plane ticket, but there was a *gun* in her shoulder bag. Duh! How stupid could she be? Suddenly the bag seemed ten pounds heavier.

She scanned the passengers in the screening queue. Gracelyn wasn't among them. She glanced at her watch. 9:40. Gracelyn was waiting awfully late to go through—or she'd gone early. Liberty took a seat under the overhanging leaves of a tropical plant and picked up a rumpled newspaper. Feeling foolish and vulnerable, she pretended to read it, keeping an eye on the shops and bars.

Speaking of bars, she figured she could watch just as well with a glass of wine. She folded the paper, laid it next to a man who was curled up sleeping, and walked across toward a dim, open lounge. She halted in mid-step. A woman in a black skirt and lavender jacket rose from a table near the entrance.

Gracelyn Rodgers, bar ticket in hand, walked to the counter to pay.

What would Liberty say to her? What would she do? *Where* were Jack and the detective? Jack was supposed to be shadowing Gracelyn. Had she shaken him so easily? Some gumshoe!

Gracelyn strode out, raincoat folded over her arm, roomy traveling bag over her shoulder. She headed in the direction of the gate.

Liberty shadowed her quarry, mind whirling with her next step.

When Gracelyn approached the security line, Liberty stepped into her line of sight. "Gracelyn," she said. "We need to talk."

The woman's eyes widened, but she corrected herself quickly, and the eyes narrowed, resolved and calculating. Keeping her regal posture, Gracelyn glanced around coolly for a way to escape. She could not run in the airport. That would definitely crimp her plans of boarding that plane to New York.

Then her features relaxed. She even smiled. "Why, Liberty. What on earth could we talk about? Imagine running into you at the airport like this. Why aren't you at home with your family. Or in church?" Liberty didn't like the way she said *church*. "Are you expecting someone?"

Liberty gave her a pleasant smile in return. "I am," she said. "My mother's flying in from California."

"How nice for you," said Gracelyn. "I'm off to visit relatives."

Jack, Jack, where are you? "Your son isn't going with you?"

Her figure stiffened; anger flashed, and then it faded. Man, what control. What an actress. Gracelyn shrugged. "Those young people. He's going to spend Christmas with a girl."

"I know how young people are," Liberty said.

Liberty shifted from one foot to the other, glancing toward the TSA agents. The line shuffled forward, carry-ons plopping on the conveyor belt ahead. The clock on the wall opposite ticked off the minutes. Some man had well-tied shoes, and the line stopped. "It's going to be a sad Christmas without Sam, isn't it?"

Gracelyn's brows knotted in vexation. "I'm going to miss him."

"He was so perceptive," Liberty said. Now she was going to bluff. "He confided in me, you know."

Gracelyn's eyes narrowed into slits.

Liberty took a step forward and lowered her voice. "He told me all sorts of things, Gracelyn. Told me he had suspicions that someone was embezzling. Did he tell you?"

"Of course not," she snapped. "He didn't know anything about it." She caught herself and flushed but didn't change her haughty expression. "I mean to say, nothing like that happened. I would have caught anything like that."

"Would you have, Gracelyn?"

"I'm a competent bookkeeper," she said. "I was good enough. I don't see why he had to bring in someone else."

"So Kelsey made you uncomfortable? What did Kelsey find? What was the auditor going to find next month?"

A sheen of sweat broke out on Gracelyn's brow, and a thin film of moisture formed on her upper lip. Her features contorted. "Don't throw accusations at me. I could throw some back at you. You and he were sinning. I know you were sinning. He deserved what he got."

"We were not doing anything of the kind."

"It was God's punishment. Now leave me alone."

Liberty, now angry, grabbed her arm. The woman tried to push Liberty aside, but she held on. "Is God watching you, Gracelyn? Thou shalt not . . . *steal*."

"I need to get in line," she snapped. "I'll miss my plane."

She broke loose and shouldered past Liberty, almost hitting her with the *People* magazine poking out of the side pocket of her carry-on. Liberty looked frantically toward the entrance. *Where were Jack and Hogan?*

Gracelyn joined the back of the shortest line. Liberty caught up to her and grabbed her shoulder. "Get your hands off me," Gracelyn snarled. People turned and stared, but said nothing, loath to interrupt some personal quarrel. A woman security guard ambled across the far end of the room. She hadn't spotted them.

Liberty thought of the gun in her bag. How utterly useless!

But then again, maybe it wasn't.

The queue shuffled forward, closer to the metal detectors. "Goodbye, Liberty," Gracelyn said, smiling. Liberty stepped back as if beaten. "Goodbye, Gracelyn." She slipped the firearm out of her bag, concealed by her jacket sleeve. Then she sidled closer to her quarry. "I forgot to tell you something. Something important."

"Stop bothering me, you bitch," Gracelyn said, hissing. "Go away or I'll call a guard."

"Have it your way." Liberty lunged forward and shoved the gun into the pocket of Gracelyn's carry-on, then turned and race-walked away. "Have a nice flight," Liberty called.

She looked over her shoulder just in time to see Gracelyn dig into the pocket to find out what Liberty had dropped, pull it out, and stand looking at it, stunned.

Listening to the screams from the ensuing commotion, Liberty took a quick exit, keeping an eye on the escalators fetching people from the train. She spotted a taffy-haired woman in jeans, high-heeled boots, and fur-trimmed jacket among the passengers, and then there was more screaming—by the taffy-haired woman. "Liberty Jean!!"

Liberty went to greet her mother, while guards hurried toward the security line from every direction.

Chapter Thirty-Six

Being Real

"There they are!"

Right after Gracelyn had been taken away by airport security, Liberty spotted Jack and Hogan elbowing their way through the crowd. She made her way toward them, Paloma clip-clopping behind on high heels.

"There you are!" Liberty said.

They had the good sense to look abashed.

"Where on earth have you been?"

"Liberty, this is my pal Detective Hogan," Jack said. "We were planning to be here an hour ago, but Hogan's car had a flat tire. But more to the question, why are *you* here?"

Liberty gave her best Cheshire-cat smile. "If I hadn't been here, our suspect would be in the air right now, trying to leave the country."

Paloma straightened and gave the men a bright smile. "My daughter hasn't introduced me, gentlemen. I'm Paloma Morgan, and I'm *ever so* happy to see you."

"Well, how about that," Hogan said, "I watch that show, *Hometown Criminals.* You're great!"

"Me too," Jack chimed in. "Pleasure to meet you, Miss Morgan. Now Hogan and I need to go to Security and try to get this mess straightened out. Stay at the airport."

Liberty sighed. She'd be up half the night at this rate. "We'll be at Starbucks." She called Dallas, and, crossing her fingers, told him that Paloma's plane was late.

It was after midnight by the time Jack and Hogan returned to the women and their peppermint lattes. Let's go," Jack said. He looked tired.

"So what happened?" Liberty asked, afraid that Gracelyn had walked.

"Hogan booked her on a weapons charge, and he's going to question her again about the arson. Donovan too."

Hogan spoke. "That'll keep her out of commission for a day or so, but we've got to find more evidence. She'll get a lawyer, but she won't find one tonight."

"You go ahead and collect her," Jack said to Hogan. "I'll meet you at the car. I want to escort the ladies to theirs."

Walking beside him, Paloma pulled out all her charm for Jack. "Gavin would've eventually gone into PI work if he'd lived," she told him. "He said that was his dream, to retire early and open his own agency."

"Your father," said Jack, looking at Liberty.

Liberty nodded, throat full. She almost couldn't get out the words she'd been holding in, and then she blurted, "I have evidence that Sam was murdered. I've had it all along." She told him what she'd found out about the manuscript.

Paloma walked beside them listening, saying not a word, her Botoxed face a mask, and when Liberty had finished said, "You mean Gracelyn put penicillin on the manuscript? She knew his habits, that he licked his fingers and turned pages?"

"That's right," Liberty said. "She'd been reading *The Name of the Rose.*"

"That's my girl." Jack hugged her, and she felt that Jack would have whirled her around right there in the parking lot if her mother had not been standing right there. The giddy feeling faded when she realized she'd have to say good night to Jack and drive her mother to her house, just the two of them.

Jack ushered the two women into the car, made sure their belts were buckled, and closed the door gently on Liberty's side. She could tell he wanted to kiss her, but she couldn't let that happen. She gave him her hand and he kissed that instead. "Au revoir," he said, winked, then turned and walked away with the cool swagger of Humphrey Bogart.

The trip home, under those orange lights that winked by in the tunnel, past the city skyscrapers with their holiday lights, seemed like the longest trip Liberty had ever taken. For the first few miles a dark silence filled the space between them, so much so that when her mother finally spoke, it startled her. "Tell me things," she said. "Tell me about your life now. It wasn't as perfect as you pretended it was. I thought you were so lucky, and I was happy for you."

"I was acting, Paloma," Liberty said. "I guess I'm more like you than I realized."

"Why did you hide so many things from me? What happened tonight is the end of a long story, isn't it?"

"You didn't have time to listen before," Liberty said. "Maybe I'll tell you someday."

"I'm sorry, baby," she said. "Life is complicated."

"Complicated? It was always some man or other, wasn't it?" Liberty said. "You couldn't spare a little time for your only child?"

Paloma took a deep breath and, with her perfectly manicured fingers, raked her tousled taffy hair away from her eyelashes. "I went through a bad patch," she said. "Out there it's easy to go off on the wrong track. I think you know what I mean. I'm clean now. I did a lot of things I wasn't proud of. I'm in television work now, you know."

"Yes, that's great." Liberty hadn't ever watched the show. It might have been different if her mother had just picked up the phone to tell Liberty about it. "Why did you speak of my father just then? You forgot him soon enough."

Paloma shook her head. "Oh, no, no. I never forgot him. I was trying to, but I couldn't. Something about that man Jack reminded me of Gavin."

She must have seen her daughter's skeptical frown. "Oh, no, not in looks—your father was a taller man, and heavier—but just in the way Jack carried himself, the way he looked. He's confident, sure of himself." She paused, appeared to be thinking about how to frame the words. "Where I live, it's all about illusion. Nothing is real. Maybe that's why I like it. But Jack Ford is real. And I have a feeling he cares about you."

"I don't know what's going to happen," Liberty said, "but I do know one thing. No more acting. It's going to be real or nothing."

Paloma's voice grew wistful. "It's a real Christmas here, cold weather and all. It never seemed much like Christmas in LA, and in Florida it was always so funny, those fake sleighs on the lawns under the palm trees. I wondered why people bothered."

"There was a man named Sam," Liberty told her, "who said that symbols are important, and so are rituals."

Paloma nodded. "Your father was a big one for rituals. I think I never married again because I was looking for someone like him, and there *was* no one else like him."

"Not in Hollywood." Liberty fought her urge to shout *Wasn't I enough? Why couldn't you live for me?*

"No," Paloma agreed, "not in Hollywood. But it was too painful to stay where I'd be reminded of him every day. Work was the best medicine."

Yes, Paloma had her work, and she had succeeded, in her own way. Would Liberty have wanted a pitiful widow for a mother, a woman with no life of her own, with no interests but her one child, waiting by the phone for a telephone call? But surely there was another way?

Liberty wheeled off the ramp, down a deserted boulevard. People were snug in their homes by now, waiting for the sun to rise on Christmas Day. She glanced over, and her mother looked old and tired. Having run a long race and not won the prize. "But the chase, Paloma—Mother—you still had to search, didn't you? Looking for another Gavin?"

She smiled crookedly. "That's life, isn't it?"

The light turned green and they headed for home. Liberty's bitterness dissolved. It would be a while before they worked out all the kinks, but now Liberty was glad her mother had come. Now she only had a murder to wrap up.

Mama Jean and Papaw were waiting up for them; Dallas, too. Would her husband have waited up if his in-laws had not been there? It was after one o'clock in the morning on Christmas Day, and Emmy had been asleep for hours.

There were kisses and hugs all around, with Dallas putting on the salesman charm. Paloma did not try to flatter and amuse him, as she might have done before. She knew how things were between the two, for Liberty had told her a little of it, and this evidence of loyalty was a point in her favor.

Liberty impulsively offered to put her mother in the master bedroom, but Paloma wouldn't hear of it. The basement, she said, was just fine. She'd come on short notice, after all. As long as she had a bathroom, she was happy. This was so unlike her former high-maintenance behavior that Liberty thought miracles must be in the air.

Dallas confirmed there was a bathroom downstairs, and Paloma wanted to go to bed straightaway. She pled exhaustion and told them not to wake her until well into the morning. Mama Jean had prepared the fold-out. Paloma told everyone goodnight, flung kisses, and left.

After everyone else had agreed on dinner at two in the afternoon, Mama Jean turned to Dallas and Liberty. "Lord knows, children, we all need some sleep."

"You all go," Liberty said, looking from one to the other. "I've got one more chore."

Mama Jean nodded. Dallas shrugged and walked off as if he knew he couldn't bully her any longer.

It was a job, taking out all those pages. Liberty separated carefully the ones recently acquired from the original ones Alicia had given her. And then the tedious process began. Take a page up. Moisten a finger, rub it across the page, taste it.

When she had gone through the stack, three pages were set aside. Three pages had left a bitter taste on her tongue: the pages Gracelyn Rodgers had brought to Sam that night.

She sealed the three pages in a fresh plastic bag, gallon size, and put them away.

When she finally crept into the bed, thankful that Dallas was already asleep, she drifted away at once. It seemed just a few minutes before she was awakened by Emmy's excited shouts. The little girl pattered into her parents' room and tugged at her mother's hand. "Santa came! Can we open pre'tents?"

Liberty opened one sleepy eye and smiled. She tucked Emmy's hair behind her ear. "I'm coming now, sweetheart."

Dallas lurched out of bed and into the shower. Liberty rose, tied her robe, and went down into a kitchen of heavenly aromas. Coffee was ready, and a surprise Christmas coffee cake complete with red and green cherries, was warming in the toaster oven. Mama Jean grinned. "Merry Christmas! I brought it in my suitcase!"

For the space of one blessed morning, Liberty felt they were a happy family, sitting in a blue-sun kitchen on Christmas Day, the house spicy and warm with love, and old hurts forgotten. Yet, after this day was over—this brief space—what would happen? Had anything really changed?

The investigation would go on after she'd turned in the evidence, she knew. When the lab reports came back, tests would show traces of poison in Duff's body, and they'd find out that when he'd come over to the church, Gracelyn always brought him his coffee.

Of course, Gracelyn had planned to be out of the country by the time all the test results came back. And if they wanted to go back to check into Wick Rodgers's death . . . well, that was long ago and far away.

It would be a long, hard road ahead for Liberty. But there would be no connection between her and the night she'd found Sam. Or so she thought. There were still those footsteps upstairs. And the mysterious woman. But what if . . .

She called Jack Ford, and he answered on the first ring. "I'm sorry to call so early . . ."

"I sort of hoped you'd call," he said. "Merry Christmas."

"It is merry," she said. "I know who the person upstairs was."

Chapter Thirty-Seven

THE LAST COFFEE
DECEMBER 27

Two days later, Liberty hurried to meet Jack in the bookstore coffee shop with mixed emotions. She'd just seen Paloma off at the airport, at last feeling a warm glow toward her mother, and strangely, sadness had drawn a black border around the warm glow. She didn't know why. The case had been turned over to the police, and they were in charge now. She felt glad for what she had done to help solve the crime.

She made her way through the bargain-hunters and the shoppers with gift cards or exchanges to the coffee corner, where Jack, seeing her, rose from a booth. She blinked when she saw his smart plaid shirt, khakis, and tweed jacket. And loafers.

He grinned at her. "I'm not on duty today."

"Not on *duty*?"

He winked, rose, and went to get her coffee, and came back with two mugs and a scone with jam for each of them.

When they had each taken a bite from the delectable scones, he said, "I wanted you to see I'm not always so kooky. I like dressing like that, and it's also good cover. Nobody notices what I look like—they only notice the clothes."

Liberty had to smile. "Acting—just like me," she said.

"What do you mean?"

"It's a long story," she sighed. She wasn't sure she'd ever get a chance to tell him, so better not start. Better change the subject. "What's happening with the case?"

He filled her in on the police investigation and told her that a homicide detective would come by her house to collect the evidence of the manuscript papers and start building a case against Gracelyn.

"What about Donovan?" Liberty wanted to know.

"He and his mother fell out over Kelsey. The lady was becoming unhinged. She wanted him to kill Kelsey, and he refused. You know, Donovan found he was really in love with this girl, and her goodness made him ashamed of what he'd done."

"You've talked to him?"

"Yes. He's been carrying a heavy burden all these years, and when his mother tried to involve him in the embezzling scheme, it got too much for him. He went to Sam and made a confession that he saw his father and mother fighting in the boat. He saw her push him over the side after he'd had maybe one too many drinks. Talk about a traumatic experience."

"He didn't say anything to *anybody*?"

"He was too stunned. His mind rejected what he saw. It was a case of denial."

"And Sam confronted Gracelyn?"

"The boy thinks so. He believes that Sam asked her to turn herself in. Maybe Sam even told her his own story."

"So why kill Sam? He was trying to help her."

"Because she couldn't kill the only person she'd ever loved, her son. With all that Sam knew, she was done for. She needed to get him out of the way."

"She killed Duff for the same reason?"

"Yes. She was afraid Sam had told Duff about the murder that night when she came over to deliver the deadly pages. Whether he did or not we'll never know. And, of course, there was the affair Duff and Gracelyn had. Revenge for breaking it off?"

Liberty grew angry. What a waste. Sam and Duff, good people. And this twisted woman, full of greed and wishing for revenge, taking their lives. Even her son finally saw her as she really was. "Will the son be charged with anything?"

"If he enters evidence they can get a plea bargain," he said.

Liberty was silent, sorry for Donovan, sorry for Kelsey, sorry for the whole world and all the messes people get themselves into—herself included. And now there was one more thing to ask. "What did Melvin say?"

"It took a little persuading, but he admitted he was upstairs that night."

"I felt it had to be him, from the way he acted. But why?"

"Same reason you came over. He wanted to grouse to Sam about something or other and couldn't get him on the phone. He walked over, found the door unlocked, came in and saw the body. Right afterwards, you drove up and he hurried upstairs. He didn't know what had happened and thought it might be the killer coming back. Then later, he stayed quiet for fear of being the prime suspect. You remember they'd quarreled about the attempted dog poisoning."

She looked down then and fiddled with her wedding ring, which she usually did when she was nervous. "Will he give me away?"

Jack shook his head. "He likes you."

She said a prayer of silent thanks, hiding her emotion behind a sip of coffee.

"What will you do, Liberty?" Jack slid his hand over hers.

She bit her lip and left her hand where it was. "I don't know." She knew he was talking about Dallas, and she changed the subject. "I wish we could find that mysterious woman."

The silence between them hung like a curtain. "Wouldn't you like to think it was Sonia? That she tracked him down? That they made their peace before the end?"

"Yes," Liberty said. "I'd like that."

And she liked Jack a lot—too much. She liked the feel of his comforting hand on hers. But she had a duty, didn't she? The duty to repair her marriage, to give her child a happy family. Now there was nothing else to say, and she withdrew her hand. "Maybe we'd better call it a morning," said Jack, half-smiling. She realized she'd hurt him, and something twisted inside. Now she knew what his sadness was about.

She might never see him again, and that thought brought an anguish that she tried desperately to overcome. She touched his wrist gently, hoping he'd stay just a little longer. "Wait," she said. "Tell me something. What happened with you?"

He shook his head. "Not now. Maybe someday."

"All right," she said, feeling her body warming. "Someday." She looked down. "I don't know what will happen with Dallas." The words were hard to get out. "There's Emmy. I have a duty." She managed a weak smile. "And I've got to set a good example for my mother."

"I know," said Jack. "And I admire you for it. That doesn't mean I like it." He rose and lifted his tweed jacket off the back of his chair and slipped it on.

Outside the weather was changing again, that Janus-faced weather at the end of the year. Fog was swirling all around as they walked to her car. Jack touched Liberty's arm. "Hogan said to tell you that you could have your gun back after the questioning, if you can produce a permit."

She laughed. "If my father's up in heaven he's looking down right now and having one good laugh. I can hear him now. *What the hell have you done, Biddy?* That's what he called me."

Jack looked at her with a lopsided smile. "Biddy? A chick. It kind of fits." He leaned over and kissed her then, softly, so wispy it almost wasn't real, and for a moment she couldn't breathe.

He shouldn't have done it . . . but she was glad he did. When he pulled away, she felt marooned on a raft in a sunless sea.

"Take care, Liberty." He touched her cheek, then turned and walked off into the fog.

Someday . . .

She stood and watched him go as the fog turned into drizzle, as tears ran down her cheek. She felt as though she'd just turned the last page of a book she didn't want to end. The drizzle kept coming down, plastering her hair to her head. She glanced down at a crack in the curbing, where a tiny green plant was pushing through, looking for life wherever it could find it, reaching for the beautiful rain.

Notes and Acknowledgments

This novel was written some time ago. Feeling the time was not right for it, I put it away. Then, while *Wildwood Flower* was underway, my longtime friend and beta reader Anna said, "Whatever happened to that book about the dead preacher? It was good." Thanks, Anna! (Thanks also to my other beta readers, who wish to remain anonymous.)

Since, like *Wildwood Flower*, *Things Left Undone* is about a clergyman, I hesitated. Did I want to be another James Runcie? (Grantchester) Well, no. But I loved my characters and decided to go ahead. There might possibly be a sequel (ahem).

This book owes a lot to my daughter, Virginia, who was born with Down syndrome. Bringing her up was a challenge and a joy, and she taught me a lot about compassion and patience. Thanks also to "Just" People, where she lives now, especially Becky, Kelli, Lisa, and case managers over the years, who have expanded her horizons and helped her with independence.

Thanks also to my writer's group, my friends at Sisters in Crime, my Episcopal church friends, my brothers and cousins, my classmates and hometown friends, and so many others who have helped and supported me, especially my extraordinary husband, my daughter Camille, and my son Jay.

And of course, many thanks to Words of Passion: Nanette Littlestone for excellent editing and Peter Hildebrandt for a great layout and cover design.

THANK YOU

Thank you for buying this book!

I hope you enjoyed it. If so, it would be wonderful if you'd write a review so that others can find it. These reviews mean the world to an independent author, and I'd so appreciate it.

If you'd like to know more about me and my books, please visit my website at www.annelovett.com. If you like cooking, my other site www.mamanellsrecipes.com features favorite recipes from my late mother, which I made for my family. I'd like to share them with you.